FOR LOVE

&

BASKETBALL

A MATCHMAKERS' BOOK CLUB
NOVEL

NICOLE VIDAL

COPYRIGHT

TABLE OF CONTENTS

KEEP IN TOUCH WITH NV

Facebook (http://fb.me/NicoleVidalAuthor)

Instagram (http://instagram.com/nicolevidal_author)

Amazon (https://www.amazon.com/Nicole-

Vidal/e/B082DJHPXP?ref_=dbs_p_ebk_r00_abau_000000)

My website (www.nicolevidal.com)

Pinterest (http://pinterest.com/NicoleVidal_Author)

Goodreads

(https://www.goodreads.com/author/show/19827329.Nicole_Vidal)

PROLOGUE

CARLY

"I would like to call this meeting of the Matchmakers' Book Club to order. Let's get the business out of the way and then focus on the fun," I state from near the fireplace at the Ramirez home.

The ladies' chatter decreases upon my announcement, and they gather around the living room.

"I would like to welcome our newest member, Rosalina Gugliotti. Lina captured the heart of one of our community's most eligible bachelors and has been invited to join our sorority of sorts."

Shock materializes on Lina's face. "The list is a real thing?"

The group of ladies laugh, and Willa adds, "Welcome. We pride ourselves on keeping our matchmaking a secret."

Lina turns to her sister-in-law. "Were you in on it the entire time?"

"I may have offered a nudge here or there. However, you and Tino didn't need our help at all," Willa replies.

The group erupts in laughter.

I continue, "For those of you who are new to our group, allow me to share our purpose. Initially, our group started as a gaggle of nurses and EMTs to de-stress from the rigors of our profession with a book club and girls' night in. Over the years, it evolved into a girl gang of epic proportions. Not only do we host events for the local children's charities, but we keep tabs on the most eligible singles in our community. Our matchmaking book club was created in good fun, and the tradition has continued for the last five years."

"Along with the purpose of our group, the rules for inclusion on the list have evolved. Inclusion consists of a few factors balanced against one another. First, an attractive package is a must. Also, candidates and admitted bachelors or bachelorettes must be a member of our first responder community, including police officers, firefighters, and EMTs. Most importantly, we attempt to keep the list secret until after he or she has been legally wed. It has come to my attention a few younger members of the YPD are aware of our group and have attempted to learn the inner workings. So far, they've failed. The secrecy must be maintained. The last thing we want is our fun to be thwarted. Now I open the floor to all members to suggest additions to the list."

"I realize this is my second time joining you, but I suggest Callan Craven of the YPD to replace Gugliotti," Scarlett suggests. Scarlett is an exception to the legally wed rule. She warrants an invitation due to her profession as well as her engagement to Zack Smithson, an honoree on the YPD list.

"Any other suggestions?" Carly asks.

The room is silent.

"With no other potential candidates or objections, Callan Craven will fill the YPD list vacancy. Now the floor is open to suggestions for our next couple. The group shall discuss amongst themselves, and we'll vote silently on the way out. The chairperson will then enlist members to foster the selected honoree."

"Séamus Penn," one member suggests aloud. "He would be the first EMT we've attempted to match."

Several members nod in agreement. The smaller groups in the room break into discreet conversation.

As I walk around, I hear Kelsey inform Rosalina, "We have the list, and we work from that. If we see an avenue to assist a person on the list, we do."

"I have a suggestion, but it may seem off the wall to you," Willa whispers.

Maggie and Kelsey speak in unison, "Davis."

"How…?" Willa asks.

"Tabi is your lifelong bestie. Of course you want her to be happy."

I make my way around the room, listening for suggestions. I overhear other names, like Lachlan Hagen and Landry Reed. A smile blossoms on my face. It would be nice for my brother to find a partner.

Before I call the ladies to order again, Kelsey Ramirez pulls me aside. "I received a request from a community member. How they know about our group, I don't know, but the suggestion is coming from an outside source, not someone in this room." Kelsey shares the information, and I ponder how to pull off the special request from an unlikely source.

"It's going to take some extra members to pull it off, but I think it's doable."

"Good, they both deserve it, and for the requestor to see their connection and be willing to push them along, it'll be worth it," Kelsey replies.

"I agree."

Kelsey retakes her seat.

I call the group to order again. "We have received a special request unlike any we've had before. I'll speak to those who are in a unique position to assist this couple and allow voting on other suggestions as well. The suggested honorees are here by the box. Please vote on your way out." I share the book for next month and the sign-ups for the charity football game hosted by Santino Gugliotti, which is being held in the late summer instead of early fall this year.

"I shall read the names, and then we can move on to our book discussion. The list of potential honorees reads as follows: The York Police Department list includes Callan Craven, Zachary Smithson, Lachlan Hagen, Donovan Davis, and Piper Montgomery. Former honorees are William Ramirez, Grant Washington, Luca Cappelli, and Santino Gugliotti."

Kelsey Ramirez, Maggie Washington, Willa Cappelli, and Rosalina Gugliotti smile as I read their husbands' names.

I continue reading aloud, "The York Fire Department list includes Bradford Collings, Alden Rhodes, Aidan Madden, Landry Reed, and Mia Arden. No former honorees to date. Lastly, the EMTs in York County include Séamus Penn, Jude Pascal, Hollis Booker, Lexington Soren, and Lacey Ransom. No former honorees to date."

We spend over an hour chatting about the book selection and then go our separate ways with the understanding of our united goal to pair up unsuspecting members of our community.

CHAPTER ONE

CALLAN

I hustle to the precinct and meet up with my partner for the day. Lately, Cap has been sending Gugliotti with me to the high school since Smithson was promoted to the detective division. Today though, it's me and Smithson.

"Let's go, Smithson. We can't be late."

He grumbles, "Craven, you're too much of a morning person."

I shake my head. Honestly, mornings are not my favorite, but I relish in completing my workout before shift. "You were as well until your engagement to a certain stunning brunette."

Smithson smiles at me. "You'll understand when you find the right woman. The last thing I want is to leave Scarlett in our bed for a long morning run. There are plenty of other more… pleasurable ways to pass the time before work."

Jealous. I'm straight up green with envy. "I hope you're right."

"You would have to go on a date or two to find the right woman."

"Do I? You knew Scarlett was the one for you when you spilled coffee on her."

"True."

"Yet it took you nearly two years to make a move."

"Also true. I guess the question is… who's your unsuspecting coffee girl?"

"Haven't accidently spilled coffee on her yet." I'm looking for an all-encompassing love that brings peace to my heart and soul. Sappy, I know.

Smithson laughs and drives toward the school where he checks in with Michelle at the front office. Today we're hanging with the students for an end-of-the-year breakfast and planning for the summer. The student council, along with the athletic boosters, have provided an enormous amount of food and beverages while the kids hang out or play basketball and volleyball in the courtyard. Gugliotti has requested we recruit some of the rising seniors for his charity flag football game. It'll help with the manpower as well as earn them community service hours for their graduation requirement.

Smithson and I split up. As always, I'm drawn to the basketball game. It's my favorite sport to play and watch. Cap purposely assigns me extra duty at the high school games when he can. I appreciate it.

"Hey, OC, you joinin' us today?" Caden calls from the top of the key with a ball set against his hip. He's the star point guard heading into his senior season at York High. Caden deemed "Officer Craven" overly formal when we met, so he calls me "OC" instead.

"Sure, if you're willing to go easy on me."

Caden and Kyla laugh.

"No need for us to go easy on you. You can hold your own despite your age," Kyla quips. She's the point guard for the girls' team and a highly touted recruit for a perennial top twenty-five school.

"Exactly how old do you think I am, Miss Walton?" I set my phone on the player bench.

She shrugs. "Maybe thirty?" The question in her voice indicates her belief she may have offended me.

"Close. Thirty-one is old? Good to know."

Both grin, and Caden checks the ball to me.

"For the record, it's unfair to have both of you on the same team," I admit.

"She's not *that* good," Caden goads her.

"I'm better than you," Kyla retorts and rolls her eyes.

They're dating, and he's trying to knock her off her game. Frankly, their skill sets are strikingly similar.

"Prove it. You can switch teams with James," Caden throws down the challenge. Kyla and James trade places.

I pass the ball to Caden who passes it back. It takes Caden one swipe to steal the ball and dribble out to the three-point line. Kyla is in his face almost as fast as he stole the ball from me. Caden fakes right, but Kyla doesn't bite. He pulls up for the jumper, and Kyla blocks the shot. Their classmates cheer for Kyla and jeer Caden.

The couple continue to play one-on-one for a few plays until the principal calls the students over for an announcement. Mrs. Kisel raises her hand to quiet the groans for interrupting their morning fun.

"Thank you. A few brief words, and I'll let you get back to your breakfast and activities. Detective Smithson and Officer Craven are here to chat about the charity flag football game and opportunities for the upcoming school year to prepare for college with the resource program. Please speak to them before you head into class."

A chorus of chatter surrounds us. We have nearly an hour before the students need to head inside. I appreciate her assistance.

"So, OC, what do you need for the flag football game?"

"We need some volunteers to help set up, man the concession stand, distribute team jerseys, and collect the donations."

"We're in," Kyla answers for both.

Caden laughs. "We should see when it is first, Ky."

She wrinkles her nose at him. "True. When is the game?"

"It's July 15th."

"That's on a weekend, right?" Caden asks.

"Yup."

"We're in," Kyla repeats.

I grin at them. "Here's my card in case you don't already have one. Please email me so I can send you the community service slip for your parents to sign."

Caden takes the card. "Thanks, OC."

"You're welcome."

I see a lot of myself in Caden—not only the basketball prowess but the desire to achieve something great for his family. I've only seen his mom, an older gentleman, and another older woman. His mom is a fixture in the stands and impossible to miss. I don't think she's ever missed a game. She keeps to herself, despite her son's athletic ability. She's a professional of some kind, always dressed in a suit or dress clothes, complete with high heels. Her strawberry blonde hair is similar to Bella Thorne or Isla Fisher. In short, she's stunning from a distance. We've never actually met. I put them together when she joined Caden on the court for the all-league, all-state, all-region celebration over the wildcat logo at center court at the end of last season. Some would say she's standoffish. I prefer to think she's private. One look at her and I see a strong woman who has overcome an obstacle—or a few—in her past. Obstacles she refuses to allow to define her future.

The bell rings and pulls me back to the present. The students grumble but dutifully head into the building for class.

Smithson jogs across the court. "How many did you wrangle?"

"Two. You?"

"Same. Now we can focus on team practices instead of logistics. We need to win this year. The guys from the fire department can't win twice in a row."

I laugh. "Truth. When is the next practice?" It's more like a light workout and drinking under the guise of flag football.

"Saturday at noon, I think," Smithson answers.

"Are you going to be able to get out of bed?"

"I'll do my best."

I chuckle as we enter the building and take a stroll through the halls in opposite directions. Near lunch we meet in the cafeteria and hang with the students. After some not-so-great food, I head to our office adjacent to the guidance department and take a seat.

Smithson joins me shortly thereafter. "Are the days here always like this?"

I frown. "What do you mean?"

"Fulfilling and fun."

"Yes to the first part, sometimes to the second part. What happened?"

He shares the story of his chat with a group of sophomores looking to set up a peer group for students in need of support for summer employment.

"Sounds great, except this summer might be tight considering it's already late May," I share.

"I agree, and they're aware. They plan to have it ready for next summer."

"I'm impressed with their desire to find employment, as well as their understanding this year will be difficult."

"Me too. I didn't care about any of that when I was in high school."

"Same. I was only worried about basketball and girls," I admit.

"No kidding."

We spend the rest of the day chatting up the charity game and secure three more volunteers for Gugliotti. Overall, it was a great day.

With the funds from last year's game, we were able to provide open gym time and an intramural basketball league for those who simply want to exercise or lack the skills to earn a varsity spot. With the support of the park department, we held a hiking trail cleanup in the spring. We also coordinated assistance from a college counselor to help with entrance essay writing as well as paying application fees after a show of need by any student. We helped ten students apply to college who otherwise wouldn't be able to afford to do so. The plan with this year's donations is to expand those programs.

The community resource officer position was Luca Cappelli's. However, he moved to the crisis unit with the state police. Davis, who was Luca's partner, lacks passion for the position. It's simply an assignment to him, so Cap has been assigning him elsewhere. Davis also applied for the same position as Luca, but there hasn't been another opening. Since then, I have been working with Gugliotti. When I joined the force, it was to help people. While I have other shifts too, I enjoy these at the school the most.

After the last bell rings, Smithson and I make our way back to the precinct.

"Yo, Craven!" Greyson shouts as I enter the locker room.

"Hey, Greyson. How was desk duty today?"

"Not bad at all. I snagged a date with a hottie from the university for tonight," he replies. "Wanna tag along for her friend?"

Hell no! I'm too old for a college girl. "No, thanks. I have plans." I don't, but I'll create some to avoid the position of Greyson's wingman.

"Suit yourself. She's hot."

"Maybe next time." Never going to happen.

I change and drive toward the gym, despite going for a run this morning. The temperature outside has me changing my mind. I opt to shoot hoops at the court near my townhouse instead of lifting. Ideally, I'll have the court to myself for an hour or so before the pickup games begin. Nearly two hours later, drenched in sweat, I exit the court and head home. I have a shift tomorrow and Saturday but have Sunday off. Perhaps a solo hike of Mount Agamenticus will pass my free time.

CHAPTER TWO

ALANNAH

The school year is wrapping up, and I've been working hard to set aside time to visit colleges with my son. That doesn't include his basketball options. He has two offers before his final season. He isn't sold on either school. In his words, one is too far away and the other doesn't give him good vibes. I'm glad my love of the game rubbed off on him. It makes sense, considering he was present at every open practice and home game when I was in college. If you told me how my life would turn out, I wouldn't have believed you. My son is my world, and I have limited time left with him before he goes to college.

I climb the stairs after my light workout and check on my son. He should be up by now. "Caden, ready for school?" I knock lightly on the door.

My son groans. "Ugh! My exam is at ten."

"Sorry. Are there buses or do you need to come to the office with me?"

"Ky is going to give me a ride." Kyla is a sweet girl who my son has been dating for the last two years. They're both excellent students and talented athletes.

"Okay. Sorry. Good luck."

He sits up. "Don't worry about it. There's a permission slip for the charity flag football game on the island. Can you sign it?"

"Sure. See you tonight. Love you."

"Love you too, Mom."

After showering and dressing for an office day, I head back to the kitchen. While my coffee is brewing, I review the slip, sign it, and mark the calendar. I recall hearing about this game last year, but I thought it was in the fall. Caden talks about the programs the community resource officers added from the inaugural game. I'm proud he's helping out this time. He doesn't need the services, but he certainly used the open gym time to his benefit. His foul shot has greatly improved, as did his defense, despite having a hoop at home. Although, I think Kyla has a lot to do with his improvement.

I pull out of the driveway and head toward the office. When I walk in, my assistant takes my bag and ushers me into the conference room.

"Morning, Alannah. Mr. and Mrs. Spencer reached out about a mediated divorce on Saturday. Rather than wait, they showed up this morning," Cara, my part-time assistant, informs me. She's in her midtwenties and has an interest in the law but no desire to be an attorney herself.

"Okay. I'll fit them in before my scheduled appointment with the first selectwoman."

"I'll bring them in and gather the pertinent information for your meeting with the selectwoman about the lot line issue," she replies.

"Thank you." I swallow a gulp of my coffee and paste a huge smile on my face as my new clients are shown into the room. "Mr. and Mrs. Spencer, good morning. How can I help you?"

I spend the next hour sorting out their marital issues and how they plan to divide their assets. I schedule a follow-up in a few weeks to execute the petition before escorting them out with a bare minute to spare before Joan Bickel arrives for her appointment.

Once I allay her fears about the boundary issue and how it can be addressed with an affidavit, I take a seat at my desk for the first time today. I glance at my inbox. Only fifteen emails, not terrible. Before I get started, Cara steps into my office and sets a stack of files and phone messages on my desk.

"I took the liberty of ordering them by urgency."

"Thanks." I finish the last swig of my now cold coffee and tackle the messages. I don't have a chance to dive into them deeply before my cell rings.

"Hey, Del!"

"Hey, girl! Are we still on for lunch?"

"Ugh! I'm swamped. Can you come to the office instead?"

"Sure. I'll have chef make us something and head over."

"Please say hi to everyone for me."

Delilah and I have been friends since grammar school. She's the only person who knows the actual roller coaster my life was in the early years after…. I push my negative thoughts away. I don't wallow; it isn't good for me or Caden. Del works for Maggie Washington at Morgan's. August Morgan is the owner and chef.

I spend every second of my time before lunch culling down my action items. When Del arrives bearing delicious grub, I only have three more emails to address before an estate intake this afternoon.

"It's been too long!" I hug my bestie.

"It has!"

"How are things with you and Scott?" I ask her. Scott is a local guy who works in construction. They met while Harborside was being renovated. Harborside is the banquet hall attached to Morgan's.

"Good. Really good. He's a great guy. We should talk about you. Any recent dates?"

I shake my head. "I don't have time to date. You know this."

"Not true. Caden is perfectly capable of caring for himself for an evening. Plus, is he ever home? Your son's dating life is better than yours."

I laugh. "You aren't wrong. They make a gorgeous couple, and they have common interests." Daniel and I did as well… sort of.

"Nope, do not go down the Daniel rabbit hole. He's in the past, the ancient past," she says, interrupting my thoughts. As I mentioned, Del knows all the gritty details about my life. "When was your last date?"

"Six months ago… I think."

"Lan, I love you, but you need to get laid."

I snort my water through my nose. "We aren't talking about how long it's been since that happened."

"How long are we talking exactly?"

"Really, Del, it isn't important."

"Yeah, it is. If it's more than a week, I get the twitches."

"With a man or with my purple vibrator?"

"Will the answer be different?"

I stick my tongue out at her. "No, the answer is the same. Since Greg, so a little more than a year. I'm not opposed to dating, Del. I thought—"

"You thought you would've found your person by now."

"Yeah. Maybe Daniel was my person, probably not. All I know is no one is willing to start a relationship with me where I am."

"Because of Caden?"

I frown. "Not always."

"What was wrong with Greg?"

"He didn't want kids, not even a nearly grown one."

"Jerk! Who was before him?"

"Robert didn't make it past the appetizers. His issue was my profession. Kenneth was before Robert. He was on two dates at once."

"Will you let me fix you up? I have a few ideas. Some of Scott's friends are hot as hell and handy."

"No, but thanks."

Del drops her head. "Lan, I'm giving you a few months, and then I'll do it anyway."

"Fine." Despite the content of our conversation, it's nice to catch up with Delilah. "Can we do lunch again in two weeks?"

"Yes, we can." After a hug, she's out the door, and I tackle the rest of my day.

After my intake, I check my texts.

Caden: I'm at the courts at the park off Rogers with the guys.

I check the time. It's from about an hour ago.

Me: Thanks. Need a ride home?

Caden: Yeah, Kyla dropped me off. Whenever you're done working. I need

to study tonight.

Me: I'll be there.

I finish up for the day and drive over to the courts. I park, hop out, and lean against the trunk of my car. Caden signals he sees me. While I wait, I reluctantly reopen one of the dating apps I've used in the past. Only this time, I tweak my bio information to hopefully eliminate anyone not interested in a single mom—teenage or otherwise.

When I look up, I notice Caden talking to a fit man at the court. I unabashedly look my fill of him, which takes a decent amount of time. He's tall, moderately built, and his smile from afar is breathtaking. My instinct is to go rescue my son until I see the YPD symbol on his shirt. After a clearly practiced handshake, Caden points in my direction in response to his question. Then he trots over to the car and waves back.

"Hey, bud. Who was that?"

"Hey. That's OC."

I raise an eyebrow in question before reversing out of the parking spot.

"Sorry, Officer Craven. He's one of the school resource officers."

"Cool. OC?"

"It's a nickname I gave him because calling him Officer Craven is a lot and his first name isn't respectful enough."

"Got it. How was your exam?"

"Not bad considering it was my most difficult."

"Which one is tomorrow?"

"My last one of junior year." He laughs. "Calculus at 8:00. Can you drop me off?"

"Sure. Are you taking the bus home?"

"Either that or I'll take the bus to your office."

I pull into our driveway and head inside. "Why don't you shower while I cook dinner?"

"Sounds good."

In the time since I reactivated my account and now, I have four messages. Ignoring them for now, I start an easy stir-fry for dinner.

Caden rushes back into the kitchen as I'm adding extra sauce. "Smells good."

"Thanks. Can you get drinks?"

"On it."

I laugh, and we enjoy a quiet dinner.

"Go study. I'll wash."

"Thanks."

After cleaning the kitchen, I change out of my work clothes. When I return downstairs, I curl up in the window seat. Our house is a cute Cape with three bedrooms and an office. It's cozy and bright in each room, except Caden's. I gave him free rein for his fourteenth birthday. His room is gray with muted blue linens and dark furniture.

I scroll through the dating app messages and reply to one, mark one unread, and block the other two. I'm not looking for a GQ cover model with a bajillion dollars, just a normal guy with a career who shares a common interest or two and is willing to work on a relationship with me and my son. I'm worth it. *Right? Yes!*

I sigh and glance out into our backyard. The setting sun paints the sky a kaleidoscope of colors. I enjoy the beauty before checking the locks and falling into my bed alone.

CHAPTER THREE

CALLAN

The last month has passed quickly, and the flag football game is upon us. The team practices we've had generally devolved into the guys hanging out and drinking beers to relax. Have we done enough to defeat the fire department this year? Not sure. By the end of the day, we'll find out.

I hurry out the door with a coffee and my bag. I make it to the high school with a minute to spare and narrowly avoided a lashing for lateness from Gugliotti. I zigzag through the cars toward the football field.

"Hey, Craven," a familiar voice I can't immediately place calls from behind me. Mrs. Lina Gugliotti. She married my coworker a little over six months ago.

"Hi, Lina. How can I help you?" I set my bag and coffee on the ground.

She thrusts a large box into my arms and adds a second on top. "Santino needs these near the registration table."

"Got it." I take two steps and realize I left my bag and coffee.

"Need a hand, OC?"

I don't need to look to see who it is. "Thanks, Caden."

A sultry voice from the same direction glides over me. "You take a box. I'll grab the bag and coffee."

"Got it." Caden lifts the top box and falls in step with me toward the registration table. He sets it down and then takes off running back in the direction of the parking lot, where Kyla is getting out of her car.

I turn to the woman beside me carrying my bag and coffee. "Hi. You must be Caden's mom. I'm Callan." Her soft hand slides into the hand I've extended toward her. Awareness and a sense of calm unlike anything I've ever felt before floats through me.

"Alannah. Pleasure to meet you."

My observations of her from afar weren't close to accurate. In business wear, she appears buttoned up and professional. On a random Saturday morning with little makeup, cutoffs, and a V-neck, she's stunning with a sexy name to match her sultry voice.

"Likewise. I can take those." I point to my cup and bag.

"Oh, of course." She hands them over as the kids join us, hand in hand.

"Sorry, Mom."

"It's fine. Morning, Kyla."

"Morning," she greets in response to Alannah. "Officer Craven."

"Officer Gugliotti is near the snack shack with your assignments," I inform the teens.

"Thanks. Are you staying, Mom?" Caden asks.

Say yes.

"Is there somewhere I can help out?" she asks me.

Yes! "There can never be enough volunteers. I'm sure we can find somewhere you can help." My reply comes out cool and nonchalant... at least I hope it does.

"I'll be around, Caden."

"'Kay," her son replies before he and Kyla take off toward the snack shack.

Alannah addresses me again. "As long as it doesn't require extensive knowledge about flag football, I'll be fine."

"Not a football fan?"

"Don't know much about it at all. I prefer basketball."

I look around us and lean in a little closer. Her scent, a mixture of vanilla and flowers, surrounds me. It's downright intoxicating. "Don't tell Gugliotti, but basketball is my favorite too."

She smiles and laughs softly. "I'm pretty sure he already knows."

"Fair enough. Why basketball?"

"I fell in love the instant I picked up a ball at five and never looked back."

I set my hand on her lower back and guide her across the field. "Really? I went to college on a basketball scholarship."

"Me too. Where did you play?"

"Southern New Hampshire. You?"

"Boston College."

"Sweet, but... never mind." How did she play division one basketball with an infant? Unless she's much older than she looks.

"You can ask. I may not answer."

"It can wait for another time."

"I would like that," she replies as we reach the registration table.

"Me too." My thoughts tumble for a moment. Did she just agree to a date?

"About time you joined me," Gugliotti says without looking up. When he sees the beautiful Alannah beside me, the ribbing stops cold.

"Gugliotti, this is Alannah. Can we use another volunteer at the registration table?" I suggest, knowing full well it's where he assigned me.

A sly smile curves the corner of his mouth. "Sure. Maybe she can keep you on task until it's time for you to play."

She may be a distraction of the best kind. A smart, beautiful woman with long, toned legs capped off with perfectly painted pink toenails will absolutely keep me on task. "Great!"

Gugliotti continues, "Here's the roster of teams. It includes the location of the first game. Smithson set up signage for the later rounds. The jerseys are separated and labelled. You need to collect the donations and waivers before handing over the jerseys. Cap or I will pick up the donations and tally them before the championship game."

"Got it." She takes the clipboard from him and turns on her heel back the way we came.

Before I can walk away, Gugliotti looks at me with questions in his eyes, so many questions. I shrug before rushing to catch up with her.

"Did I get you in trouble?" she asks.

"No, not at all."

"Good. What time is the first game?"

"Eight. The players should be arriving in the next fifteen minutes or so. Then the second pair of first round games are at ten. Then noon for the semis, and the final is at two. Why?"

"Since you're playing, you must know something about flag football. Could you give me a crash course? Then the game will make some sense when I watch later."

"Sure, right after we check in the first team. Morning, Booker. Penn."

Séamus Penn grouses, and Hollis Booker zeroes in on Alannah.

"Morning. Team captains for the EMTs. I believe it's listed under Ransom," Penn informs her.

I move closer and scan the list at the same time as she does.

"Found it. They're green. I need your waivers and donations, please," Alannah asks them.

Penn hands over the envelope while Booker takes the jerseys from me.

"You're on the far field for game one," she directs.

"Thanks, Antoinette," Penn states.

"Séamus, nice to see you."

Two sets of eyes bore into mine. It's a warning, as if Penn and Booker know something I don't. Perhaps they do. It's been less than an hour since I met Alannah. All I know is I want to learn what the warning is about and every detail she's willing to share.

"Antoinette?" I ask when they walk away.

"It's my first name, but it was also my grandmother's name. When I was younger, it mattered. Then it didn't. By the time it didn't, I was used to answering to my middle name, Alannah."

"Alannah suits you better."

Her cheeks flush pink slightly. "Thank you."

We check in the rest of the teams with early start times before I start to explain flag football. "Do you know anything about regular football?"

"The basics, sure."

"Okay. It's nearly the same, except there's no tackling. Instead, we grab one of the flags strapped around our opponent's waist. There are some more differences, but mostly there's limited to no physical contact between the players. We modified the rules a bit as well for this tourney. We don't kick field goals or extra points, although they're allowed within the regular rules."

"Cool. When is your first game?"

"Ten. We should be able to watch some together from here before I need to join my team."

"Even better."

Soon thereafter, the teams on the field closest to us line up to start their game. We take a seat on the bench against the fence. Her focus is on the game, but mine is on her. She asks a few questions.

After her most recent football question, I ask, "How long have you lived here?"

"I was born here. You weren't though." She's astute.

"No, I'm from Connecticut. After college, I went home, attended the academy, and worked in a midsized city for a few years."

"Why here?"

"I liked the pace of the area around my college but also the small-town feel of home. You can't beat access to the shoreline either. Here is the perfect mixture. Did you not love Boston?"

"Boston is a great city, rich with history and culture, but I didn't want to raise Caden there. My childhood here was idyllic. Not even the influx of tourists each summer could keep me away."

"I agree with the idyllic part. However, I prefer the offseason. I mean, who wants a line at Dunne's?"

She laughs softly. "True. What's your favorite flavor?"

"The Maine blueberry is delicious and has its place, but I'm only slightly nontraditional. Chocolate chip is my favorite. Yours?"

"I'm nearly a purist then. Chocolate is my flavor of choice."

"Straight up or do you go for chocolate with even more chocolate? Cap's daughter is a chocolate extreme fanatic."

"Straight up, no extras. Val is super cute and precocious. The perfect combination of William and Kelsey."

"She is."

"Yo, Craven! You playin' or what?" Greyson shouts from ten yards away.

I glance at my watch and realize we've been talking for nearly two hours.

"I'm sorry," she whispers.

"Don't be. I would rather stay here and talk to you than play. However, I committed so…."

"Me too, but I understand maintaining your commitment."

"Consider yourself relieved of registration duty."

"Thanks."

I decide to take a bold step. "Are you free tonight?"

"Yes."

No hesitation in her answer but a slight hitch in her voice. "We're having a postgame meal at Endzone Draft and Barrel. Would you be interested in joining me? Caden too if he wants." The postgame meal is a group thing. I won't be alone with her despite my desire to be.

"Sure. What time?"

"Not sure. When we're done cleaning up."

"Craven, let's go!" Greyson impatiently shouts again.

I wave him off.

"I'm going to stay for at least the first game." She pulls her phone from her back pocket. "What's your number?"

I take a step closer and share my number with her. Moments later, my phone vibrates against my thigh.

"Text or call when you know the rest of the details."

"I prefer calls for anything longer than a word or two."

"Okay, a call. Have fun, Callan."

"Thanks." I have an overwhelming urge to kiss her—a notion I consider sharing but quickly decide against before I jog toward the field with my bag in hand.

When I make it to the warm-up area, Smithson is the first to ask about her. "Coffee girl?"

"Potentially," I reply, and he drops the topic. Perhaps I found my plus-one for his wedding. I set my bag on the bench and add my keys and wallet. Before I drop my phone in my bag, I check my texts and save her number. My reprieve doesn't last long.

"Is she why you begged off last night?" Greyson asks.

"No, I met her today." I refuse to admit to him she intrigued me as far back as four months ago when I connected her and her son.

"Damn, you move fast."

I attempt to ignore the insinuation in his words but find I can't. "Are you always disrespectful to women?"

"Yes, most of the time he is," Smithson adds from my left, arms crossed over his chest.

Greyson clams up and walks away.

"Thanks."

"He deserves it. Pulled the same thing with Essie and Scarlett. We may not deck him, but someday his words will piss off someone enough. Then he may learn his lesson."

"Thanks again."

"No problem."

I take a few more minutes and stretch before the referees call for the captains. Our opponent is a team of dads who play in a weekend league for fun during the fall. Ideally, they're rusty and we can advance to the semifinals.

Gugliotti reminds us of the lineup. Hagen takes the quarterback spot since he's the only one of us with experience. Many of my coworkers ran track or played baseball. How and why we have a football game for charity, I'll never understand.

The aptly named "Team of Dads" are terrible. Within the first ten minutes of play, we've nearly eliminated all their receivers. Finnegan Blake, a rookie, steps in as a sub for me. As casually as I can, I sweep the stands for Alannah. I find her surrounded by a sea of blue-line wives. Kelsey is beside her, and Maggie and Willa are on the bleachers in front of her. Scarlett, though not a wife yet, is also speaking with her animatedly while Caden and Kyla laugh at something on their phones.

I'm not concerned. Yet I wonder, if these women know her, how have she and I not met before today? As far as I know, Alannah only knows Kelsey, at least from our conversation so far. Everyone knows Kelsey. Her pastries are the best around. I shake the thought away and refocus on the game. The team of dads resign at the midway point of the second half. We huddle up for a brief postgame chat. When I look up into the stands, she's gone.

I grab my stuff, and the guys usher me to the concession stand for hydration and a snack. I check my phone and find a text from Alannah.

Alannah: I'll be back. I had an errand to handle.

Me: Thanks. See you later.

I eat a deli sandwich before our rematch with the fire department. Even though it's the semifinal match, it's for bragging rights. YFD won the inaugural title, and we need to defeat them to restore the natural balance. If we're lucky enough, we'll bring the cup home after winning the finals as well.

Midway through the first half, I find Alannah in the stands with Caden and Kyla. Her attention is riveted on the game. More realistically, her attention is on me with her limited understanding of flag football. When I cross the goal line, the three of them are on their feet cheering. It's pretty awesome. Moving here was the right choice for me, but I'm a few hours away from my family. Their support is welcome, especially since I met Alannah today. We handily defeat YFD and move on to the finals.

After the game ends, I make my way to the fence. "Thanks for staying," I say to all of them, but my focus is on Alannah.

"It's fun," Kyla offers.

"This is cool, OC!" Caden replies.

"I already volunteered to help next year."

I raise my fist to him. "Awesome!"

"Kyla and I are heading to the beach and then to the bonfire at her grandparents'. I'll see you around or at the courts over the summer."

"Sounds fun! Have a great time and be safe." The words hit a bit differently today than before. I've said those exact words to him and many of his classmates, but my interest in his mother amplifies their meaning.

"Bye, Mom. I'll be home on time."

"Have fun, Caden."

Caden curls his arm around Kyla's waist, and they head toward the parking lot.

I take a step to the right. Now I'm directly in front of Alannah. "What do you think so far?"

"I'm glad Caden didn't take a liking to tackle football."

I laugh. "My mom had similar sentiments for me and my brothers when we were younger. Are you staying for the finals or do you need to go home?"

"Will I have time to change after the game before the postgame celebration?"

Nothing wrong with what she's wearing right now. Nothing at all. "Definitely. The last thing anyone wants is a large group of smelly participants at Endzone. I'm thinking Leo wouldn't let us in." Leo is the owner of Endzone and engaged to Lily Cappelli.

She smiles and laughs. "Then I can stay."

"Sweet. I need to get to warm-ups before Greyson yells at me again. He gets a kick out of having one up on any coworker outside of the precinct."

"Good luck, Callan."

"See you after." I take a step away but turn back. "Thank you for staying."

"I may not understand it all, but it's fun. You're welcome. Go. Don't get in trouble on my account."

"It would be worth it." I wink at her and jog to the other side of the field. I would bet no one has put her first in quite some time. As I near the scorer's table, Penn and Booker—who are on the opposing team—stop me.

"What's going on with you two?" Booker asks.

"I don't know yet. I met her this morning."

Penn acknowledges the information. "She's special. Don't hurt her. She's been through enough in her life already."

His opinion is markedly correct, and I barely know her aside from her love of basketball, her amazing son, and tangentially her profession. Those attributes pale in comparison to my unyielding physical attraction to her. "Not my intention. I saw your warning earlier. Care to clue me in?"

Penn shakes his head and continues stretching. "Not my story to tell. She'll share when she's ready."

My analytical brain is spinning theories and ideas faster than before. After a few moments, I push the thoughts away. "Thanks, guys."

"No worries. Ready to lose?" Booker asks.

"No chance." I fist bump them both before heading over to my bench.

Smithson steps beside me. "Consorting with the enemy?"

"No. They were asking my intentions for the lovely Alannah."

He tilts his head in question, urging me to share more.

"Seems like a big brother/old friends thing rather than a 'stay away from my woman' warning."

"Understood. Did you invite her to join us later?"

"I did."

"Well, let's win this game so you can get to your date."

"Not a date. More like a group thing."

"Are you sure?"

His question makes me wonder and then makes me anxious, which is completely out of character for me.

From the initial snap, things fall into place for the EMTs. They run all over us, and by halftime, we're toast. The only bright spot is Alannah sitting in the stands cheering when appropriate. By the time the final whistle blows, our team looks disheveled and downtrodden.

After the congratulatory high fives and trophy presentation to the EMTs, we break down the remaining items, then go our separate ways to meet for dinner.

CHAPTER FOUR

ALANNAH

The YPD was crushed in the final game. It wouldn't surprise me if Callan wants to beg off the party at Endzone. I intend to help clean the remaining items, but the guys have it handled by the time I make my way across the field.

"Thanks for not running at the half," Callan states as he approaches.

I grin at him. "Honestly, I considered it. But this is better than what I planned to do this afternoon."

"Which was?"

"Cleaning and laundry."

"Happy to give you an excuse. We're meeting at seven."

"Sure. Casual work?" My mind scans my closet. I need Del.

He falls into step beside me and escorts me to my car. "Yes." When I stop near the driver's side, he reaches for the handle and opens my door.

"Thank you." I nestle into my seat.

"I'll pick you up at a quarter of seven."

"Okay."

He carefully closes the door and takes a step away.

Lowering my window, I ask, "Don't you need my address?"

He turns and flashes a sexy grin in my direction. "I know where you live."

I raise an eyebrow.

He answers the unasked question. "It was on the community service form for today. I certified them for Gugliotti."

"Okay." Hesitation is evident in my voice.

He returns to the door. "I remember basics about everyone from forms and reports. It helps with my job."

His explanation is reasonable. The sheer amount of information I have access to in my client files is off the charts. "You didn't need me to give you my phone number earlier, did you?"

Callan leans closer. "No, but I'm glad you sent it to me." He pauses. "Feel better?"

"Yeah. I'll see you later." Before I get worried again, I pull out of the spot and use voice commands. "Call Del."

"Hey, Lan, how was the game?"

"Fun. Do you know Officer Craven?"

"Ooooh, girl! He's hot! Blond, built, dreamy light-colored eyes. He's one of Grant's coworkers, right?"

His eyes are a unique hazel—light brown with golden flecks. "That's disturbingly accurate, Del. Yes, he is."

"Why are you asking?"

"I think I have a date with him tonight."

I imagine my bestie's eyes widening.

"You think? Pour it out even without the virgin margaritas." We stole the term from the first season of *Sweet Magnolias*. The main female characters spill the good and the bad of their lives at the end of each episode over margaritas.

I share our conversations from the day and how I thought it was a group thing that morphed into a date.

"Do you want it to be a date?" she asks.

"Yes...."

"But?"

"He's the community resource officer and has a preexisting relationship with Caden."

"Nope, not enough. The fact he knows about Caden is a tick mark in the favorable column in my opinion. It also means Caden likes him. What else? What scares you about him?"

True. Everything. "When he shook my hand, I swear—"

"Did the earth move under your feet?"

I burst out in laughter. Only Del would quote Carole King lyrics in everyday conversation. I turn onto my street. "Something like that. The air between us is electric, and when we were chatting, it was easy, for lack of a better adjective."

"Date or not, you should go and have a good time. If it isn't a date and you want one, ask him. You're a catch, girl!"

Every woman needs a bestie like Delilah. A no-holds-barred, tell-it-like-it-is cheerleader extraordinaire.

"Thanks, Del. What do I wear?"

"Awww. You're nervous too!"

Off the charts.

"Go with dark jeans and either the emerald V-neck or the peach, open-back top but bring a cardi."

"You're my rock, Del! Love you."

"Love you back. Have a good time."

I end the call and make my way inside. I switch the single load of laundry from the washing machine to the dryer. With a glance at the clock, I calculate if I have enough time to dry my hair. If I hurry a little, I can pull it off.

With five minutes to spare, I hit the bottom step, wearing the peach shirt Del suggested with my booties in hand as Callan rings the doorbell. I peer out the sidelight, then open the door. "Hey, come in. I only need to put on my shoes."

"No need to rush. I'm early. I'll wait."

I hop into the kitchen, tugging on one bootie, and grab my phone. Leaning against the island, I pull on the other. As I rejoin Callan in the foyer, I take in his attire. Dark jeans hug his muscular thighs, and his pale blue shirt fits like it was specifically tailored for him.

"All set?" he asks, his voice deep and smooth.

"Yes, but… can I ask you an off-the-wall question?"

"You can ask anything you want. First, you look lovely."

"Thank you. You do as well." I feel my cheeks heat with my poor choice of words.

Of course, he picks up on my physical reaction, steps closer, and sets his hand on my forearm. "Lovely is a fine adjective."

He listens well.

I shake my head. "I assure you, I'm normally more eloquent."

"Except when you're nervous?" He's perceptive too.

"Yes, except then."

"Why are you nervous? Do I make you nervous?"

I lift my eyes to his, and they pin to mine. "Yes, but not for the reasons you may think. Is this a date?"

He drags his free hand through his hair. "Smithson said my invitation wasn't clear. My intention was to spend time with you and then ask you on a proper date. A proper date would include much more planning and flowers."

"Okay."

He extends his hand to me, and I take it. After I lock the door, he tucks my hand around his arm, holding it in place, and leads me to his SUV. Not a date but... his manners are impeccable. After opening the passenger door for me, he hurries around the front of the vehicle and hops in. "Have you been to Endzone before?"

"No."

"It's a craft brewery and whiskey distillery. The food is amazing. Gugliotti set up a buffet for us."

"Awesome."

Callan reaches over the center console and covers my hand with his. Thankfully, my palm is down. Otherwise, my body would confirm I'm still anxious. It appears the trembling is enough to concern him.

"Want to share why you're nervous? We don't have to go to the party. We can do something else, or I can take you back home."

I shake my head but say nothing in response. Callan pulls into the lot for Short Sands Beach and parks along the sidewalk lined with benches facing the ocean.

"Do you want me to take you home?"

"No." I exhale sharply. "You're the first man who didn't run the other way."

He shifts to face me and takes both my hands in his. "Meaning?"

Where to start? I can't divulge our entire story right now. "Caden. You already know I'm a mom."

"Yes. A smart, vibrant, capable, and beautiful one. Caden is a great young man. You've done well raising him on your own."

"Thank you."

"Why does me knowing about Caden worry you?"

"From the outset, I know we could make it past tonight. A second date—first actual date in our case—never happened before, and its uncharted territory for me."

Surprise crosses his face. "You've never been on a second date because of Caden?"

"Pretty much."

"We don't have to call spending time together dates if it assuages your fears."

"I appreciate the offer, but I needed you to know. Talking with you today was…."

"Effortless," he supplies.

"Yes, and our potential scares me a little."

"Good."

"Good?"

"When you chased your dream of playing college ball, were you scared?"

Terrified at the prospect of playing division one basketball with an infant. Good grief. "Yes."

"When you took your first step into law school, were you scared?"

"Yes."

"When you put Caden on the bus for kindergarten, were you terrified for him to be out of your sight for so long?"

"Hell yes."

Callan's sexy laugh echoes around me. "If it isn't scary, is it worth doing?"

"No, not at all." Before I think better of it, I lean forward and press a chaste kiss to Callan's cheek. "Thank you for sticking with me."

"You're welcome. What do you want to do?"

"We should go to the party, or people will talk. They may already given our late arrival."

He winks at me. "Let them."

"I'm more of a low-profile person these days."

"Same actually. We can set them straight if necessary."

"Okay."

Callan shifts back into the driver's seat but doesn't let go of my hand. The party is in full swing when we arrive at Endzone. Luckily, everyone is too busy enjoying themselves to notice us.

His hand skims the exposed skin of my lower back and sends warmth through me. It's a virtual impossibility for Callan to miss my physical reaction, especially since he picked up on my nervousness earlier. Callan leans in and asks, "What can I get you to drink?"

"A Sprite, please."

"I'll be right back." He leaves me near a table against the back wall. I scan the walls and the brewery. Half of the walls are decorated with football memorabilia, but it's elegant not tacky.

"Hey. Fancy seeing you here."

"Hi, Séamus. Congrats on the win."

"Thanks."

I'm grateful Callan arrives before he can ask any questions of me. I wouldn't know how to answer them.

"Penn."

"Craven." I take my drink, and Séamus takes off to talk to some of his teammates. "Something I said?" Callan quips.

"No, he's basking in the glow of the win." I dig my fingers into the nape of my neck. "Sorry, I didn't mean that how it sounded."

"It sounded accurate. I would be if the situation were reversed. Hungry? The buffet is open."

"Sure. Lead the way." We follow through the line and heap food onto our plates. Callan finds a table on the patio tucked in the corner. A few bites into the delicious food, I ask, "Tell me something basic about you."

"Basic? I love coffee but don't like donuts."

"The stereotype doesn't apply to you? How do you take it?"

"No, not at all. Now if you happen upon the Perk and a savory scone is available, that's my pastry vice. I'll drink it black, but I prefer some cream and one sugar. You?"

"Same actually. The coffee, not the pastry. I'm more of a chocolate-filled croissant type of girl. Kelsey's are unmatched."

"Most everything she makes is. Who are the most important people in your life?"

I pause. "Caden, obviously. Uncle Paul and Aunt Clem. I wouldn't be where I am without them. What about you?" Ideally, he won't call me on the fact I didn't mention my parents or siblings, at least not tonight.

"My family. My parents are amazing and supportive. They raised the… my siblings and I to find our passions and run with them wherever we would end up." His response is flat, no true emotion behind his words. Intriguing.

"You mentioned brothers."

A blip of sadness cast over his face. "Yes, I have two brothers, Patrick and Liam."

Like he didn't press me, I don't press him. There's more to his family story than he shared. I completely understand.

He continues between bites. "Patrick is an architect. He's divorced, and his twin daughters are ten. Liam works in construction."

"Both older than you?"

"Yeah. Why law?" His question is thwarted when a younger guy approaches our table. I saw him at the field earlier today but don't know his name.

"Craven, my man! Why are you hiding your gorgeous woman out here? I would be showing her off to everyone."

Callan rises from his seat and positions himself between his coworker and me. He isn't aware, but I can take care of myself. Yet his ingrained protective gentlemen is sexy as sin. "Greyson, I'm going to call you an uber. Go home and sober up before shift tomorrow."

"I'm off tomorrow."

Callan looks over his shoulder at me. "I'll be right back."

Silently, I nod.

He grabs Greyson's bicep and handily escorts him away. I grip the edge of the table and settle the warring thoughts in my head. People like Greyson and his behavior is one reason I avoid bars and clubs. It isn't enough to forgo alcohol. I don't like other's drinking around me either. I don't ask anyone to refrain for my comfort though. I noticed Callan opted for soda as well. Callan's reaction to Greyson is similar to what mine would be if I knew Greyson personally—pissed off and unrelenting.

I'm not sure how much time passes before Callan rejoins me at the table. The remainder of his food is cold.

"Sorry about him."

"Nothing for you to be sorry for. He needs to own his actions, and no one else."

Keen and unadulterated understanding meets my gaze. Basketball may not be the only thing we have in common. Tragedy, it would seem, has scarred us both. The deeper question remains: was it personal or on the job for Callan?

"You asked why law before we were interrupted."

"I would like to hear the answer, but would you mind if we leave first?"

"No."

He's back on his feet beside me. His hand settles around my waist as he guides me through the crowd. When we near the bar and the space to walk decreases, he draws me closer, his other hand gripping my hip. Despite the reason for our hasty exit, his hands on me feel downright perfect.

Lachlan Hagen calls out, "Craven, you good?" Hagen is a YPD officer and a client. I assisted him with purchasing his home and legal paperwork for his daughter.

"Yup," he replies. There's an edge to his response, which leads me to believe my observation is wholly accurate.

We step outside into the humid air.

"You all right?" I murmur when we reach his SUV.

He nods tightly and opens my door. By the time he reaches the driver's side, he's calmed a bit, but he's still not the same guy he was before Greyson interrupted our conversation.

"Do you still carry court shoes with you everywhere?"

His interest piqued, he replies, "Yes. Where do you have in mind?"

"My place."

"I didn't see a hoop."

I smile widely. "We have one. It's in the backyard. When Caden was young, I needed to be sure the ball wouldn't roll into the street."

"Are you willing to lose?" he asks.

"I may be rusty, but who do you think taught Caden?"

"I won't go easy on you."

"I expect nothing less than your best. Then, when I win, you won't have any excuses."

"I'm gentleman enough to admit defeat, if necessary."

"I believe you." Then he gifts me with a wide, heart-stopping smile. Somehow, I have a feeling this game of one-on-one is going to be harder than I anticipate.

CHAPTER FIVE

CALLAN

Our drive to Alannah's gives me time to filter my anger toward Greyson. I'm not angry with him exactly. His behavior set me on edge. Even all these years later, drunken behavior sets me off. I park along the side of her driveway.

She moves to open her door.

I set my hand on her arm. "I'll get your door."

A look of appreciation and perhaps surprise splashes across her face. I can see her objection to being taken care of immediately, yet she doesn't voice it. One thing I would bet is true about Alannah, she'll speak her mind if she feels it's necessary. She also knows when to refrain as well. It probably makes her a talented attorney. The notion a woman can't be independent and her man—that's a stretch—is a gentleman seems contradictory to me. Her independence is sexy as hell and increases my desire to care for her and her son. Knowing when to let her lead will be key in the long term.

Her hand slides back into her lap. "Thank you."

I hurry to the trunk and pull out my bag with court shoes and a spare set of workout clothes, which I determine are clean after a discreet sniff test. Dropping the bag on the ground, I open her door and extend my hand to her. When she stands, the tiny space between our bodies sparks with tension and desire. Swallowing hard, I take a step back and close the door without releasing her hand. I scoop up my bag, and she leads me up her front steps. The middle step wobbles when I reach it.

"I've been meaning to fix that. Haven't had the time," she mutters and continues inside.

Isn't she full of incongruent surprises? On one hand she's a tough-as-nails attorney—at least our community seems to think so. Yet she's also a hardworking single mom, former division one collegiate basketball player, and apparently capable of fixing a broken staircase. What other impressive traits does the exceptional Alannah possess?

When I was here earlier, I didn't truly take in her home. It's a large Cape, cozy and bright. Exactly like her, at least in my eyes.

"I need to change."

"There's a bathroom around this corner, and the kitchen is straight ahead," she offers.

"Thanks." I change and take a seat in the kitchen. It appears newly renovated or updated. She incorporated the formal dining room and created a massive eat-in kitchen. It has stainless appliances, including a double gas range with separate double oven, light gray cabinetry with a massive island, and prep sink. In short, it's a chef's dream. Lost in my cooking daydream, Alannah appears beside me.

"All set?" Her words draw my focus to her. While the dark jeans and peach top were perfection—particularly since they provided the ability to feel her warm skin beneath my fingertips when I guided her out of the brewery—she looks equally as good in shorts, a threadbare T-shirt, and sports bra with her hair piled in a messy topknot.

"Yes. Lead the way." I would be lying if I said I wasn't watching her walk in front of me. She's statuesque, but her curves could make any man weep. If I thought the kitchen was amazing, the backyard is an oasis. We step onto a large patio complete with a firepit surrounded by six Adirondack chairs. There's an outdoor cooking area covered by a pergola. The inground pool is off to the right, but the full-size court rivets my attention. "Do you ever want to leave your home?"

She smiles at me over her shoulder. "Not if I can help it." As she walks, she rolls her shoulders, circles her arms, and twists her taut torso.

The court is stellar and painted in white and blue on one half for Caden and maroon and gold on the other for her.

"There's a rack of basketballs in the box behind you."

As if the other features aren't enough, she flicks a switch near the far hoop and the entire court is illuminated as if we're indoors.

"Wow! This is sweet."

"Thanks." Silently, she grabs a ball and takes a shot. It rims off the edge, and she chases it down. After a few more stretches, she shoots from behind the three-point arc. *Swish.*

"Shooting guard?" I ask.

"Yeah. You?"

"Forward." I dribble toward the basket and take a layup. Then I skirt around her back to the top of the key. I square up and shoot. The shot pings off the backboard toward Alannah. She skillfully catches the ball before releasing her own shot.

"Impressive." The more shots I get off, the calmer I become. Alannah may be as attuned to me as I am to her. It's nothing short of shocking. "How did you know I needed to play?"

"It still works for me when I need to settle my mind or work out a client issue."

I set my ball on the rack and make my way across to her. "Did Greyson offend you?"

"By calling me gorgeous and yours? I haven't taken the time to dissect his words, truthfully. I was more concerned about you." She checks the ball to me and guards me loosely as I drive to the basket.

"I feel a sense of responsibility for the younger guys. It isn't logical, I know. We're supposed to be an example for the community, and he was drunk and disrespectful to you. Me too when I consider his words more. His disrespect irked me more than it should for how long I've known you. It makes me want to deck him, not protect him from his own stupidity."

I move back to the top of the key and drive to the basket. This time she guards me tighter, but I still make the short-range jumper. There isn't a doubt in my mind she's more focused on our conversation than the game.

"You should tell him when he's sober and willing to listen." She easily steals the ball when I lazily attempt to make my way back to the top of the key. Alannah checks the ball to me, fakes a jumper, and maneuvers around me flawlessly, then sinks the layup. She returns the ball and hustles to midcourt.

I send the ball back to her. "You going to shoot from way out there?" I goad her.

"I could, but I won't... at least not yet." She dribbles toward me and spins around me like I'm invisible and drains the bucket. "Ready to actually play defense?" The smirk on her face leads me to believe I severely underestimated her skills—not because she's a woman, but because she's humble. Other than indicating she taught Caden, she hasn't mentioned basketball. A search of the Boston College women's basketball records might help me going forward. Her career statistics to begin with.

"How skillful are you?"

She lifts her shoulder and winks at me. "Defend and you can find out. Perhaps you should forget I'm a woman for a little while."

Never going to happen. "Impossible." If a higher power built my dream woman, it would be Alannah—from her sharp wit and admirable profession to her killer body and unusual skill set.

Her reaction to my reply is the smallest chink in her demeanor. Our attraction is mutual without a doubt. My response affords me the slightest opening. I steal the ball back and sink the layup. She hangs her head.

"Perhaps you should forget you like me for a little while as well."

"Also impossible."

Over the next twenty minutes, I figure out how to push my emotions and feelings about Greyson to the sideline. We start a fresh game, and she easily takes the lead, draining long-range shots with a few easy jumpers and layups mixed in. It would be a lie to say this is my best game. It isn't.

When defending, she doesn't care about anything but defending. Our attraction doesn't matter in the slightest, nor does the undercurrent of lust each time her body is surrounded by mine and her perfume envelopes me. Not even when I guard her and her full breasts are at eye level does it matter to Alannah. Finally, when I think I have the upper hand for a possession, she traps me in the corner. I'm out of options, she knows it, and I'm about to concede.

"OC, baseline pass!" Caden shouts.

Blindly, I pass the ball around her, and he shoots a layup.

The pout on Alannah's face is priceless as the ball swishes through the net.

"Hi, Mom. I'm home!" Caden fist bumps me beneath the basket with the ball perched on his hip.

"How did you know it was me?" I ask him.

"I saw your SUV earlier today. I don't believe anyone else around here has a SNHU sticker in the window."

"Well played, Callan." She glances at her watch. "You're early. How was the bonfire?"

"It was okay. Too many people not acting right, so I left."

"Proud of you," she states.

"Thanks. I am too. You both up for a game of H-O-R-S-E?"

"I'm in," Alannah replies.

"Why do I get the feeling we're both going to get schooled, Caden?" I ask him.

"Mom and I are fairly matched as long as you don't shoot threes. She will obliterate us both."

I lean closer to him. "That information would've been helpful a bit earlier tonight."

Caden laughs. He makes his way to the bench and sets down his phone and hoodie.

I pass the ball to Alannah who is positioned at the top of the key. Without a thought, she rises and drains a long-range three. Both Caden and I are at H after missing the same shot. We continue playing, and despite our intention to be as creative as possible with our eyes closed or behind-the-back antics, we're losing. Neither of us can match Alannah's stroke from downtown; Caden is close, but I'm pathetic in comparison. She's sitting at H while Caden is at R, and if I miss this shot, I'm the loser.

"Told you, OC. She's amazing! Do you still hold the record, Mom?"

Record? He's right, though, she is amazing, but not just at basketball. However, that is not an appropriate sentiment to share with her son.

"Not sure. Haven't checked," she answers.

Caden trots over to his phone and promptly searches. "You still hold the record."

Alannah nods curtly. Her athletic achievements are bitter for her somehow. Another layer of this unique woman I ache to peel back.

I take the shot and miss. Game over. I lose.

"There's always next time, OC," Caden offers.

"Not sure I plan to play H-O-R-S-E with either of you again."

The three of us laugh, clean up, and move inside for refreshments. After downing a sports drink and cereal, which would make my stomach turn eaten at the same time, Caden clears his bowl and heads to bed.

"Later, OC."

"Bye."

"Night, Mom. Love you."

"Good night, Caden. Love you." Alannah retrieves a second water before calling me on my facial expression. "You seem surprised."

"Only because he said it with me here."

"Fair. Unfortunately for him, he isn't taller than me like most of his friends are to their moms. There's no throwing his arm over my shoulder to show his feelings or prove he's grown. I'll take any words of affection or hugs I can get from him, especially the unsolicited ones."

With my water empty as well, I add the bottle to the recycle bin near the trash. "I should get home. I'm on shift tomorrow."

"You didn't have to stay to play."

I eliminate nearly all the space between us, set my fingers beneath her chin, and lift until our gazes meet. "I wanted to. As you correctly determined, I needed to release the tension. I had a great time today in spite of our expeditious exit from Endzone."

"I did too."

"Still interested in an actual date?"

A small smile curls at the corner of her mouth. "Yes, I am."

"I'll know my schedule for the next month tomorrow. Then we can pick a day."

"Okay."

I press a sweet kiss to her cheek. With my bag in hand, we walk toward the front door. "I'll call you tomorrow."

"Good night, Callan."

"Good night, Alannah." I step onto the porch and wait for her to engage the two locks before climbing into my car.

CHAPTER SIX

ALANNAH

While it's only a promise of a date, last night after Callan left, I shut off the dating apps I recently rejoined. I truly never wanted to use the apps as a means of meeting dates anyway. Besides, I've only received inappropriate pictures and direct messages. If Callan and I don't work out, I'll succumb to Del's incessant pressure to fix me up.

I opt for a short run this morning since we were playing basketball late last night. Callan fits with us. I can't explain it, but he does. When I round the final corner of the three-mile route, I notice a car pulling out of my driveway. Concerned, I pick up my pace instead of slowing down.

The bag on my stoop is recognizable from the street. The Perk. Curious, I eliminate the space, grab the bag, and read the attached note.

Alannah,
   Hopefully this arrives before you have breakfast. Have a great day.
   I'll
call you later.
Callan

As if he wasn't already in the forefront of my mind, he has breakfast delivered. I scoop up the bag and accompanying coffee and step inside.

"Sweet! You went for goodies." Caden reaches for the bag.

I shake my head and shield the bag. "I didn't. They were delivered. I don't know what's inside."

"Who sent you breakfast?"

"Callan."

"Oh."

I peer inside the bag and find not only a chocolate croissant but a Fruity-Pebbles-topped donut. "Did you by chance mention your favorite donut to Callan?"

"Of course. We talk about tons of things. Mostly basketball, but we talk about Kyla, school, favorite foods, and pizza toppings. Why?"

I pull the donut out of the bag and hand it to him.

"Wow, he remembers that?" He takes a huge bite.

"Is it weird for you?"

Caden replies with a full mouth of cereal sprinkled donut, "What?"

"Having Callan here. Me potentially dating him."

"No. He's cool. What do you mean 'potentially'?"

"He asked, and I said yes, but if it'll be uncomfortable—"

"You should've said yes. You two have a lot in common."

"Like?" I might as well use the resources I have.

"Both of you love basketball, think I'm the coolest guy on the planet, and read thrillers."

I smirk at him. Shock doesn't begin to cover my internal response to my son's reaction. Instead of pressing him for more similarities, I let it go. I would rather learn from Callan. I send him a quick text while my breakfast warms in the microwave.

Me: Thank you for breakfast.

Callan: You're welcome.

I savor each bite before starting the tasks I should've completed yesterday. It was worth it though. Near one, after I'm nearly done with the main rooms, Caden bounds into the kitchen.

"Can I go to the village for some pizza with the guys?"

"Which ones?"

"Jonah, Silas, and Tiny." As you might expect, Tiny—whose name is Anthony—is anything but tiny.

"Sure. Don't forget to fill out the coach request form for camp. We need to leave first thing next Sunday."

"I'll get it done tonight when I get home."

"Have fun and drive safely."

"Thanks. Mom?"

I shake my head. "Bring me my purse."

Magically, it appears before me as if a genie conjured it up for him. I dig out my wallet and hand him some cash.

"Thanks. You're the best!"

I shrug, and he's out the door. For the first few months, I freaked every time he pulled out of the driveway. My panic is significantly less now but will likely never dissipate.

I finish cleaning, shower, and collapse onto the couch. As I'm about to doze off, my front door sails open. It can only be one of two people, and one just left.

"Hey, hey! I'm here to get the lowdown with snacks!" Delilah shouts.

"Hey, girl. Did I miss a text?"

"Nope, I knew you wouldn't spill over the phone, so here I am."

She's right. Del comes prepared. With snacks and my favorite strawberry lemonade, we curl up on the patio. After a few crackers topped with fixings from her homemade charcuterie board, I start to share details from yesterday in painstaking detail.

"He said 'it would be worth getting yelled at to spend more time with you'?" Del reacts.

"He did."

"I like him already."

I finish sharing the rest of the night and attempt to leave out my reactions to him, but Del calls me on it.

"Spill the rest. Caden isn't here."

I sigh. "Spending time with Callan is… effortless. I don't mean a relationship wouldn't be work. It would be with anyone, but we—"

"Mesh well. You know I want the dirty details, Lan, not the sappy ones."

"There aren't any. Not really. After my mini-breakdown, I kissed his cheek. Before he left last night, he did the same."

"Okay, fine. Only you could manage to find a rare, true gentleman. But is there fire?"

Hell yes! "More than I've ever felt before, and we haven't kissed." The awareness coursing through my entire body when he's near me is unmatched.

"Even with Daniel?"

"Especially with Daniel. Daniel may be Caden's father, but the sex was inexperienced, rushed, uncoordinated, and frankly unfulfilling. I've gotten myself off better than Daniel ever did." I sigh and continue, "Then, Caden was in school, I was working to build my practice, and my status as a single mom became problematic. Never mind the fact I didn't have any time to myself. I love Paul and Clem, but asking them to watch Caden so I could date didn't seem appropriate. Only Callan hasn't run."

My phone ringtone breaks into our conversation, and I answer, "Hi, Callan."

Del is keenly attempting to listen to my conversation. Thankfully, his voice is quiet.

"Are you going to be home tonight?"

"Yes."

"Perfect. Can I stop by and fix the front step?"

"You don't need to do that. I can do it myself."

"I know you can, and your fierce independence is sexy. However, it needs to be taken care of. You're welcome to help."

"Will you be here whether I consent or not?"

"Alannah, I may have met you yesterday, but I am who I am. I want to fix the step for you."

In my head, he ran his hand through his hair when he said my full name. I heard the underlying sentiment too. He wants to take care of me—us. "Fine. You can fix it with my help, but I'm cooking dinner afterward."

"Deal, if we're cooking afterward. I don't expect you to cook for me."

Images of the future flood my brain, but I push them away. It's too soon to think like that. "I accept your terms."

He laughs. "I'll be there in under an hour. Thank you for allowing me to help."

"Thank you for wanting to. See you soon." I end the call and turn back to Del who is bouncing on the couch like a kid waiting to be released at an amusement park.

"For the love of all that's holy, Lan, Let the man take care of you. You deserve it."

"I'm trying, Del."

"I know." She rises to leave. "I'm out even though I would love to see Officer Craven up close…. Oh my!" An image of something popped into her head. "Yes! Make sure he takes off his shirt."

"You're terrible. Get out of here!"

"You know you wanna know. Love you, Lan."

She isn't wrong. I do very much want to know if Callan's torso matches the image I have in my mind after the slightest glimpses last night. "Love you back, Del."

Uncontrollable butterflies flutter in my belly. Not only are those new territory, but a guy who understands and accepts my need to do all the things myself is going to take some effort. Settling my nerves as much as possible, I clear the rest of our snack dishes.

My phone indicates a new text.

Caden: Can I go over to Jonah's until curfew?

Me: Sure.

Caden: Thanks.

I rummage through the freezer and search for something to cook for dinner. For two. Only not the two it normally is. I transfer chicken to the fridge. Caden eats fairly well, but while I search for adult sides, the doorbell chimes.

"Hi," I greet him after opening the door and leaning against it. Yet he doesn't move. "Would you like to come in, Callan?" As I close the door behind him, I notice the bag of tools at the foot of the steps.

"Thank you." As he steps inside, he inquires, "Is Caden here?"

I tilt my head in question. "No, why?"

"Verifying where the boundaries are." He steps closer to me, curls his arm over my hip, and draws me close. Heat settles over me. His other hand slides up my arm and rests against the nape of my neck.

The simple fact he asked puts him far above any other man I've ever met. Unmatched chemistry buzzes between us. Eliminating nearly all the space between our lips, per Alex Hitchen's instructions in *Hitch*, Callan pauses a hairsbreadth away from me. Meeting his gaze, desire strikes me in the center of my chest. I steal the remaining air and press my lips to his.

At first our kiss is sweet and nearly chaste until I pull his lower lip between my teeth. His hand tightens perfectly around my neck so he can direct my head where he wants it to be. The penetrating, steal-my-breath kisses are knee weakening and make my heart pound in my chest. It's as if the rest of the world fades away and only Callan and I remain. We kiss and kiss some more on a winding path from tender to passionate and back again until we're both panting.

"I wanted to kiss you properly last night," he murmurs, the tips of our noses skimming one another.

"Properly feels amazing. How does improperly feel?" The volume of my voice drops as I finish my question.

Callan adds a sliver of space between us. "Small steps first, beautiful."

"Small steps," I repeat and brush my lips across his. "How was your shift?"

"I was on desk duty. During the summer, it's typically boring. What about you?"

"I had an impromptu takeout breakfast. How well do you know my son?"

He lifts an eyebrow. "Well, why?"

"The donut was a nice touch. He was legitimately surprised you remembered his favorite."

"Well, I plan to keep doing it, if you'll allow me to."

"Doing what?"

"Taking care of both of you."

"Starting with the front stairs?" I question.

"Exactly. Well, breakfast and the stairs. You're going to need shoes if you want to help. We wouldn't want to risk your cute, pink, pedicured toes."

He noticed the color of my pedicure. "Okay. There are tools and tread in the garage. I can meet you there," I suggest.

"I'll wait."

I grab socks and sneakers and rejoin him near the front door. After a trip to the garage and an assessment of the front steps, we rip off the middle step.

"Do you have an extension for the drill, so we don't have to remove the rest of the treads?" he asks.

"I believe I do. I'll be right back."

When I return, Callan seems shocked I got the correct item or I have it, I'm not sure which. He resecures the stringers to the base of the porch, then asks, "Who taught you to repair things?"

"Me. Well, YouTube mostly." I inhale sharply. "I need you to understand, it's only been me for the last... for too long. I'm not used to someone, especially a man, who is willing to... help, accepts me—"

"And Caden?"

I drop my head slightly.

"I know. If I pushed too hard, I'm sorry. You're not only a talented, record-holding basketball player—a fact you failed to mention—a respected attorney, and a single mom, but you're self-sufficient. It's insanely attractive, and most men would assume you were taken even without a ring on your finger."

"I never really thought about it that way."

"Can you hold the other side?" he asks before he cuts the tread to size.

I move to the far side of the tread as he cuts off the excess. After verifying it fits, Callan attaches his side and hands the drill over to me. I repeat on my side of the stairs. We stand back and inspect the finished repair.

"My help wasn't so bad, was it?" he asks.

"Now for the other things on the 'to fix' list."

"Lay it on me." No hesitation in his words.

This man could be everything I ever wanted for myself and for Caden. I press a kiss to his cheek and laugh. "There isn't a list. I'm joking."

"Alannah, would you share if there were?"

I turn more fully toward him, cup his jaw with my hands, and meet his emerald-tinted hazel eyes. "Yes, now I would. Thank you for allowing me to help."

"I should be thanking you for allowing me to help."

"Ready to clean up and cook?"

"Sure." We clean up the front walkway and head inside. He pauses near the guest bathroom. "Do you have a non-guest towel I can use?"

Warmth cascades through me. I may not have met his mother yet, but she taught him right. Then again, his manners are unparalleled. It begs the question, is he a gentleman in the bedroom too? How well he kissed me would lead me to think he may not be. I clench my thighs together and push the thought out of my mind. "Yeah. I'll get you one."

I pull one from the closet and hand it to him.

"I'll only be a few minutes. Then we can focus on dinner," he states after taking the towel.

"No problem. Water, iced tea, or lemonade?"

"Iced tea, please."

I force my feet to move toward the kitchen. I exhale slowly as I wash up a bit before pulling down two glasses and filling them. The creak of the bathroom door draws my attention to Callan, his shirt not fully pulled down.

"You didn't need to hurry." Although I'm grateful for the visual confirmation of the lower third of his torso. The divots and ridges of his abs are precisely as I imagined, as is the coveted V leading southward. Now to get my hands on him as soon as possible. *Small steps.*

"What are we cooking?"

"Caprese chicken with balsamic glaze, asparagus, and crusty bread."

"Sounds good. Where are your saucepans, vinegar, and brown sugar?"

It takes me a minute to figure out what he plans to make. "I have glaze in the corner cabinet. You don't need to make it from scratch."

"Mine will taste better, I promise." He kisses me lightly and expectantly awaits my response to his question.

After I guide him to the ingredients he needs, I prepare the chicken, season it, and set it in the oven. While it bakes, I halve the cherry tomatoes and slice the mozzarella. "A closet chef?" He has expertly made a glaze from scratch.

"Yes, actually."

"Why are you a cop instead? I promise to try not to interrogate you as if you're a witness."

He offers me a panty-melting smile. I'm confident he doesn't realize how it affects me. "I haven't interrogated someone in quite some time, but same." He turns off the burner, removes the saucepan from the heat, and shifts around me to cut the bread. "I love cooking. Baking, I'll leave for Kelsey. I didn't want it to be my career and end up hating it."

"Your logic is sound."

"Why law? I don't recall ever getting an answer."

"I didn't answer you. I was busy beating you at basketball." I smirk at him and pull the nearly cooked chicken from the oven. I add the cheese atop the meat and add tomatoes to blister, then continue. "I wanted to save the Hawksbill Turtle. I figured the best way to accomplish my goal was to become an attorney and protect their environment somehow. When I finally reached law school, I realized my plan was filled with roadblocks and politics, which I despise. The reality was much more difficult than I imagined, but I fell in love with the intricacies of the law."

The timer sounds, and I pull the pan from the oven.

"Where are the plates?" he asks.

"Above the dishwasher."

He sets two plates on the island, and I serve chicken and veggies on each one.

"Ready to throw away your store-bought glaze?" he asks.

"Depends."

His head lifts in question. "On?" Expertly, he drizzles the dark glaze over both servings.

"If it wows me and you would be willing to teach me to make it myself, then yes, I'll exchange the bottle for the real thing."

"I will teach you, but I'll happily make it for you whenever you want it."

A sense of comfort and... familiarity spreads over me. "Why does it feel like we've known one another for longer than we have?"

"I don't know, but I like it."

"Me too. I accept your offer. Let's eat." I grab both plates and weave around the island to the dining table. I set down the plates and turn back for silverware. When I return, he's standing behind a pulled-out chair. He takes a seat beside me instead of across from me and waits for me to try the chicken.

"Oh my... Callan. This is amazing!"

A slight redness creeps onto his face. "If you think the glaze is amazing, wait until I cook you an entire meal."

"Tell me when and where."

"A second date before the first one even happens, I'm in."

I laugh.

"Would you be interested in scheduling a third one as well?"

"Bold, Callan. I like it. When and where?"

"Smithson's wedding. It's the first Saturday of November at the Cliff House."

"Are you in the wedding?"

"I am."

"You clad in a perfectly tailored tuxedo, I'm absolutely in."

"I knew you liked me a little."

It's more than a little, but I won't admit it, at least not yet. I laugh again and dig into my plate. We eat and talk about anything and everything from the basic favorite season—both of us love fall—to the benefits of using fouls to extend a game. There we disagree. With clear plates and clean dishes, we move outside onto the rattan couch. Callan sits against the arm, and I face him with one leg bent in front of me. We banter more, covering a myriad of topics until Caden arrives home.

"Mom?" my son calls from inside.

"We're out here." I don't think he could miss Callan's SUV but just in case he does, I said 'we're'.

"Hi, Mom. Hey, OC."

"How was Jonah's?"

He shakes his head. "It was fine until Fiona stopped over uninvited."

"I thought they broke up," Callan states.

I cast a look at him. He knows all the high school gossip. I'm not truly surprised; he was at the school daily.

"Me too. Jonah thought so too." Caden's knowledge of the situation has been officially exhausted. Thus, ending the conversation. "Well, I'm gonna eat and then fill out the form for camp."

"Okay," I reply.

The screen door slams as he heads back inside.

"Should we add the screen door to the phantom 'to fix' list?"

I laugh. "Do I need a list to get you to visit?"

He leans forward, brackets my waist with his hands, and hauls me against his body. "No list required." His warm mouth is on mine, and he kisses me breathless again. Like before, his kiss makes me melt into a puddle, except nothing about this kiss is tentative. Callan moves with precision, and his skillful mouth leaves me wanting more… much more.

"Good."

"What camp?" he asks as if his breathing is normal.

I share the information about the basketball camp Caden's attending starting this weekend.

"I volunteered at the camp for a few summers after I graduated. It's a great camp for recognition. I'm not on shift, would you mind if I join you for the drive?"

"No, company would be nice."

"Does he want to play in college?"

"He's hard to gauge. His love of the game rivals mine, but he knows he isn't going to play professionally. He's realistic. I've encouraged him to keep his options open."

"Would you mind if I talk to him about it?"

I appreciate the request more than he knows. "Thank you for asking. Not at all. Maybe he'll share more with you because there's no expectations or reactions from his responses."

He nods. "Are you cold? Do you want to go inside?"

"Not even a little as long as I don't have to move."

"You in my arms is preferred."

We remain cuddled in our spot talking, laughing, and kissing—mostly kissing until Caden turns in for the night.

"I should go as well. I'll call you tomorrow." After hands down the best good-night kiss I've ever experienced, Callan slips out the front door.

CHAPTER SEVEN

CALLAN

At the end of my shift a few days later, I run into Greyson in the parking structure.

"Hey, Craven. How was your date?"

Before speaking, I push down the anger boiling within me. "Greyson, do you recall anything from the party at Endzone?"

"Not really. I was high on the ladies and solidly buzzed."

I'm not surprised he doesn't recall his actions, but his honesty is shocking. "You disrespected her and me. You owe Alannah an apology, me as well, but I'll settle for hers. We don't know one another well outside of this building. Very few things make me angry to the point where I need to remove myself from a situation. Your words and drunkenness definitely top the list."

He's stunned speechless.

"Yo, Greyson! Ya comin'?" Davis calls from the far end of the lot.

"Yup!" He turns without another word.

I take a few deep breaths and opt to hit the court rather than run off my anger. There should be a few pick-up games already started by the time I arrive. In the summer, as expected, the court is filled with players of all ages and skill levels and extras waiting to join in. Hopping out, I make my way around to the trunk and start to pull out my bag.

"Hey, OC! The guys and I are headed to the house because it's crowded. Want to join us?"

"Sure, thanks. Need a ride?"

"No, I'm set."

"I'll meet you there."

The ride isn't far. Plus, I haven't seen Alannah since Sunday. We've exchanged brief texts each morning, usually initiated by her, and we talk each night. She's been working late on an upcoming tumultuous divorce trial. I note Alannah isn't home yet when I park, but I don't question Caden on the house rules. Whatever the rules are, he appears to be following them. The boys don't go inside the house. They walk around the garage to the side gate. Caden parks in the garage and waves me inside. Alannah must have updated the house rules recently.

"You're allowed in the house. Some of those guys aren't," he informs me.

"Thanks. I'll be right out."

I set my bag on the floor near the island and grab a water. I step outside and join the game. The boys left me a spot on the opposing team from Caden. My age becomes readily apparent after a full court game with him and his friends. Thankfully, three of the other guys beg off to go home, so I duck inside to clean up. I pull a fresh towel from the linen closet and step into the guest bathroom. After tugging off my shirt, I step back out for my bag.

When I turn toward the bathroom again, I hear, "Hi, Callan." Her voice is shaky.

"Hi." I step closer to kiss her. "What?"

She pauses before whispering, "Have you looked in the mirror lately?"

My cheeks flame, and I decrease the space between us even more. "I don't need to see you shirtless to ask you the same question. Although I want to."

Now her face is as flushed as mine. I slide my hand up her arm and cup her face. Tentatively, her soft hands rest flat on my chest. I would stake my life savings that I'm not imagining her clenching her thighs together.

Curling my fingers around the nape of her neck, I kiss her like a man starved. Frankly, I might be. Four days is long... too long. True, we've talked each day, and our first date is on Saturday night, but I would prefer to see her each night. I understand her need to work on her case. It doesn't change what I want. Mid-kiss her fingernails score my pecs with half-moon marks and a muffled groan seeps from her lips when the sound of footsteps on the porch is unmistakable.

I add some space and ask, "How was your day?" as if the world doesn't fall away when I kiss her.

She takes a moment to respond. I'm ecstatic the world seems extinct for her as well. "Not too bad. Yours?"

"It was pretty good until I ran into Greyson again. I went to the courts, but Caden invited me here with the guys instead."

Our encounter with Greyson likely flashed through her mind. "Do you want to talk now? We didn't last weekend."

"We can, but later."

"Okay."

"You don't have to share when I do."

"It's only fair you should know at the same time I do," she offers.

I skim my lips over hers and return to the bathroom. The last woman I dated—hell, the last two—weren't as honest and forthright as Alannah seems to be. It makes sense, especially if no other man has seen her for what she is—everything any man could want or need.

When I exit the bathroom, the kitchen is swarming with teenage boys. I recognize Jonah, Silas, and Tiny. The other four, I don't know well. Their faces are familiar, but they haven't used the resource office at the school. They are likely who Caden meant when he said some of the guys aren't allowed in the house without Alannah here.

"Yes, six cheese pizzas, cheesy bread, and buffalo wings, extra hot," I hear Alannah order. She turns to me and mouths, "Anything else?"

I shake my head. Our pizza preferences appear the same if the wings are for her.

"Okay, guys, the drinks are in the fridge. I'll bring the pizzas out when they arrive."

A chorus of thank-yous echo in the kitchen, from "Thank you, Ms. Kramer" to "Thanks, Caden's mom." Per her request, the boys head back outside after grabbing waters and sports drinks from the fridge.

"Pizza work?" she asks.

"On one condition."

"Which is?"

"You share your wings with me."

"How do you know the wings are mine?"

"Extra hot." I grin at her. The double meaning fits perfectly.

Her response is simply dropping her head. It has become a passion of mine to remind her daily how I see her.

"Can you give me a few minutes to change into more comfortable but appropriate clothes?"

I frown. "You look perfect."

"Maybe in your eyes."

"I'll be right here."

What feels like an eternity later, but is realistically only ten minutes, Alannah returns wearing leggings and a long, off-the-shoulder shirt covering too much in my opinion. Her exposed shoulder shows a fitted tank top.

"Comfy?" I ask.

She shrugs, rounds the island, and starts searching for something.

I follow her and offer, "How can I help?" I set my hand on her waist and feel her vibrating with concern. "Alannah?"

She turns and snakes her arms around me. I slide my hand over her hip beneath the shirt and hold her against me. The softness and warmth of her skin nearly short-circuits my brain. Minutes pass, and she says nothing.

Knowing we have limited time before the delivery interrupts, I ask, "What are you nervous about?"

"Sharing my—our—story with you."

"You don't have to."

"I should. It'll give you the option of cancelling our dates."

"Nothing you say will make me change my mind about pursuing a relationship with you."

"Perhaps you should reserve your statement until you hear what I have to say."

"I'll repeat it again after you share how you and Caden got to today, word for word."

"Promise?" she asks weakly.

A man—or a few men—truly made her doubt her worth based solely on her son. Nothing could be farther from the truth in my eyes. "Promise." I kiss her lightly as the doorbell chimes. "I'll grab the pizza."

She nods and turns toward the tall cabinet. I hear her release a jagged breath as I walk away.

I answer the door and accept the pizzas. After depositing the wings and one pizza on the island, I follow Alannah, who located the paper plates and napkins while I was answering the door. The boxes barely touch the table before the ravenous bunch throw open the top one and dig in. It's rare for silence to surround a group of teenage boys, but feed them and you can achieve it for a about five minutes.

"We'll be inside," Alannah informs them.

"Thanks, Mom. OC."

"Welcome," she replies.

We each take a seat at the island, and she offers me the first pick of the wings. I take one and wait for her to choose.

"Wow! These are hot!" I admit after my first bite.

"Too hot for you?"

"Never! They must know you, because mine are never like this when I order them from the same place."

"The owner is a client. I'm sure my orders have stars to make sure they get it right."

"I see. Do you want to talk now or wait until the boys leave?"

"Now is fine if you still want to share," she replies.

I take a few minutes to gather my thoughts. "When you asked about my family—"

"You edited your words midsentence."

"I did. Why didn't you call me on it?"

"You didn't call me out on why I didn't mention my parents."

"You're right. I didn't. I saw the omission as purposeful." My eyes briefly close. "Omission isn't the right word. You weren't ready to share."

"I saw the unmistakable sheen of sadness when you corrected to brothers. You had a sister?"

I take a deep breath and share my family story for perhaps the second time to a woman with long term potential. "After three boys, my parents tried once more for a girl, and Sadie was born three years after me. She was a true tomboy. She had fiery red hair and sharp green eyes. She played sports with us and refused to wear a dress for longer than my mother would like to admit. When she was nearly thirteen, she begged to spend the weekend with her bestie's family at their cabin. Reluctantly, my parents agreed."

I hadn't realized it, but I stopped eating when I started sharing. Alannah threads her fingers with mine, urging me to continue.

"While on their way home, they were in a car accident. My sister didn't survive."

She lifts our linked hands to her lips and kisses the top of mine. "I'm sorry, Callan."

"Thank you. Unfortunately, there's more. Her bestie's dad was legally under the influence when the crash occurred, but later we learned his medications adversely reacted to the single drink he had at lunch midway through their trip home." To me, it doesn't matter.

"That's why you don't drink."

"Yes. What happened to your parents?"

Her fingers briefly tighten around mine, and she inhales sharply. "Sharing this will tell you nearly everything about me and Caden."

"I will never lie to you, Alannah. I'm not going anywhere."

The back door opens wide, and a few of the boys pop their heads inside to say thank you again and goodbye. Then Caden comes inside with a pizza box filled with trash. He empties it and trashes the box. After another trip, he says, "I'm going to practice outside for a bit."

"Okay," Alannah manages.

I feel her tense before she speaks again.

"The recruiters started watching me play basketball when I was a sophomore. I had a full ride offer from a perennial top twenty-five school by the end of the season. Three more filtered in by the time my junior year ended. I narrowed it down to the University of Connecticut and Boston College. I made an official visit to Boston College, and I loved it." Her eyes flutter closed.

I twist on the stool and pull hers closer, bracketing her thighs with mine, our hands still linked between us. "Take your time," I whisper and set a kiss to her forehead.

"At the time, I was dating Daniel. He was sweet to me and understood basketball was my life. I saw him at school and maybe once every other weekend, especially during the season. Near the end of my senior season, I realized I was pregnant, and had been for most of the season. Daniel and I talked about getting married so we could raise Caden in a two-parent household like both of us had. We also decided to keep the baby a secret as long as possible."

"You were afraid the colleges would pull their offers?"

"Yes. Did I broach the subject to find out? No, I didn't." She gathers her thoughts for a moment and then asks, "Will you take a walk with me?"

"Anywhere, anytime." It's in this moment I wonder how much Caden knows.

She informs Caden, and we're out the front door within a few minutes. With our hands intertwined, we walk down her tree-lined street. The sun is setting, and the summer humidity is dipping. When we reach the next block, she starts sharing again. "My parents, Daniel, and I visited UConn. The facilities were top notch and the coaching staff exemplary. I liked it enough and knew it was probably the best choice for my career. The next morning, I walked the campus with Daniel, hashing out what to do. He was the king of pros and cons lists. He was willing to attend school wherever I chose so we could raise Caden together."

"You chose UConn that morning?"

"I did, but I didn't share my decision with anyone other than Daniel."

We round the corner and make our way to a small community flower garden and take a seat on one of the benches. Her hands tremble in mine, and I lift her into my arms.

"Whatever happened wasn't your fault."

She nods against the curve of my neck, and her tears slide down my skin. She takes a deep breath and adds space between us. "On our way home, we were struck by a drunk driver. Only I survived the twisted mass of metal and broken glass. Caden and me."

I take a moment to digest the depth of her loss. Her parents and the father of her unborn child were all killed at the same time, leaving her to raise her son and make a future for them both all by herself. "You're the strongest person I've ever known." I kiss her hard and deep, hoping to absorb some of her pain as my own, knowing exactly how she feels losing a family member. Penn and Booker's warning makes sense now. They're locals and saw the aftermath of the accident in real time.

I also know without a doubt, the pain doesn't go away. It ebbs and flows based on the day and the situation. Sadie has been at the front of my mind daily since the party at Endzone. That isn't to say I don't think about my sister normally. I do. Attending the party was a rarity for me. Bars and clubs don't hold any allure for me, never have. Plus, avoiding similar establishments allows me to protect my story until I choose to share it. Generally, people don't simply take "I don't want a drink" as a sufficient answer.

"I'm not. Caden is."

"You both are. How much does he know?"

She snuggles deeper into me. Her hand settled around me, digging into my shoulder.

I tighten my hold on her. Pushing off my physical reactions to her is a virtual impossibility despite the tenor of our conversation. "Do you want to walk back? Are you cold?"

"Not yet. No. I need a minute. Then I'll answer any questions you have."

I kiss the top of her head and murmur, "I'll hold you for as many as you need." Sharing any more with Alannah will likely scare her away. If her son is the only skeleton she's worried about, then I'm in to learn the rest. She very well could be the one for me to grow old with.

After nearly fifteen minutes of me memorizing the curves of her frame, she lifts her gaze to mine.

"Thank you for being true to your word."

"You're welcome. Want to start walking back?"

"Sure."

Reluctantly, I set her on the ground and rise from the bench. The moonlight highlights the unique color of her hair. It's mesmerizing. Before we move, I draw her flush against me. The feel of her in my arms is unmatched by anything I've ever felt before. I lower my mouth to hers and kiss her until our lungs ache for oxygen. I lift her hand to my lips, kiss the back, and link our fingers. We start our walk back to her home.

"To answer your question, Caden knows broad strokes about the accident. I've shared details about Daniel with him, and he sees his grandparents maybe twice a year. Susan and Martin moved to South Carolina soon after the accident. I disclosed my pregnancy, and neither school pulled their offer. I changed course to Boston College because I needed help with Caden. Uncle Paul and Aunt Clem, my mother's sister and her husband, were all I had left. They took me in and were tremendous help during my college career. During the basketball season, they moved in with me and Caden in my off-campus apartment. Every home game, they were courtside. Away games in March, Caden stayed with them here."

"You amaze me."

"I did what needed to be done to meet my obligations and raise Caden."

Our pace slows as we turn down her street. Despite our heavy conversation, I don't want tonight to end. "He's exceptional, Alannah."

"There isn't an appropriate response other than thank you."

"Can I ask you a favor?"

"What?"

"Will you let me continue to take care of you and Caden?"

"Yes." One small, seemingly inconsequential word. It's a few steps forward. This intelligent, gorgeous woman and her son are burrowing their way into my heart faster than I ever imagined possible.

CHAPTER EIGHT

ALANNAH

My nerves are off the charts. I have a date with Callan in a few hours, and I'm freaking out. It's been a few days since I spilled my family drama with him, and he didn't flinch. Losing his sister in a similar manner, though difficult to handle at the time, gives him a deeper understanding. Why am I nervous? He knows the deepest, darkest recess of my soul, and he's still here.

A beat later, my heart reminds me why. *He could be everything I ever needed for myself and wanted in a partner.*

Me: I need you. Are you off today?

Delilah: On my way for date prep.

Me: LOL. Love you.

Less than fifteen minutes later, she busts through the front door. "Hey, girl! How much time do I have?"

"He's picking me up at six," I say. "Thank you for coming."

"Always. It's been nearly a month, and you're happier than you've been in a long time. Where is he taking you?"

"Out for dinner, but he didn't tell me where. He said dressy but not work clothes."

I can almost see Del scanning my closet in her mind. "Do you still have the sexy, emerald sundress and strappy, nude sandals?"

The dress she's referring to is ankle length with a thigh-high slit and nearly open back. It's perfect.

"Yeah."

"Outfit chosen. Go shower, and I'll get some snacks."

"You're the best bestie ever, Del!" I scurry upstairs and shower as instructed.

We spend too much time laughing and chatting, but I'm ready. My makeup is minimal, and my hair smooths over my shoulders in waves expertly crafted by Del.

"Before Callan arrives, where's Caden?"

"He's with Kyla and her family. They're hanging out since he's heading to camp tomorrow for a week and then the following week Kyla will be away at one herself."

"Whoa, two whole weeks. It's a lot for a young couple."

"It's a long time for any couple, but good practice for next fall if they end up at different colleges."

She nods in agreement. "Have a great time, Lan." She throws open the door and straddles the threshold.

"Thanks for the moral support, Del."

"Always. Don't forget protection!"

My skin heats at her words, not because of the possibility of being with Callan, but because he likely heard her. He looks hot in navy pants and a crisp white shirt with the sleeves rolled up, exposing his forearms, as he steps out of his SUV.

"Hi, Callan," Delilah says, stopping beside him.

"Have we met?" he asks.

"No, but Maggie Washington is my boss and speaks highly of you. Take care of my bestie."

"Pleasure to meet you. I will." As he climbs the steps, his gaze sweeps over me from the hem of my dress to my face. "You look gorgeous, Alannah." He hands over a huge bouquet of flowers, including sweet avalanche, Miranda and Darcey roses, and calla lilies mixed with cream and pink orchids.

"Thank you. These are lovely. You do as well." Again with the typically female compliment. I shouldn't be surprised at his attuned response.

"No need to be nervous, unless you're worried about what I overheard. Even then, no need to be nervous. Can I kiss you, so you forget I overheard your bestie strongly suggest we move faster than small steps tonight?"

"Yes, please."

He smiles, steps inside, closes the door with his foot, and immediately surrounds me in his arms. I set the flowers on the console table in the foyer and slide my hands around his neck. The pull of him is unlike anything I've felt before. The desire in his eyes mirrors mine, and he kisses me. His kiss is dangerous to me keeping my wits intact. His right hand rises on the bare skin of my back, and I feel the heat of his touch. The tips of his fingers lightly press into me. He should come with a warning label, and I've only seen him shirtless. My body is on fire from my toes to the tips of my ears.

Nearly breathless, I tug his lower lip between my teeth and draw back slightly.

"Do I have time to put these in water?"

"Sure."

He follows me into the kitchen. I set the flowers on the island and tug a stool around to the tallest cabinet. With a quickness I never noticed before, he covers my hand before I can climb onto the stool.

"I'll get it for you."

My initial inclination is to huff and do it myself. The more time I spend with him, the more the walls of self-preservation around my little family crumble. He shifts or removes a brick with each thoughtful and endearing act to take care of us, and yet it isn't overbearing at all.

He climbs onto the stool and pulls down my vase, one that hasn't been used for far too long—a fact that makes Callan stand apart from the other guys who scored a first date. He's different in many other ways though. My independence isn't a drawback for Callan; it's a benefit. Perhaps it's the quality I haven't found before. A man looking for a partner, not a pliable woman to fit into his life.

"Thank you."

With the flowers snipped and arranged, we head out the front door with our hands linked.

"Where are we going?" I ask.

"Did I not share?"

"No, you didn't. However, I'm sure it was by design."

He opens the passenger door and waits for me to settle inside. "We have dinner reservations at Clay Hill and then dessert reservations elsewhere."

"An air of mystery, I appreciate it."

A tiny smile curls at the corner of his mouth before he replies, "Thanks," and rounds the car.

When we arrive, I wait for him to get my door, which takes patience I'm learning, not only because I'm capable, but I appreciate the chivalry. When I slide off the seat, most of my leg is exposed from the high slit. His eyes widen before he casts his gaze skyward.

"You have a leg thing?" I ask, hoping to add some levity. Our heated kisses barely took the edge off the tension between us.

He levels his gaze to mine as he brands my back with his hand. His whispered response near the shell of my ear causes goose bumps to erupt on my skin. "I have a you thing."

I'm officially a puddle of mush in his large, capable hands. "Good."

"Good?"

"We wouldn't want to waste our terrifying potential, would we?"

He tucks my arm around his and closes the door. "No, we wouldn't."

The restaurant is surrounded by gorgeous gardens. Callan wasn't kidding when he said a proper date would take planning.

The hostess leads us to a private gazebo. "Your server will be right with you."

I take a seat in the chair Callan pulled out. "This is beautiful."

"Never been here before?"

"No, and I doubt you're surprised."

He takes my hand in his and brushes his thumb along the back. "More like shocked and grateful."

"Why grateful?" I ask as our server arrives to take our order. We order our meals but request she wait to put in the entrees until after our appetizer is served.

"Your previous dates walked away from you without taking the time to learn how exquisite you are, inside and out."

The same applies to him. "Thank you. Where have you been hiding?"

"Not hiding. I'm a simple, private guy. Like you, I don't frequent bars and clubs. The first time I saw you—"

Our server, though quite pleasant, has horrible timing. She sets my salad and his bisque on the table, refills our waters, and slips away. We each take a few bites.

"When was the first time you saw me?" I ask.

"I saw you the first time Cap assigned me to the boys' basketball games at the beginning of last season. You're impossible to miss. I didn't connect you and Caden, who I met on my first day as the resource officer, until the end of the season celebration when you joined him at center court. Have you ever missed a game?"

"No. My parents never missed mine. I need to give the same to Caden, especially since it's only me."

"It isn't only you anymore."

My chest tightens and my stomach flip-flops. "I'm still getting used to the idea of not being alone." The loneliness doesn't need to be said. It seems to follow, at least in my mind. No partner equals lonely.

"I'll keep showing up for both of you until you are tired of me."

I tilt my head. "I don't foresee me ever getting tired of you."

"I'm glad. Neither do I."

Julia, our server, removes our plates and replaces them with our entrees. Callan chose the prime rib, and I opted for the lamb. After a few bites, Callan asks, "How were your parents? You mentioned wanting to raise Caden in a similar home."

Conflicting feelings bubble within me. Marrying Daniel would've been the right thing for Caden, but I would've been miserable. I never wanted to go through Caden's formative years alone, but…. As if my thoughts are plastered on my face, Callan threads his fingers into mine atop the crisp, white tablecloth.

"My parents were best friends. They had mutual likes, but also had their own separate passions. Mom was a teacher, and Dad was a bank manager. She was an avid gardener—flowers not veggies. Dad was a tinkerer, mostly small clocks and other items he might be able to fix. We had enough. Being an only child has benefits and drawbacks. At least one of my parents was always present, usually both until they weren't." I don't need to fill in the rest out loud.

"Did you want more than one?"

"Yes, so in the unlikely event something happened to me, Caden wouldn't be alone like I was. My mother was the youngest, and Clem the oldest. My cousins were out of the house for about five years before they took me in."

"Do you still want more children?"

"Yes, but there are other factors at play. You?" I want at least two more, but my age isn't helping matters. Sure, some women have kids into their forties, but the what-ifs are heavy.

"The short answer is yes. I can't imagine not having my brothers when we lost our sister. My parents sound like yours, but for a while, they were oppressive in their manner of watching over us after the accident. Looking back, I understand. They questioned their choice to allow her to go and tightened the reins on my brothers and me."

"It makes sense. One of the hardest things I've done is allow Caden to find his own way. Even basketball was his choice. Do you regret moving away? I only had my aunt and uncle. I would think more family would be helpful."

"No. I needed to find my own life. My childhood hometown is small like this one, and everyone knew our tragedy. I needed to figure out who I was outside of the poor boy who lost his sister."

"Understandable."

"We have a knack for having hard conversations, don't we?"

I smile. "Yeah, we do."

"Ready for the next part of our date? I promise no hard conversations."

"Either way works for me, but a break would be nice."

Callan pays for our meal, and we stroll back to the car. After about a fifteen-minute drive, he parks alongside a gorgeous home near the shore.

"Where are we?"

"Smithson lives here. He and Scarlett are away for a prewedding weekend, and I exchanged use of his beach for checking on the house."

"How could you know I love the beach?" slips out before I can stop it.

He turns to face me. "I didn't, but I'm glad I chose well." After a sweet kiss to the tip of my nose, he's smiling as he rounds the car. "You may want to carry your shoes or leave them here."

I slip off my sandals, leaving them on the floorboard while he removes his shoes and sets them on the ground.

"Aren't you worried about bugs?"

He shakes his head. "I wasn't until you mentioned it." He sets his shoes beside mine and offers me his hand.

"Chose well" doesn't begin to cover Callan's planning. I have no idea what part of this setup is always here and what he created; either way, it's perfection. There's a platform with a cushioned lounger that is only open to the shoreline. A private cabana would be an apt description. After he flicks a switch, string lights illuminate the cozy spot with an appropriate amount of ambiance.

"Why did they need to go away when this is their backyard?"

"Not sure. I wouldn't need to leave either." He escorts me over to the lounger. "Do you want to walk, have dessert, or sit?"

"Three times, Callan. Impressive."

He draws me against him and sets a light kiss on my lips. "Three?"

"You're exceptional at planning dates. The flowers, dinner, and this... three."

"I will do this and so much more as long as you'll allow me to."

I drop my head briefly to sort my thoughts. "Walk." We turn left down the beach with our hands linked between us. "How did we not meet before now?"

"I keep asking myself the same question. We have plenty of mutual friends. Perhaps it wasn't the right time."

I wrap my hand around his bicep and sidle closer. "Maybe not." The sun is showing off tonight. A canvas of purple, red, pink, and orange streaks across the sky as we walk along the shore. When the tide reaches our feet, we shift closer inland. We walk along the sand in comfortable silence.

"Ready to see what Auggie created for you?" he asks as we round the last corner. August Morgan is the executive chef and owner at Morgan's where Delilah works.

"Your attention to detail is—"

"Details, even seemingly unimportant ones, are the mortar of a solid foundation to build a relationship."

"Like knowing my son's favorite donut."

He guides me to the lounger and takes the spot beside me. "For starters, but I didn't seek those details out. I used my knowledge, sure, but paying attention to your answer to my random question was key. Your single answer yielded a breakfast delivery and this confection." He opens an insulated bag and pulls out two bottles of water, two spoons, and napkins. Then he opens the lid of the Morgan's box with a flourish. "Have you ever had a chocolate *mille-feuille*?"

"Can't say I have."

I scoop a spoonful and savor the decadent, flaky layers and chocolate. Containing the satisfied moan is impossible. "Ohmigod, this is...." I slide the spoon through the layers again and offer it to him.

"That's really good," he admits.

I take my thumb and swipe along his lower lip to remove some of the filling. The warmth of his jaw beneath my hand has me leaning forward. A mere inch between our lips, he takes the spoon from my hand, then surrounds my waist with his arm, and slides me into his lap. I draw my tongue along his lips before kissing him deeply. Ignoring the throbbing between my thighs with him hard beneath me is more difficult than I anticipate. Our lip-lock ratchets up to feverish. Callan sets a row of kisses along my jaw and down the curve of my neck. A shiver of pure, unfiltered desire passes through me. I set my hands on his shoulders and start to shift.

"Who's there?" A deep voice echoes from behind us to our left.

"Craven." Callan's eyes meet mine.

I shift to beside him instead of straddling his thighs shortly before Captain Ramirez rounds the cabana.

"Cap," Callan greets him.

"Antoinette, pleasure to see you. I didn't mean to interrupt, but Smithson is away, and the lights caught my attention."

Callan nods. "I offered to check on the house for use of the beach."

"And now I see your car. My apologies. See you on Monday." Cap retreats as quickly as he arrived.

I bury my head into Callan's arm.

"Sorry about the interruption. I forgot he lives a few doors away."

"Not your fault. I knew too, but I didn't think he would investigate random string lights." I chuckle.

"What time is your curfew?" he asks.

"At or around Caden's, which is midnight tonight. Why?"

He glances at his watch. "Would you prefer to take another risk at your house or go to mine?"

I don't even think about my answer. "Yours."

CHAPTER NINE

CALLAN

We clean up the cabana area and kiss our way back to my SUV. The ride to my condo is silent in words, but not in actions. Alannah doesn't fix the slit of her dress this time, and most of her toned thigh is exposed. I can't resist drawing my hand along her smooth skin.

"Gentlemanly small steps are going to be difficult if you keep looking at me like that," I murmur as I pull into my garage.

"Can we speed up to medium steps and improper kisses?"

"We can, but large ones are going to have to wait."

"Why?"

"We don't have all night." Her half-lidded eyes meet mine, and she attempts to respond, but I continue, "Yes, it's going to take *that* long."

I let my words marinate in her head while I get her door and escort her inside. We don't make it far. Our kiss ramps up again before I can close the entry door from the garage. Her fingers move deftly down the column of buttons on my shirt. Once my chest is exposed, she presses a row of kisses from left to right. I dig a woman kissing my chest, though I would prefer the roles reversed. As she moves, I gather her silky hair into my hand. When she switches direction, I tug on her hair and lower my mouth to her now exposed neck. After each kiss, we travel one step further into my house.

Without discontinuing my exploration along her neck, over her collarbone, and then down the plunging neckline of her dress, I dance her to the edge of my couch.

Releasing her hair, my hand slides down her side and gathers the skirt of her dress to her hip. I dip my fingers under the fabric, guide her long, toned leg around my back, and allow the satiny material to fall toward the floor again as my fingers grip the flare of her hip.

Next, I attempt to push the fabric hindering me from sucking her breast into my mouth out of my way. "How does this come undone?" I murmur against her skin when the fabric doesn't allow me access to her breasts.

A small giggle echoes around me. She draws a zipper on the side of her dress down. I curl my fingers around the strap and slide it over her shoulder and follow with a trail of soft kisses.

Goose bumps skitter across her skin following each press of my lips. I explore the valley between her breasts and draw circles with my tongue around her taut, rosy nipple. She arches closer and steadies herself with one arm around me and the other gripping the couch. The heat of her against me is miles beyond my imagination. Her movements are slow and deliberate. Matching her pace, I move southward, skipping over her toned but still clothed belly. Every few inches, I kiss or nip her leg until I reach the top of her foot. Traveling in the reverse direction, I lightly caress her calf and her inner thigh before dragging my thumb over her lace-covered core.

She trembles with each pass of my thumb. "Callan." My name a plea and a prayer for more at once.

I repeat my movement a handful more times before dipping a finger beneath the edge of her panties. She's soaked. "When was the last time?"

"Me, a few days."

I lift an eyebrow in question but draw my finger from her puckered hole to her swollen nub twice.

A shiver passes over her. "You realize you're hot as hell, right?"

"Your candor is refreshing." It probably wouldn't shock her to know I used an image of her before I picked her up tonight to take the edge off. The men around here are seriously stupid to overlook her. A woman like Alannah deserves to be cherished and worshipped regardless of how her past played out.

All talking is replaced by panting and mewls when I increase the pace of my fingers. Her inner walls pulse, and she scores my flanks with her fingernails as the pressure builds.

"Damn, not even I'm this good at…." Her words trail off as she flies over the edge of bliss.

Before the contractions around my hand cease, I brand her lips with mine. "I'm not done with you yet." Not today, next year, or maybe for the rest of my life. I lift her into my arms and sit on my couch with her straddling my lap. I coax another orgasm from her while she expertly draws one from me. I don't recall the beginnings of a relationship being as satisfying when I was younger. I was in a hurry to get to the grand finale. It never felt like it does with Alannah. Reluctantly, I allow her to move off my lap and I lead her into the bathroom. After we clean up, we return to the living room.

Much to my dismay, it's time for our evening to end. "Ready to go home?"

She wrinkles her nose. "No, I would like to be irresponsible and continue our evening, but I need to." She moves out of my arms and searches for her sandals. I'm conflicted as well, but I understand.

I pull into the driveway right before Kyla. After a pause to greet Caden, we slip inside while they take a seat on the front stoop.

"That didn't look good," I admit. Kyla's shoulders are slumped, and Caden looks stunned.

"No, Caden looks upset about something."

"I agree. What time do we need to leave tomorrow... later today?"

She smiles, and it warms me from the inside out. Showing up is the easy part of a relationship in my opinion. Figuring out how to handle differences and conflict can be difficult. "Registration starts at eleven."

"I'll be here at nine thirty." I eliminate nearly every inch of space between us. After a perfect kiss to cap off our amazing first date, I pull away, which is the absolute last thing I want to do. "Good night, Alannah."

"Good night, Callan."

Caden steps through the front door and asks, "What time do we need to leave tomorrow?"

"No later than ten," she answers.

"Okay. Night, Mom. OC." Whatever he and Kyla discussed wasn't easy or not resolved to his liking.

I reach back for her hand and lift it to my lips. "Want me to stay until you finish talking to him?"

"I do, but not for him. You shouldn't though. He won't talk tonight. He ponders and dissects before he talks about things, especially his relationship with Kyla."

"Okay." I kiss her temple and head home. More than once I consider turning around and camping out on her front porch. I know she's more than capable of reading her son and caring for him. I merely want to be within arm's length to take care of her. After shucking my clothes and washing up, I decide to share my sentiments.

Me: I would prefer to be there with you.

Her reply is nearly immediate.

Alannah: I would too.

Me: Good night, beautiful.

Alannah: Night.

Nearly seven hours later, which feels like two, my alarm startles me awake. The last time I looked at the clock, it was near three in the morning. With my head not truly in it, I push through a lifting set and then make my way to Alannah's with breakfast. Lightly, I knock on the front door.

"Morning," she greets me, but she looks tired. Alannah is showered and dressed in jeans and a fitted shirt.

I kiss her to the brink of improper, then offer her a coffee. "Did you sleep?"

"I tried. Does that count?"

"It counts, but why you didn't is important as well."

"You are why I didn't sleep."

I set the pastry bag and my coffee on the console in her foyer and draw her against me. "Me?"

"Yes, you."

I tilt my head in question. "For a good reason or a bad reason?"

She lowers her mouth near my ear and whispers, "A sexy reason."

"I see. Well, we can revisit your reason when we get home this afternoon. First, you need to eat."

She pulls back and meets my gaze. "Thank you. I will, but I need to drag Caden out of bed. I'll be right back." With a quick kiss, she bounds upstairs. I hear a knock and muted talking as I make my way into the kitchen. I search for a small plate and warm the croissant for Alannah.

"Please sit and eat," I request a bit more forceful than I mean to when she returns.

If she's taken aback, it isn't showing on her face. She takes a seat on one of the stools, and I set the warmed pastry in front of her. "Thank you. Did you eat?"

"Yes. I attempted to wait until I got here, but the aroma was impossible to forgo."

She laughs softly and takes another bite. Caden ambles into the kitchen. Wordlessly, I extend the bag in his direction.

"Thanks, OC."

"You're welcome."

With a few bites, the first donut is gone and he's working on the second.

After a few minutes to allow the sugar rush to reach his brain, Alannah asks, "Do you have everything you need?"

"Except pizza money," Caden reminds her.

"Right, of course. I'll give it to you before we leave."

Fifteen minutes later, Caden thrusts his bag into my trunk and climbs into the back seat. Without thinking, I take Alannah's hand in mine as we drive toward my alma mater. I catch Caden's eyes in the rearview mirror, but he doesn't react to the display of affection. Throughout the drive, we chat about baseball, which Caden loves to watch, and the camp itself. There is no mention of Kyla or their conversation last night. After the drive, I park and we walk Caden into the arena.

"Callan? What are you doing here?" my college coach's son asks.

"Hey, Manny. I'm here with my—"

Thankfully, Alannah jumps in. "Hi, he's here with us. My son is attending camp this week."

Manny extends his hand to her and welcomes Caden.

"What are you doing here?" I ask him.

"I took over for my dad about six years ago."

"Good for you!"

He's called away, and we continue through the registration process. With his dorm assignment and schedule, we set him up.

"I'll be back on Friday for the final game and closing ceremony," Alannah informs him.

"You comin' with her, OC?"

Without hesitation, I answer. "Yes." I have plenty of vacation days to take.

"Love you, Mom. Later, OC."

"I love you too, Caden. Have fun."

"Bye, Caden." I close his door behind us and link my hand with hers. "Up for a walk before we head back?"

"Sure."

We walk away from the arena toward the quad in the center of campus. The silence stretching between us is unbearable.

"Please share what's going on in your gorgeous head. I mean from in the arena, not earlier this morning."

"It isn't important."

"If it's bothering you, I'm sure it is."

She shakes her head and pulls to a stop. I don't think Alannah has ever been at a loss for words. Nervous, sure. Stumbling over word choice because of her nervousness, yes. At a loss, no.

I speak instead. "I wanted to claim you both, but I wasn't sure how you or Caden would take it."

She cups my face and kisses me hard with a possessiveness she's never acknowledged before. "How you can read and settle me so soon after we met is unfathomable. I'm completely on board with whatever label you want to use for you and me. As far as Caden, you'll have to talk to him."

I tighten my arm around her and turn us in a circle. "I can work with that. Where to now?"

"I don't have plans."

"Interesting, neither do I. What are your thoughts on Thai takeout and a movie at my house?"

"Sounds perfect, but I draw the line at horror."

We curl up on my couch and watch a drama with an excessive amount of food. Our evening is comfortable and exactly what I want in my future.

CHAPTER TEN

ALANNAH

All I feel is warmth. I reach over my shoulder, and when my hand meets Callan's chiseled jaw, I realize we fell asleep on his couch at some point after the movie. I haven't slept as soundly as I did in his arms since... ever. Carefully to avoid falling off the couch and waking him, I twist around.

Holy hell, he's equally attractive while he sleeps. The lines of his jaw are quiet and his unique hazel eyes lightly closed. I rotate my wrist to check the time. It's a little after six.

Callan's hand on my hip grips tighter before he mumbles, "Please tell me it isn't morning and I can go back to my blissful sleep with a stunning strawberry blonde in my arms."

I snuggle closer and skim my lips across his. "I wish I could."

His eyes open, and he studies my face. "You're more exquisite fresh from sleep."

This man sure knows how to make me feel good. Words fail me, but I kiss him deeply in appreciation of his compliment. Ignoring the buzz between us, especially knowing we both need to work, is more difficult than I anticipate. "When do you normally leave for work?"

He draws me inexplicably closer. "Never."

I giggle, then attempt to wiggle away. *Sweet mercy!* I fail miserably and find myself suspended between disbelief, responsibility, and a deep, aching need to touch him again. For the second time, my brain trips and calculates the likelihood Callan is well-endowed. He stills at the same time I do.

He swallows hard and meets my gaze. "By seven thirty, but earlier today so I can take you home first."

I slowly extricate myself from his embrace. "Do you mind if I make coffee?"

"Not at all. I'll be down in about twenty."

I fumble around the kitchen to find what I need. For a man who loves to cook, his kitchen could use some updating. I chastise myself for making assumptions. The house is an older craftsman with gorgeous woodwork and trim. I locate the mugs and set the first one beneath the brewer and start it. While the coffee maker drips morning nectar into the mug, I grab a spoon and the cream from the fridge.

"Find everything?" Callan asks when he returns.

I never fancied myself a woman who would swoon over a uniform, but… I was wrong, so wrong. "Uh-huh" is all I can manage.

"What?" He checks himself as if something is out of place, then surrounds me with his arms.

"It's nothing."

"It's something, sweetheart. You're flustered, which means you're nervous. Spill it."

My face heats. I haven't the slightest clue why I'm embarrassed to admit the thought in my head.

"I don't need my extensive training on reading people with you, never did. I know something is up. The sexy blush on your face is unmistakable."

I exhale and mumble, "I've never seen you in your uniform before." I probably saw him from afar at a game but didn't know it was him.

"Really? The uniform does it for you?"

I bury my face into his shoulder. "It certainly doesn't hurt." My words are muffled by his shirt.

"If we're voting on the version we like of one another best, I still vote for fresh from sleep you."

This man. I lift my head to look at him. "I can't say my answer is definitive yet. I still have more research to complete."

"When?" Then it dawns on him. "The wedding. I'll allow you to have a tentative answer, counselor." He kisses me deeply and thoroughly before adding, "As much as I don't like it, we need to go."

I frown but acquiesce to his request. Waking up with Callan was beyond words, adding in a firing squad wasn't on my agenda this morning.

"Who is that?" he asks of the couple standing on my front porch.

"My aunt and uncle. You don't have to meet them now if you need to get to work."

"I need to meet them. I hurried you out of my house so you would have enough time to get ready here. Then I could take you to work."

"Why? I can drive, Callan."

"I know, but if I drop you off, then I need to pick you up."

My heart constricts. *I want you too.* "Yes, I want to see you after work, but you don't need to be my chauffeur. Plus, I need my car today."

He winks at me and hurries around to open my door.

I approach my front porch and greet them both with a hug. Uncle Paul is the quintessential older gentlemen. His daily uniform includes khakis, a polo, and boat shoes. I would bet he has a polo in each color of the rainbow in his closet. Clem, short for Clementine, is a bit trendier. She opts for jeans and a floral, scoop neck shirt most days.

"Did I miss a breakfast date?"

"No, dear. We thought you might be lonely with Caden at camp, but I see that isn't the case. Hello, I'm Clem, and this is my husband, Paul. And you are?"

His wide, infectious smile will be the death of me. "Callan. Pleasure to meet you both."

"I would keep him to myself as well, young lady," Clem states, covering her mouth near my ear, but fails miserably if she intended to be discreet. "I see you're a police officer. Are you a local as well?"

"I'm not a local. Please don't hold it against me."

I have to give it to Clem. Her attempt to gauge if he knows about my past is smooth.

Clem replies, "Never. I'm merely establishing if you're good enough for my niece."

"A local need not apply?"

Paul responds definitively, "No, they think they know everything about our family despite the many passing years. They don't."

To end Clem's interrogation of Callan, I interrupt. "Okay, on that note, would you like to come in for coffee?"

"No need. We wanted to check on you, and it appears you're not lonely at all. It was a pleasure meeting you, Callan." Clem replies.

"You as well. Have a lovely day." Callan extends his hand to Uncle Paul, who takes it. Aunt Clem though, she throws her arms around him as best she can. Callan has no choice but to hug her.

After releasing Callan, she states, "He's muscular, nice strong arms."

If the ground would swallow me whole, that would be fantastic. "Auntie," I say in warning to get her to stop. "Thank you for checking on me. Have a nice day."

"We will. You too, dear," Clem replies, adding some emphasis on the you before they drive away.

There's nothing I can do but shake my head.

"She's a spitfire," Callan offers after closing my front door.

"That's an apt description. I'm so sorry about them, but mostly her."

He hauls me into his arms again. "Don't be. I mean it isn't everyday an older lady feels me up. Oh wait, aren't you older than me?"

"Callan!"

"I'm joking. It's true, but I'm joking." He kisses the tip of my nose and loosens his hold on me. "Where is your appointment outside of your office today?"

The protectiveness of him is exactly enough. "I'm going to So Elegant at lunch to get a dress for the wedding. Any chance you know what color the bridal party is wearing?"

"No, sorry."

"What time will you be home?"

"No later than six," I reply.

"Invitation still open?"

"Of course, if Clem didn't scare you away."

"Never. She's protecting you with humor."

"Have a great day."

After a sweet but chaste kiss, he replies, "You too," and heads out the front door. Thankfully, my morning appointment isn't first thing.

After hustling through the shower and throwing together a simple lunch I can eat while I work, I rush to my office.

"Morning, Alannah," Cara greets me.

"Hi, Cara. Sorry I'm late."

She glances at the clock. "You're the boss. Mr. Brinson is set to arrive in fifteen minutes. Here's the mail and a fax from earlier this morning."

"Thanks." I plop into my comfy desk chair and tackle my inbox. I'm able to reply and sort through it before meeting Mr. Brinson to file his late wife's estate. Afterward, I usher Mr. Brinson out of my office and hand the file over to Cara.

I spend the next hour wrangling with the opposing counsel for my divorce trial next week. Ideally, he can get his client to budge on a few small property distribution items and we can avoid the trial altogether. At the end of my call, I check my text messages.

Delilah: Available for lunch to dish on the date?

Me: Can't. Dress shopping.

Delilah: Next week?

Me: Sure.

A knock on my door pulls my attention away from my phone as it chimes. "Hey, Cara."

"I'm headed out. Mr. Brinson will be returning to sign the estate paperwork on Thursday morning."

"Great, thanks. See you tomorrow."

Cara heads out, and I finish checking my texts.

Caden: Hi, Mom. Just checking in.

Me: Hey. I'm good. You?

Caden: Yeah. Coach Manny is pretty awesome. He has stories about OC from his college days.

Me: Interesting. You'll have to share when you get home. I'll see you on Friday. Love you.

Caden: Oh, I will. They're funny. Love you too.

When I finish texting with Caden, I head out to my appointment. I give myself a little extra time and park in the farthest spot in the beach parking lot. It's balmy and slightly breezy today near the shore. Surprisingly, the beach isn't crowded today. When I reach the store, I press the bell.

A woman with a pink pixie cut answers the door. "Hi. Welcome to So Elegant. I'm Poppy. Who is your appointment with?"

"Billie."

As if she heard me, Billie steps through the break in the counter, shielding her slightly round belly. If I recall correctly, this is her and Peter's second child. They have a boy named Morgan who is about three. Billie is Scarlett's sister-in-law, I think. Savannah, the bride's sister, is married to Billie's older brother. "Alannah, so nice to see you."

"You as well. How are you?"

"As big as a house," she quips.

Not even close. Billie is a tiny woman with the baby bump. "When are you due?"

"We're having a little girl in late September."

"Congratulations!"

Billie smiles. "I pulled some dresses for you and hung them in room two. Scarlett and Zack are keeping things small but elegant. Let me know if you need any assistance."

I try on three dresses before I find the perfect option. It's a maxi dress with a flowy skirt in red.

Billie calls from outside the room, "Does the maxi dress need to be hemmed or taken in anywhere?"

I smile. "You have skills, Billie. Yes, the bodice needs to be taken in a bit."

"Step on out here. I'll get my pins," she instructs.

Poppy answers the door again while I move onto the pedestal for Billie. "Are you Alannah?"

"Yes, why?"

"This is for you." She hands me a red box and a small gift bag.

When Billie returns, she hums while she pins my dress. It takes her longer than I expect for her to ask who sent me a gift and what it is. "What's in the bag?"

I shrug. "Didn't open it yet."

"Who's the lucky guy?"

I smile. "Callan Craven."

"The best man?" Billie asks.

"Yeah, I guess. He mentioned he was in the wedding party but not his role."

"He's hot! You're a lucky girl."

I am.

Billie continues, "I'm set. Once you change, we can discuss pickup."

"Thanks." I'm giddy to dig into my package but don't want to do it here. I set an appointment to pick up my dress and head out the door without sharing the contents of my gift. I stroll slowly back to my car, enjoying the late summer sun. My self-control is through the roof right now. Instead of tearing into the package, I wait until I get back to my office.

Since I have no more appointments, I lock the outer door. It forces walk-ins to knock and allows me the option whether or not to answer.

Finally, I tear open the larger box and find chocolate covered strawberries. I laugh because he's being cheeky about my hair color. The other gift though is a heart stopper, especially so soon. The small box contains a delicate necklace with a C linked in it. At first, I think—bold—although he isn't wrong, I do have strong feelings for him. Yet after reading the note, I realize it's a sweet gesture.

Alannah,

I thought you might be missing Caden even if you aren't alone.

xoxo, Callan

The necklace is a gift from a father to a mother. The sentiment hits me square in the chest despite the short time we've been together. Without another thought, I send a text just in case he isn't free.

Me: Can you talk?

Instead of a reply, my phone rings. "Hi, gorgeous."

"Hi. Thank you. It's perfect."

"You're welcome. I'm glad you love it."

Unspoken feelings stretch between us on the telephone line. He had to order it sooner than today, and the thought scares me a bit.

"Did you find a dress?"

"I did."

"What does it look like?"

"You're going to have to wait."

"Will you at least share what color?"

I shake my head. "It's red. You failed to mention you're the best man."

I can hear the smile in his voice. "I didn't want you to say no because I'll have things I need to do aside from warding off every single man in the room."

"What are you worried about?"

"Someone trying to steal my girl while I'm being a great friend."

His. I like it, a lot. "No one has taken a chance on my son and I until you. You're safe in your spot beside me as long as you want it." I pause, replaying my last sentence in my head. "Please tell me I didn't say the last part out loud."

"I promised I would never lie to you, Alannah."

I sigh heavily. "Please ignore those words for now."

"Can't unhear them, sweetheart. No panicking required. Your spot is safe on one side of me and Caden on the other."

Floored. "I don't know what to say."

"Nothing more to say right now. Unfortunately, I need to get inside. I'll see you later. Bye, sweetheart."

"Bye, Callan." I bite into one of the strawberries and then clasp the necklace at the nape of my neck after ending the call.

A promising email from opposing counsel comes through near four, requesting another call tomorrow morning to hash out a few more details. I respond and set a conference call for ten tomorrow morning. Then I reconfirm with my client what her bottom line is for her settlement agreement with her future ex-husband. After another read through of the draft agreement and notes from my conversation, I head home for the evening. The smile on my face grows wider the closer I get to the house. Unfortunately, my plans for the evening are canceled with a text from Callan.

Callan: I'm going to be held over at a car accident. I'll call you later if it's not late.

Me: Please call anyway.

I'm sad our plans changed, but I understand. I change into leggings and an oversized shirt and curl up with my latest book on my patio until the bug population forces me inside. So far, I haven't found an adequate method for reduction or elimination in my yard.

CHAPTER ELEVEN

CALLAN

I park near the barrier and send a text to Alannah. Should I text her now? It's a gray area, at least in my mind. I refuse to allow her to worry when I'm late, especially if I'm held over at a call. More importantly, I'm not in any danger. I didn't expect a response, though I got one asking me to call her anyway. Instead of pondering the what-ifs of her request, I hop out of my cruiser and take instruction from the scene commander. He puts me on crowd control. I push the crowd back further with my coworker Blake.

When I complete the task, I turn toward the scene. It's one of the worst I've seen. The car is right side up. However, it appears to have rolled at least once, coming to a stop near a concrete barrier. The passenger side appears concave, and the hood resembles an accordion. When I see the teen driver, my thoughts immediately go to Caden, despite knowing we dropped him off at camp a few days ago. *We.* The thought nearly brings a smile to my face at an inappropriate time. Once I push my concern from my mind, I focus on the passenger whose blonde hair is glued to her face with a stream of blood from her head wound—Kyla.

A myriad of questions float through my mind, and none of them are good for her. Is she hurt? If yes, how badly? Is this guy, the driver, why she and Caden were arguing? I won't be able to answer any of those questions anytime soon. Nor are the answers any of my business, except as it pertains to Caden.

"Craven, move it," Penn shouts as he arrives on scene.

I step back and continue to monitor the crowd. A loud commotion has me looking across the street.

"That's my son! Let me through," a woman shouts.

I shift a few steps in her direction to offer assistance to Blake if necessary. The rookie successfully prevents her from breaching the scene. I nod in his direction.

The rescue crew extricates the driver who I now recognize as Andre Sims. He's the star running back for the football team. When Penn reaches his rig, Andre's mother and another woman approach and receive instruction from Lacey.

Almost simultaneously, Jude, the other EMT on scene, guides a conscious but woozy Kyla to a stretcher after putting a collar in place to protect her neck. The blood from her head has slowed, but she's holding her arm. Once the occupants of the vehicle are loaded into ambulances, the crowd starts to disperse.

The responding officers congregate around the scene commander to await further orders.

Blake steps beside me.

"Well done with the mother, rook."

He nods. "Thanks."

Nearly an hour later, we're dismissed from the scene. I consider heading to the hospital, but without Caden here, it doesn't make sense. Plus, I don't have any details. For all I know, Andre and Kyla are friends. Mindlessly, I swap my cruiser for my personal vehicle and drive home. Yet I don't find myself at home when I park. I drove to Alannah's.

I pull out my phone and call her.

"Hey, Callan."

Her voice alone settles me. "Hi, beautiful. Still up for company?"

The dash clock glows almost nine.

"Yours? Always." She swings open her front door as I approach.

Uncharacteristically, I surround her with my arm and step inside without words of invitation and her in my arms.

"Was the call that bad?"

Instead of answering her, I back her against the wall and kiss her deeply and thoroughly. We kiss and explore until we're both panting.

Part of me can't see my future without her and Caden, which makes me want to spill the details, but the rest considers if it's my place to cast aspersions on her son's girlfriend. "It hit me differently than any other. Perhaps because I know the occupants personally."

Her phone trills from the console table beside us. "I need to answer the call; it could be Caden." She reaches out with her left hand and answers the call.

I can hear someone talking, but I can't make out the words. While she talks, I walk us to the couch and guide her into my lap.

"Were you at the scene of Kyla's accident?"

I nod tightly.

"That was Shelby, Kyla's mom. She didn't want Kyla to call Caden without warning me first."

"Understandable. Is she going to be okay?"

Alannah lifts her shoulders. "Eventually. Camp next week is certainly out with a broken arm and serious concussion. You mentioned it hit differently because you know her, why?"

"For starters, she's Caden's girlfriend. I care about him." I care about Alannah as well, but I don't voice it in this moment.

Her hand cups my jaw. "Haven't you been to other accident scenes?"

"Yes. I've never had a personal connection until tonight since…."

Alannah kisses me softly with understanding. "Don't you know the report for your sister's accident inside, out, backward, and forward?"

"No. I haven't read it." I expect shock to mar her gorgeous face. How many police officers would choose not to read the report of a fatal accident of a family member? I'm sure it's a small number. In fact, Grant studied the report of his brother's shooting in excruciating detail.

She murmurs, "Me either," against my neck. "Clem and Paul shielded me, and once Caden was born, I never wanted to look back. Why didn't you?"

"My parents grew stricter for nearly a year after the accident, as I mentioned. By then I didn't want to plunge them back into the darkness they fought their way out of since her death. We were the boys who lost their sister. People never discussed the circumstances, but they walked on eggshells around us. I focused on basketball, and when it was time to decide on college, I wanted a fresh start."

"Yet you went back. Why?"

"I hoped it would feel like home again after the passing years. It didn't. Classmates and their parents continued to treat me as if I were fragile, especially after graduation from the academy."

"I would've preferred fragile," Alannah whispers.

The sheer pain and anguish behind her words guts me. I thought she was exceptional before. More so now. "How was it for you?"

"I didn't realize until years later, but the fake smiles and pity became more evident. At first, I was the pregnant teenage orphan doomed to single motherhood. Nothing else about my life or accomplishments mattered at all. Until it was time for me to leave for college, Paul and Clem were firm but loving. They screened all information I had access to and who I spent time with. Once Caden was born, I didn't have time to focus on anything other than him and basketball."

"Yet you came back as well."

"Before I lost my parents, my childhood was idyllic. They were always there, volunteering at school and interested in my life. Summers here were the best. Each day my mom and I would camp out at the beach and talk or read. The summer before they died, I was at a turning point. I preferred to spend my summer days with my friends. Mom understood, but being in the same position now, I know it hurt to let me go. Caden deserves the same upbringing. Is it different? I'm sure. Paul has done a great job acting as a male role model for Caden. The looks changed after college when I didn't shrink away. I won't lie. Law school with a preschooler was difficult, but slowly their opinion of me shifted when I didn't cower and hide away with Caden."

"They started to protect you."

She raises an eyebrow in question. "Who said something to you?"

"Penn and Booker gave me a nonverbal warning at the registration table. Later in the day, Penn indicated you were special and forbade me from hurting you."

Alannah stiffens in my arms. "Did he tell you anything?"

Her reaction is understandable. If Penn shared with me, our initial conversation about our pasts wasn't genuine. "No, he told me you would tell me when you were ready. To be honest, I asked. Penn is a stand-up guy and refused to share the details."

"I appreciate your candor. Yeah, he is. He was Daniel's best friend."

"His big-brother protectiveness of you and Caden makes more sense now."

Alannah yawns as politely as she can against my shoulder.

"I should go."

She meets my gaze. "No, you should stay, but we should get some sleep."

"Okay." I follow her from the couch back near the front door where she checks the locks. She plugs in her phone in the kitchen and extends an extra charger in my direction. The main living areas of her home are comfortable and neutral. Her bedroom is similar but unquestionably feminine. The furniture is dark gray with an upholstered headboard with a crisp-white, pinch pleat duvet with throw pillows in varying hues of purple.

She disappears into what I assume is the bathroom. I set my weapon, keys, and wallet on the tall bureau and pile my uniform atop the chair across the room.

When she returns, she pauses a few steps in front of me.

"I will still go home."

She exhales sharply. "I want you to stay."

I eliminate the space between us and draw her against me. "But?"

"No but. The reality hit me, that's all. I don't care what anyone else thinks."

"Good. Me either. Any chance you have a spare toothbrush?"

She smiles. "I set one on the edge of the sink for you."

I kiss her and finish getting ready for bed. When I return, she's sitting on the edge of her bed wearing tiny shorts and a camisole.

"Do you have a side preference?" she asks.

I chuckle. "It's your bed. I'll take whichever side you don't want."

She wrinkles her nose.

"Are you a starfish?"

"No, I just haven't shared my bed with anyone in…."

Neither have I. "I'll take the left side closer to the door." With our sleeping positions settled, I slip beneath the sheets behind her, curl my arm around her waist, and press a few kisses to her exposed shoulder. "Good night, Alannah."

"Night, Callan."

CHAPTER TWELVE

ALANNAH

"I can feel you staring at me," I whisper and slowly open my eyes. At some point during the night, I shifted in my sleep. My leg is over his thigh, and my hand is settled in the middle of his sculpted chest.

"You are becoming my favorite everything."

"You are becoming my favorite as well."

After my in-kind response, Callan cages me beneath him. "Play hooky with me today."

I frown and consider my options. "I can't do the whole day, but I can after my morning appointment."

"I'll take it, and I'll plan everything. I have a few questions though?"

My interest is piqued. "What?"

"When is the last time you had fun?"

I consider my answer longer than Callan would like. "Too long."

"Unacceptable. I'm going to fix that. Are you afraid of heights?"

"No. Now I'm intrigued. What else?"

"Any food allergies or dislikes?"

"No. Are you going to cook for me?"

"Yes, I am. Technically, we're past a second date I suppose. However, I never break a promise."

"Now I wish I could take the entire day," I whine.

"No worries, beautiful. It'll give me time to prepare. Ready to get moving?"

I disagree wholeheartedly. "No. Can I admit I like waking up with you even though the reason you stayed wasn't great?"

"I stayed only because you asked."

Falling for him is a near certainty. Hell, I'm halfway there, and we haven't…. My brain short-circuits back to after our first date. I mean his kiss makes me weak in the knees. His mouth on my skin and his fingers….

"Where did your gorgeous mind just go?"

I bite my lower lip and hope to stall as long as I can.

"Sexy as hell, gorgeous. However, lip biting coupled with your flushed face and my advanced skills of reading you indicates you need to share with me. Only me."

"I would like to keep it to myself a little longer."

"I'll relent only because the last time a similar look crossed your face, I learned you prefer a slow build to an orgasm."

"I appreciate it. I would rather act out my thoughts, but I need to get to the office for my meeting." I push up onto my elbows and kiss him deeply. Ignoring his impressive morning erection and his bare chest is more difficult than I care to admit. "Callan."

"Yes?" There's a hint of mischief in his voice from knowing I'm trapped beneath him.

"I need you to let me get out of bed."

"I don't want to."

"I don't want you to, but…."

Reluctantly, he shifts, and I scoot off my bed.

"Coffee?" he offers.

"Yes, please." I hurry through my morning routine but skip drying my hair to have a few more minutes before it's necessary for me to leave for the day.

"What do you want on this?" he asks when I join him in the kitchen. Not only did he make coffee, but he's dressed, made my bed, and toasted a bagel.

"A little cream cheese works. You didn't have to make me breakfast."

He kisses me tenderly and hands me a cup of coffee before replying, "I wanted to." Then he adds the cream cheese to my bagel.

After a few sips and a bite of my breakfast, I ask, "What is the dress code for this afternoon?"

"Workout clothes. What time can you be back?"

My brain is attempting to put together his questions and the necessary attire to no avail. "Worst case, noon."

"I'll meet you here at noon."

I glance at the clock. "Damn!"

"Go, Alannah. I'll lock up."

I steal a quick kiss and hurry out the door with a huge smile on my face. The ride to my office passes in a blur.

"Morning, Cara." I barely hear her reply. Right now, I'm cursing being the boss. Over the years, calling the shots has been helpful. I could skip out early and catch Caden's games or pick him up from practice. Today in particular, I would prefer having an associate to allow me an entire day of playing hooky with Callan. Something is better than nothing I suppose.

Exactly at ten, my phone rings. "Hello, Teddy. What provisions would your client like to change?" Over the next hour, we amend the agreement to ideally avoid trial.

"Please get this signed by your client. I want to get in front of Judge Colton as soon as possible. If your client agrees, mine would like to move his vacation up a week." He means his client's babymoon. Teddy's client has been screwing his personal assistant for the last five years and knocked her up, hence the nasty divorce.

Inside I'm boiling. Teddy knows I'm not available on Friday. Perhaps I can do both. "I'll see what I can do." Unfortunately, I know my client will accept. I'll be forced to get this agreement on the record on Friday because the clerks require one business day for notice. Judge Colton prides herself on keeping her docket moving. A settlement one day early is a win in her mind. I get my client's approval and have Cara inform Teddy.

"I'll see you in the morning," I inform her as I head back out the door. If she's surprised, she doesn't indicate as much. I shake off the sinking feeling I'm going to let Caden down on Friday as I head home.

When I arrive, Callan is scrolling on his phone on the front stoop. He stands and greets me with a sensual kiss. "How does it feel to play hooky?" he asks.

"It's mixed. I pulled off the agreement, but I might not be able to get Caden at camp."

"I can handle it. Plus, it'll give us some guy time to talk about stuff."

I arch an eyebrow. "Such as?"

"Basketball, college, and Kyla."

"Really?"

"Of course. Don't worry, he'll understand."

A wave of giddiness and a bit of trepidation wash over me. Giddiness about today, but also a smidge of fear. Callan's presence touches all aspects of my life. It's scary and wonderful at once. "Okay. Let me change, and we can go."

"I need to put some stuff in your fridge. I'll be right in."

"I'll help."

He hesitates. "One condition... no peeking. Otherwise, I'll do it myself."

"Deal." I set the bag from his trunk on the island and narrowly resist the urge to look inside. Then I disappear into my bedroom while Callan puts away the ingredients for dinner.

Once I'm ready to go, he escorts me to his SUV. After he settles into the driver's seat, he links our hands. Until Callan, I never realized how much I crave physical affection. I'm calmer when he's touching me. Daniel and I were kids, and Costas was only looking out for himself. "Where are we going?" I ask.

"Have you ever been to the aerial park?"

"No, but I always wanted to try it. Caden is going to be crazy jealous."

"We can come back with him."

I've been searching for Callan since my first Barbie wedding in my bedroom. Callan's integrity is one of the most attractive things about him. He hasn't wavered in his acceptance of my son. None of the circumstances matter. He's one of a kind.

"Alannah?"

"Hmmm." As I reply, I notice he's parked. *How long was I in my head?*

"Please share," Callan requests while lifting my hand to his lips.

I twist in the passenger seat. "This is foreign to me." My free hand moves between us. "I'm afraid to mess it up. No one made it past Caden, never mind hearing about Daniel and my parents."

"It is for me too. The idea of us is scary because we feel different than anyone before."

"Yes, we do," I whisper.

"Let's feel different together."

I smile, lean over the center console, and kiss him softly. After, our lips part and I pull back slightly. "Yes."

With a silly grin, he rounds his SUV and opens my door.

We approach the teen working.

"Officer Craven, nice to see you outside of school," a young brunette greets him. She sets a clipboard in front of each of us.

"Hi, Shayna. Nice to see you as well."

"Caden's mom, right?" she addresses me.

I smile. "I am."

"How are things?" Callan continues chatting while he scans the waiver.

"Good. Working here this summer and heading to Florida for college."

"Congrats!" he replies and scribbles his name on the paperwork.

Shayna collects mine as well.

"Thanks. Jimmy will get you two rigged up. Have a great time!"

We round the building, and Jimmy gets to work on the safety harnesses and helmets. The hint of possessiveness cast on Callan's face when Jimmy verifies the safety harness is correct strikes me hard. We spend twenty minutes going over safety instructions before we're allowed to climb. The best part is Callan and I have the entire course to ourselves.

On the way to the start, Callan curls his arm around my waist and kisses my cheek. "Ready?"

"To kick your butt, absolutely!" I grin and start climbing the web of ropes in front of me. When I reach the first Burma bridge, I glance backward.

Callan's hands grip my hips. "I'm right here, gorgeous. If you keep checking on me, I will beat you."

I turn on my heels and set a searing kiss on his mouth. "Are you sure you want to skip the kissing?"

"Skip? Never. Bunch them all together at the finish line, sure." He skirts around me, and now I'm chasing him.

"That's dirty, Callan."

All I get is a wink over his shoulder as he scurries up the vertical net in front of us. I'm frozen in place watching him climb, his arms strung tight and his calves flexed. He is—

"Stop staring and get moving," he calls from above me.

Caught! With an extra burst of competitiveness, I scale the vertical net and catch up to him on the catwalk. With our hands threaded together, we move along the tightrope at a slow but steady pace. Just past the halfway point, we take a break on side-by-side swings, our hands linked again.

"Having fun?" he asks.

"Yes."

"We both need a little more of it in our lives."

I hook my legs around the outside of his, so we're facing one another. I release his hand and grip his shirt, pulling him as close as I can. "I'm in as long as we're doing it together."

"Only way I want to do anything is with you." He eliminates the remaining space and kisses me as if we aren't tethered with harnesses to a ropes course sixty feet in the air. Warmth and longing flow through me every time he touches me. Callan calms me like no one else. Breathless again, we pull apart at the sound of an airhorn, our gaze laser focused on one another. The warning sound is followed by a recording indicating we have one hour remaining on the course.

"I guess we should get moving then," Callan suggests.

"Yeah, we should." Nervous butterflies take flight in my belly. I exhale. Pulling my thoughts together right now is impossible. Even with the hiccup at work, today has been perfect so far. I haven't had a day like today before I met Callan.

"You're welcome, Alannah."

"How…?"

A genuine, breathtaking smile breaks on his gorgeous face. "Reading you and settling your nerves about chasing happiness is rapidly becoming a goal of mine."

All I can do is nod. The feelings swirling in my head and in my heart, if I'm being honest, are a lot. I'm afraid to say the wrong thing. Although, with him, I don't think I could. He understands me better than any man I've met before.

"Let's finish this, and I'll cook for you." He kisses me again, then unhooks our legs.

I swing backward and hurry to my feet. There's a tube net and another Burma bridge between me and victory. I take off before Callan is ready to move.

"Now who's playing dirty, Alannah!" he calls after me.

"Catch me, and we can do it together,." I shout over my shoulder and hurry forward, nearly missing his groaned response. I feel my face heat. Win or lose, this part of our day was amazing.

Ten feet before the slide to the finish, Callan pulls up beside me. "Caught you!"

"Yes, you did." In more ways than he could imagine.

"Ready?" He extends his hand, I take it, and we slide down at the same time. We turn in our gear and make our way to his car.

"Next time we should actually race," I suggest and set my hand on his thigh.

He covers my hand, curls his fingers between mine, then pulls into traffic. "Nah, I would never trade those sky-high kisses for bragging rights."

Me either. "Fair enough." The tension zipping between us increases exponentially the closer we are to my house. "We're only holding hands and every nerve ending is on fire. How will more feel?"

"If you're asking what I think you're asking, it'll be indescribable."

Heat and desire surround me from head to toe. "I did it again, huh?"

He pulls into my driveway and parks. He shifts to face me as best he can. "Yeah."

"I suppose the answer to unhearing my question is the same as the last time?"

"I would rather answer your question. As I said before, answering your question properly will take us until the wee hours of the morning. However, I promised you a meal."

Holy hell!

Too many beats of silence pass for his comfort. "Did I lose you? If you want to unhear my answer, I understand. We can slow down."

"Are you really real?" I blurt. *Eloquent, Alannah.*

He laughs, and the deep, baritone sounds warm me. He eliminates the sliver of space between us and draws the pad of his thumb across my lower lip. Then he pulls my lower lip between his teeth, biting lightly before kissing me. "Yes, I'm real."

I could melt into a puddle here. He presses a kiss to my forehead and jumps out of the car. After opening my door, he extends his hand to me. "Come on, sweetheart. First dinner, then we can decide if you want an answer to your question tonight."

CHAPTER THIRTEEN

ALANNAH

I slide my hand into his and follow him inside. "Am I allowed to help?"

"No, I promised to cook for you. You can sit on one of the stools and keep me company if you want."

"I'll allow it this time, but I'm not good at relinquishing control over things."

He leans into me. "I know." After guiding me to a stool, he rounds the island and pulls out ingredients for dinner. "Slowly, you're going to willingly allow me to take care of you and Caden."

"I'm trying."

He puts a pan into the oven and stirs the pot on the stove. "I know you're trying. I'm a patient man. Running away isn't an option. Any relationship takes work." Setting down the spoon, he moves back to me, turns me to face him, and stands between my thighs. "I care about you and Caden. You deserve to be first, like he does. Some days it'll be him. Other days, it'll be you. Showing you each day is fast becoming the only thing I want to do."

"I care about you. You don't have to prove it every day."

"That's how it works for me at least. If I've learned anything from my parents and grandparents, seemingly insignificant things, like paying attention to details or making sure you eat breakfast, are part of being in a relationship. You may not realize it, but you do little things for me too."

"Such as?" I drop my head.

"Knowing I needed to play ball after my run-in with Greyson at Endzone." He lifts my chin with two fingers. "Allowing me to fix the front porch. I know you're capable. You have been long before we met. It's one of your most attractive but equally frustrating qualities. Fixing it was something I could do for you. I want to…." He scrubs his free hand down his face. "I want to carry… I'm not explaining this well. I want to be with you and Caden and share everything, even the mundane, daily stuff. I want to make your life easier and add a dash of fun."

I grip his shirt and draw him close enough to kiss him. "Your explanation is perfect. A relationship like you described is exactly what I want. Having it within arm's reach is scary and exciting, but I'm willing to share with you." I press a sweet kiss to his lips as the timer sounds.

He groans and slowly pulls away. "We're going to finish this kiss later. It wasn't nearly enough for our conversation."

"Okay. Am I allowed to set the table?"

"Sure," he replies before pulling the pan from the oven and stirring the pot on top.

I place two plates beside him and grab silverware and drinks. "Will you share what we're eating?"

He winks at me. "Chicken with parmesan cheese and sundried tomatoes in a cream sauce with garlic risotto."

"I may never let you leave. My own handy, protective, sexy chef."

"You don't need to keep me captive. I'll stay willingly."

Another brick in the wall around my heart and family crashes to the ground. Each sweet gesture and kiss rapidly exposes me to heartbreak. Yet my instinct tells me Callan won't hurt me. If anything, he seems too perfect.

"Time to eat, beautiful." He brings our plates to the table and pulls out my chair.

The first bite melts in my mouth. "Which room would you like to claim? This is delicious."

"Yours."

"Deal." I smirk at him.

He laughs, but I don't think he's kidding. Then he works on his dinner. The tension in the room increases the closer my plate is to empty.

"Alannah." Callan sets his hand on mine, pulling me back into my kitchen. "Do you want me to leave?"

I drop my head, exhale slowly, and look up at him. "No."

"Remember earlier today when you were freaking out on a smaller scale than you are right now?"

His ability to pinpoint my emotions and fears is unsettling and devastating to my heart at the same time.

I nod.

"Good. We agreed to feel different together."

"Yes, but... it's been...."

"Same for me."

"I'm not sure if I should be relieved or more nervous."

He smiles and rises to his feet. "Neither. We dipped our toes into the pool on our date, right?" With our plates in his hand, he walks toward the sink.

"That was a dip?"

"Improper, medium-sized dip. Do we need to back up to proper, small steps?"

"No. There's no chance I can forget how you make me feel. I need to get out of my head. I'll wash. House rules. You cook, you don't do dishes."

A devilish grin materializes on his face. "Okay. House rules." Callan steps away from the sink too easily.

I know without a doubt, he's up to something. While I start to wash, he brings our glasses to the island. Once the plates are washed, I move on to the pans. Midway through the risotto pan, he sets his mouth to the nape of my neck while his hands roam around my waist. Tingles flow from his warm lips to his hands and back again. I grip the edge of the sink.

"Do you want me to stop?"

"No."

He reaches forward and shuts off the water. "This needs to go." He gathers the hem of my shirt and starts to lift.

Despite the enticing sensations from Callan's touch, I retreat into my head a bit. *Of course, it isn't your sexiest lingerie you haven't worn in way too long, you were climbing before dinner.*

I barely twitch, and he says, "No, forget your last thought. Stay with me."

My head falls forward in acknowledgment, not only because of his words but the fact he seems to have a direct line to my thoughts. "If mine goes, so does yours." I lift my arms, and my shirt floats to the floor. Turning, I watch slack jawed as he grasps his shirt at the nape of his neck like only men do and drags it over his head.

"Do men realize how hot that is?"

"What? Taking off my shirt?"

"Yes, but how you take it off."

"Noted, gorgeous." Then he grins at me. "It's only fair if we're both bare chested, right?"

He unhooks my bra and slides it off. My nipples tighten at the friction, then pucker more when no space between us remains. When his lips meet mine, I'm fully invested in feeling different with Callan. Our mouths swirl in a sensual dance like our feet. With precise steps, we move into my bedroom. My fingers slither beneath the waistband of his shorts. He stills briefly when I stroke him.

Before I manage another stroke, I'm flat on my back in the center of my bed with a frown on my face.

"Don't pout. If you keep touching me, I won't be able to fulfill my promise to you."

"Which was?"

Lust and desire pool in his eyes. "I vaguely recall indicating when we were together it would take until the wee hours of the morning."

"You did, but I want to touch you."

"You're a woman who likes to be in control. It's sexy as sin and intriguing. I've never met a woman like you. In here, though, please give me a little leeway so I can worship you properly. I need to put my slow-build knowledge to good use. Then you can touch me however you choose."

Much to my surprise, and Callan's as well, I allow him to control the pace... for now. He peels my leggings and cotton thong down my legs and casts them aside, along with his shorts, but he leaves his boxer briefs on. The tip of his length peeks out the top. I shimmy higher on my bed as Callan hovers over me.

With a look of unfiltered desire in his eyes, he lowers his mouth to mine again. Using precise movements, Callan explores each inch of exposed skin. Purposefully, he nips, sucks, and kisses his way down to my navel. Each nerve ending from my head to my toes is ablaze in anticipation of his next touch.

Breathe, Alannah, I remind myself. Every moment with Callan brings insecurities and vulnerabilities, real or self-perceived, to the surface. My thoughts dissipate with the first swipe of the flat of his tongue on my heated center.

Holy mother of... I surrender to the tantalizing sensations coursing through me. With my hands fisting the duvet, I arch and allow the intensifying pressure to uncoil. My entire body shudders, and stars explode in my eyes when Callan presses the heel of his hand into my lower abdomen. "Callan!" I would bet money he smiles between my quaking thighs.

Before I recover from the most exquisite orgasm of my life, he plunges two fingers into my core and sucks my clit into his mouth. I tip over the edge of another orgasm when he curls his fingers and nudges a throbbing spot within me no man has reached before. When the aftershocks lessen enough for me to speak, I manage, "Your time in control is up. Please get up here."

Does he listen? Not exactly. With measured, pleasure-filled kisses, Callan travels up my body, keeping me on the edge of carnal bliss. He shimmies out of his boxer briefs as he climbs.

A deep groan vibrates off my walls when my hand surrounds his throbbing length. When he marginally recovers, he asks, "I don't have protection. Are you on birth control?"

"Yes."

Relief washes over his features and is quickly replaced by a look of lust-addled desire. I widen my thighs, and he buries himself inch by scintillating inch. Once I adjust, he thrusts forward fully once, followed by numerous shallow ones. He repeats the same movements, except with two plunges to the hilt and less shallow ones. I'm lost in the spiraling need Callan is masterfully building within my body. One hand is clasped with his beside my head while the other digs into his obliques.

I'm hurtling toward another decadent release and tighten my grip on his hand. When I clench my inner muscles, he inexplicably lengthens again.

"Do that again, and I'll fall over with you," he groans.

I pin my gaze to his and tighten around him again. Ribbons of pleasure overcome me. His frame tenses with another thrust forward. As promised, he explodes into me. Callan lowers his body over mine with his mouth near the shell of my ear.

"Breathe, gorgeous."

"Trying." Sweet mercy! I've been missing out. There's only one explanation... him. I exhale slowly. "Callan, I have no words."

"Neither do I."

We clean up and snuggle together in my bed. After a short power nap, Callan's skillful mouth wakes me. He wasn't kidding when he said wee hours of the morning. After our third round, we both succumb to the pull of sleep we desperately need.

CHAPTER FOURTEEN

CALLAN

Dragging my hand over the dip of her waist, down to midthigh and back again, I realize I'm likely waking up alone tomorrow. The thought makes my stomach pitch. Waking with Alannah flush against me or sprawled on top of me is where I want to wake each morning, especially naked like we are now. However, I respect the fact she's raising a teenage son.

"Stop thinking so hard; it's too early." She twists to face me and sets her lips on mine.

"How much time do we have?" I ask before marking a path with my mouth along her shoulder before slowly rolling her beneath me.

She sighs. "Max... thirty minutes for you to leave on time. Me... more like an hour."

"Do you have an alarm set?" I ask, then drag my tongue over the swell of her breast.

She exhales. Her "yes" is raspy and dripping with desire.

I roll her and draw her onto her knees. As I glide my hands up the back of her thighs, she widens her legs in invitation. I align myself with her and push forward. Once she adjusts to me, I pick up my pace. She pulses and spasms around me.

"Callan, don't...." Her words trail off with her first orgasm this morning.

Smoothing my hand around her hip, I massage her swollen clit to push her toward another release while chasing my own. Her inner muscles tighten around me, and I can't hold back any longer. I fill her as she trembles and shudders with pleasure again.

Her alarm sounds within a few minutes of us catching our breath. I silence it and move to the edge of the bed.

"You go first since you have less time. I'll make you some coffee," she suggests.

I kiss her and hurry into the bathroom. Once I'm showered and dressed, I meet her in the kitchen.

"You're fast." Her face turns bright red. "I mean—"

"I know what you mean. Time to move, beautiful." I relieve her of the cup and shoo her toward the master bathroom. I calculate how much time I have left and throw together a breakfast burrito for her before I leave. I knock on the bathroom door but walk in before she answers. "I need to go. Did you tell him I'm picking him up?"

She opens the glass door enough to peek out. "I sent a text. He didn't reply. Normally, I would freak out about him not answering, but it didn't really require an answer." The pout on her face is seriously too much.

"I know you would prefer to come with me, but he'll understand."

"In my head, your words make sense. My mama heart, not so much."

"Hopefully, we can make it back for dinner. Good luck at court." I bend at the waist to meet her lips to avoid getting my clothes wet. It's difficult enough to ignore my urge for sexy shower time with every inch of her on display.

Her kiss feels different this morning, possessive but unsteady. Then it dawns on me, she's trusting me with the most important person in her life.

I pull back slightly, lifting her chin so her eyes meet mine. "Alannah, I won't let anything happen to Caden."

Her warm, wet hand cups my jaw, and she takes a deep breath. "I trust you completely. The issue is with me. I never had to choose before. Putting work over Caden is one of the most difficult things I've ever had to do. I'm grateful I have you to be there for him today. Otherwise, I would be worse off than I am."

"Thank you for trusting me." I kiss her again and slip out of the bathroom. Nearly thirty minutes into the drive, my phone rings.

"I didn't get there yet, gorgeous."

She laughs. "I'm in the court lot. Breakfast was yummy!"

"You're welcome. If you get out of court in time for the game, we can video call so you can watch too."

"Sounds perfect! I need to get inside. Thank you, Callan."

"No place I would rather be today." I end the call and continue toward my alma mater. A perk of being an alumnus is knowing where the best parking spots are. I pull into the lot adjacent to the arena and head inside to search for a seat. Before I find one, Manny approaches me.

He extends his hand to me, and we bro hug. "Hey, Callan. Your girlfriend's…." He pauses as if he offended me by calling Alannah my girlfriend. The title isn't enough but will work for now.

"Hi, Manny. It's all good. The title is fine."

"I didn't want to offend you or her. Is she here?"

"Unfortunately, she was called into court."

"Oh. Well, I should be talking to her, but given our history, I'll make an exception. Caden is talented. We could utilize his skill set next fall." Manny's words sting a bit.

I'm not Caden's father, but I'll happily take on the role if he'll allow me the honor. Alannah as well. "He's a good student and trains hard."

"Make sure he sends his footage and schedule when it comes out. We have the video from this camp, but more is always helpful. I would be interested in attending a game during his senior season."

"I'll talk to him on the ride home. Good to see you again, Manny."

"You too." He grabs some supplies and joins his staff. I stroll to center court and climb the bleachers. After I take a seat, I search for Caden among the campers. He waves and crosses the hardwood. I make my way down to him.

"Hey, OC."

"Hi, Caden. How was camp?"

He shrugs. "Where's Mom?"

"Didn't you get her text?"

He tilts his head and then hangs it. "My phone broke."

I can surmise his broken phone and opinion about camp has to do with Kyla, her injuries, and how she obtained them. "She was called to court for her divorce case. I'm going to video call with her when your game starts." As I speak, my phone vibrates in my pocket.

"Cool. Gotta go." He takes a few steps and turns back. "Thank you for coming when you said you would."

"I always will." His statement isn't a dig at Alannah's absence but appreciation of my follow-through. He's astute enough to realize he hasn't met anyone else Alannah has dated. I see no reason there will be anyone else to meet. I retake my seat and check my phone.

Alannah: I'm set.

Me: I'll call at tipoff.

Alannah: Okay.

About twenty minutes later, the closing games begin. Four teams leave the main arena for the adjacent field house for their games. After the national anthem plays, I call Alannah.

"Hey, gorgeous."

"Hi. Have you talked to Caden?"

"Yeah."

"How did he take it?"

"Fine. He broke his phone. I'll have him call you before we leave here."

She nods. "Kyla or something else?"

"The former, I think. Coach Ortega stopped me when I arrived. He's interested in Caden for the fall. Do you have an issue with me sharing with him?"

"Wow! Good for Caden. No, feel free to talk to him about it."

"That's three offers, right?"

"Yeah."

The buzzer sounds, and the game begins. I've never watched a game with Alannah, and this barely qualifies. However, she watches intently as if she's memorizing every play. Perhaps she is. Caden is fouled hard near the end of the first half. Alannah gasps. Then I realize I'm on my feet, watching nervously for him to stand from the hardwood. The trainer is on the court and escorts him to the bench. Caden walks off under his own power, but he's opening and closing his left hand and rolling his wrist.

"Callan." Her voice is laced with guilt, and concern draws my attention. Would it matter if she was here? No, the foul would've happened either way. Would she be able to check him out personally? Also, no. I turn the camera toward me.

"He appears fine." I explain what I'm seeing in more detail.

"Okay." The horn sounds for halftime, and the teams huddle up.

"How was the hearing?" I ask, hoping to get her mind off Caden and the fact she's not beside me.

"Fine. I brokered a lucrative deal for my client, considering her husband was cheating on her with his personal assistant for the last five years and now she's pregnant. They didn't have a prenup. My client ending up with 65 percent of their assets is a win in my opinion."

"Well done."

"Thanks."

As the second half starts, Caden jogs onto the court with his teammates. By the end of the game, Caden has a double-double in assists and points. The organizers share some awards, including the team captain award, which Caden won. The award was voted on by his teammates and given to the player who the attendees feel is the most well rounded. He also garnered the most outstanding player award.

Alannah smiles from ear to ear as I make my way to the court and hand Caden my phone. "Hey, Mom!"

"Great game, Caden!"

"Thanks. It was fun. How was court?"

"Fine. I'm sorry I couldn't make it."

"No worries. You're always here. I understand."

"Callan is going to bring you home."

Caden rolls his eyes and laughs. "Good plan. See you later. Love you."

"Love you too," Alannah replies as he returns my phone to me.

"See you soon," I add before ending the call. We retrieve his bags and make our way to my SUV. "Do you need to eat now, or can you make it home first?"

"I've got snacks as long as I can eat in your truck?"

"You can."

"Sweet!" He pulls chips, individual cereal packages, and two waters from his backpack.

"Honestly, how was camp?" I ask as I turn my SUV toward the highway.

"It was awesome until I talked to Kyla on Wednesday afternoon."

"Want to share?"

He shrugs.

"I won't share anything with your mom you tell me in confidence, unless it impacts your safety. She knows you and Kyla weren't on the same page last weekend."

"She broke up with me to focus on her senior season."

"I'm sorry."

"Me too. This year was going to be epic. We were going to attend all the senior activities together and have kick-ass seasons. My mom taught me to waltz for prom last year. Then...."

I wait him out.

"Then she calls me after the accident and admits she was with Andre. Kyla claims they're just friends, but I don't buy it. I'm not a jealous guy. I trust—trusted—her. I have friends who are girls; she has friends who are guys. Andre is a newcomer as far as spending time with her. She lied to me but didn't want me to find out from someone else. It's twisted."

"Because you still care about her," I suggest.

"Exactly. Does it get easier?"

"Dating?"

"Yeah."

"Eventually." Each additional piece of advice tripping through my mind would seem like I'm bashing Kyla. I give her credit. For a young woman, she was honest, at least it appears she was.

"Can we talk about something else?"

"Sure, like?"

"Basketball."

I smile. "I can talk for hours on that subject. What part specifically?"

"What was your experience playing in college?"

I share with him why I picked SNHU and having Manny's dad as a coach was pivotal for me.

"I'm sorry about your sister."

"Thanks. College ball helped me figure out what I wanted to do with my life while playing the game I love. How are you feeling about playing next year?"

He hesitates.

"You don't have to answer."

Caden shakes his head. "I didn't really want to talk about Kyla more, but... Last year after our first offers came in, we talked about how it would work if we ended up recruited by different colleges. Part of our breakup is she doesn't want to worry about me when she's making her decision."

"It's mature of you both to discuss the major choice openly and honestly."

"Didn't do much good, did it?" He's hurt, which is completely understandable.

"Maybe, maybe not. Coach Ortega asked me about you when I arrived today."

He perks up a little but says nothing.

I continue, "What did you think of the program?"

"The facilities are awesome, and Coach is firm but fair."

"Any idea what you want to major in?"

His reply is without a shred of doubt. "Software engineering and cyber security."

"Cool. Coach requested more footage and is interested in attending a game during the season."

"Really?"

I smile. "Yes, really."

"That's awesome. I can't believe I have three offers. Does Mom know?"

"Yeah. I asked her if I could tell you. She agreed."

He quiets for a minute. "You're the first guy my mom has allowed around me."

I know the truth, but I won't share with him. "How do you feel about that?"

"You're cool, and she's happier than before you met." He huffs. "I don't mean she was unhappy, but she was alone. Always alone."

"Maybe it was a choice."

Caden shakes his head. "Nah, she was protecting me. I never told her about the kids at school. The locals who know what happened to my dad, they talk and whisper. At least they did when I was younger. I think Uncle Séamus set them straight after I lost my temper with one of the Muller boys at the playground in fourth grade."

"I got one of those warnings at the game," I share.

"I'm glad you didn't run away."

"Me too. It allowed me to get to know both of you. Your mom is awesome. I don't even mind she's a better shooter than I am."

He laughs. "Truth."

"All joking aside. I care about both of you."

"I know."

I look at him to make sure I heard him right. "What?"

"You take care of her and treat her well."

"How do you know?"

"The breakfast delivery, for starters. How could you possibly know she never eats breakfast? The flowers make her smile each time she passes them. Mom takes care of me, her business, and then herself. You don't push her to rely on you, but you're available if needed, like today."

"Truthfully, she wasn't happy about missing the game."

"She hasn't missed one my entire career. Honestly, and please don't tell her, but this one doesn't matter. Mom does way more for me than other parents. Like you did today, she shows up. She welcomes my crazy friends into our home and treats them like additional kids. Whatever I need, she provides it for me, and I'm sure it isn't easy, especially when I was younger. Sometimes I wonder how different my life would've been if my dad survived the accident." He pauses and turns contemplative. "Is this weird for you?"

"No. I'm here for you and to talk about whatever you want. Your mom shared about the accident with me."

"I always end up in the same place."

"Which is?" I ask.

"Mom is a badass, and I want her to find the man she deserves, a partner."

I grin at him. "Don't call her that to her face. She might ground you for life. Your description is flawless. She is absolutely badass. The rest is pretty deep though."

He shrugs. "Raising me alone wasn't easy. Grandpa and Grandma Kramer are awesome, but they're older. Plus, Mom is stubborn. Always wants to do everything on her own."

"I hadn't noticed." Sarcasm drips from my tone.

Caden laughs, then continues. "The locals weren't nice to her for a while either. She took it, never complained, and tried to shield me. I know she has been on dates. Not a lot, but some. My grandparents or Aunt Del usually watched me. She was never smiling when she got home until she met you. I guess all I'm trying to say is… I like you for her. Please don't hurt her."

"I won't." Silence blankets my SUV for a few miles. I've never had a seal of approval from a teenager before, but I feel like I got one. I extend my phone to him. "Why don't you call your mom and see if she could order wings and pizza? I'm sure you're starving now."

He takes my phone and makes the call. "She wants to know if you want them extra hot."

I grin inwardly, grateful Caden doesn't get the inside joke. "Yes."

He replies in kind, and I can see the smile on her face in my mind. "Thanks, Mom. You should order now. We'll be there in about fifteen minutes. Love you." Caden ends the call and puts my phone in the center console. "How many extra steps do you think Mom got today pacing while waiting for us?"

I laugh. "She probably went for a run or refined her shot more."

"Possibly, or she was dancing."

"Dancing?"

"Yeah, Aunt Del… did you meet her?"

"Yes, we've met."

"Anyway, a few years ago, Aunt Del gave Mom dance classes for her birthday. I'm sure she was trying to set her up because it was partner dancing not Zumba. She learned to waltz, samba, and a few others. At first, she was angry, but then she started to like the classes."

"Cool." Another unique facet of Alannah I never would've guessed. I pull into the driveway, and we make our way inside.

"Mom, I'm home!"

She steps in from the patio and hugs Caden. When she releases him, I kiss her briefly and pull away. The questions in her eyes are priceless.

"I'm going to take a quick shower before the food arrives." Caden rushes upstairs.

I don't bother to verify Caden isn't going to catch me. I haul Alannah close and kiss her deeply. When I'm sated, at least for a little while, I draw back. "Hello, sweetheart."

"Hi. What was that?"

My smile is huge. "I think your son gave me approval to date you."

She laughs. "Are you going to share what he said?"

"No, it's between me and him." I kiss her until dinner arrives.

Caden fills her in about the camp and a little bit about Kyla between bites. Although, he shares less with her than he did with me on the ride home. It only takes him two bites per slice, it seems. I don't recall the last time I polished off an entire pizza myself.

"We can take care of your phone tomorrow, but you need to pay the insurance amount," Alannah informs him.

"Okay, that's fair." To avoid talking more about his breakup, he asks, "If I put in a load of laundry, will you put it in the dryer? There's no guarantee I'll still be awake when it finishes."

"Sure," she replies.

"Do we have plans tomorrow?" he asks us both.

"Maybe the beach in the morning. Want to come with?"

He shrugs. "Possibly."

"I'm working," I share. "Do you need something?"

He shakes his head. "It isn't urgent, but I should work on the footage for coach."

"We'll find the time before school starts in two weeks."

"Thanks, OC. Night."

"No problem. Good night."

"Night, Mom."

"Good night, Caden."

He disappears, reappears with his laundry, and then he's gone again. We clear the dishes and put away the two remaining slices.

"I should go."

She frowns. "I don't want you to leave. I love waking up with you."

"I'm not a fan either, but it's the right thing to do."

"Are you free tomorrow night?"

Now it's my turn to frown. "No, sorry. Smithson roped me and the rest of the wedding party into some hush-hush thing for Scarlett. If I could wiggle out of it, I would. As the best man, I can't."

"I know."

"Are you free for dinner on Sunday? Both of you."

"I am. I'll check with Caden."

I kiss her again and pull away before I walk her into her bedroom. "I'll call you. Good night, sweetheart."

"Night, Callan."

Caden's seal of approval makes me hopeful I might not have to leave each night for long.

CHAPTER FIFTEEN

ALANNAH

Nearly dressed for work, I knock on Caden's door. I'm greeted with an unceremonious groan. "Time to get moving."

"We don't do anything on the first day, plus it's Thursday. I'll go on Monday."

I push open his door a bit. "Not happening. It's your senior year."

He pulls the pillow over his face. "That's why you should let me!"

I take a seat on the edge of his bed, which I don't make a habit of doing anymore. "I know it's going to be tough seeing her each day again, but school isn't optional."

He pushes to sitting and throws his arms around my neck. "How do you always know what I need to hear?" A few days after camp, Caden shared his breakup with me in more detail. He's spent time with his friends but hasn't really looked to move on yet.

With a wink, I reply, "It's a gift. You've got thirty minutes tops." I finish dressing in a hurry and start the brewer in the kitchen. Each morning before work, Callan and I share a cup of coffee.

Callan: Morning, gorgeous. Can you open the door?

Confused, I make my way to the front door. Callan approaches loaded down with boxes of goodies crafted by Kelsey.

I swing the door open. "Morning, babe. Are you feeding an army?"

He kisses me lightly as he steps inside. "Sort of. They're for Caden."

I peek in the box after the coffee finishes. The donuts are decorated with a wildcat logo and "senior year" in school colors.

"I didn't forget about you." Callan hands me a chocolate croissant.

As if the donuts for Caden weren't enough for me. "You're the best!" I put the pastry in the microwave to warm.

"Only for you and Caden."

As if he summoned him, Caden shuffles into the kitchen, grumbling, "Morning."

"Morning. I brought breakfast for you and a bunch of your friends," Callan informs him, opening the top box.

"These are awesome!" Caden rounds the island and hugs him. "Can I have one now and then more later?"

Callan laughs. "Yup, I brought three boxes."

With permission, Caden inhales half of a donut in one bite. When he polishes off that one, he asks, "Will you help me put them in the car?"

"Sure."

They leave the kitchen with the boxes as I bite into my now warm, flaky pastry. The two of them have grown closer since camp. I'm glad. Callan works hard to strike the best balance between father figure and friend. It's heartwarming to watch them bond. Both rejoin me in the kitchen. Callan drains his coffee with a long gulp. Watching his throat work has inappropriate thoughts spinning in my mind for the time of day and present company. Who knew that would get me going? Certainly not me. Thankfully, Callan doesn't catch me ogling him.

"I gotta go, Mom. I'll be home after school." Caden gives me a side hug and throws his backpack over his shoulder.

They fly through their practiced and recently expanded handshake before he rushes out the door.

"I need to go too. I'll be back after shift."

His kiss will barely tide me over until the end of the day. "See you later, sweetheart."

"Have a good day." I blow him another kiss as he walks down the hall. I throw a snack in my tote and follow them. I mentally go through my calendar as I drive to the office. I have a late morning hearing for Mrs. Brinson's estate and a closing this afternoon at three. The most important entry is lunch with Del.

I greet Cara and cull my action items before the hearing, which is completed in less than thirty minutes. I exit the probate court and take a short walk to the deli a few blocks west.

"Hey, Alannah." I turn and find Kelsey and her gorgeous babies strolling on the sidewalk.

"Hi, Miss Lan," Ben says loudly, like only a small child can. "Shhh, Val napping."

"Hi, Ben," I whisper, then turn to Kelsey. "Thank you for the amazing donuts for Caden."

"Craven requested those weeks ago. It was a fun order. Speaking of Craven, how are things going with the two of you? I should apologize for my husband interrupting your date."

At best, Kelsey is an acquaintance. We did chat at the game, but I don't know her other than spending insane amounts of money on coffee and pastries at her coffee shop. I only share personal details with Del and now Callan. "No apology necessary. He was being neighborly to Smithson. Like Callan, I'm sure he can't shut off his protectiveness."

She laughs. "True."

"It was great seeing you, but I need to get to my lunch meeting."

"You too."

"Bye, Ben."

"Bye, Miss Lan!" His words startle his sister awake. "Sorry, Mama." He drops his head.

"It's okay, bud. Bye, Alannah."

I grab my order from the deli and hurry back to my office. Thankful, I didn't share anything I wasn't ready to share with Kelsey.

"Hey, girl! Cara let me in. How was the hearing?" Del is leaning against my bookshelf, gazing out the window.

"Fine. I ran into Kelsey Ramirez."

"She's super nice."

I set the sandwiches on my desk and plop into my chair. "Yeah, it was weird though. She was asking about Callan."

"Maybe she was looking out for him. I mean, he does work for her husband."

"I guess. I'm not really a sharing kind of person. That's all."

"Only with me, and I'm grateful." We laugh and eat our lunch.

"Are you free the first Saturday of November?" I ask.

She pulls out her phone and checks her calendar. "Yup, why?"

"Can you stay at the house with Caden?"

Her smile is nothing short of giddy. "Ooooohhhh, an overnight date."

My blush forces Del to push for more details.

"Wait, did you…?" She pauses to see my reaction, which gives her nothing more. "Pour it out, right now!"

My eyes snap closed. "Nope, no details will be shared."

"That good or that bad?" she presses.

I hesitate a moment, then share, "All I'm going to say is mind-blowing good."

"Hell yes, girl! Good for you!" She raises her iced tea in my direction. "Happy for you, Lan."

No further comment is necessary. Del is my bestie, but behind closed doors, details became a no-go zone when Caden was young. I wasn't with anyone and, therefore, handling things myself. Midway through lunch, I notice an ivory envelope with an embossed Boston College logo on top of today's mail. Intrigued, I pull it out and open it.

"What's that?" Del asks.

"Don't know. It looks fancy though." I read the card and set it down on my desk.

Del picks it up and reads aloud, "The Boston College Athletics department and Carol Sowell cordially invite you…."

I tune her out. I read the details.

When she finishes, Del states, "You have to go!"

"No, I don't."

"Of course you do!"

"Why, Del?" I trust her judgment. Any event with people from my past, I avoid like the plague.

"Coach invited you to kick off her farewell season. She wants you there. Plus, you're a shining example of hard work, dedication, and overcoming obstacles. You deserve to be acknowledged for still holding the three-point shooting record fifteen years later."

Del, my cheerleader extraordinaire. My shoulders drop as I exhale. "I'll think about it."

She points at me, holding the invitation in her hand. "Promise you'll share with Callan too."

I give her the side-eye. "No."

"If you don't tell him, I will."

"You wouldn't."

"I will. I love you, Lan. He's good for you and Caden. You're happy and taken care of. You let him in deeper than any man before. This event is a big deal. You're a big deal. You deserve to be celebrated."

"I'll consider it, Del."

"Thank you."

After her warning about sharing with Callan, I'm not great company. The rest of our lunch passes mostly in silence. Del won't push me more yet, but she will tell Callan if I don't.

"I gotta get back. See you next week. Please consider the invitation, Lan."

We hug, and I reply, "I will." I lock the door behind her and review the files for this afternoon. I sleepwalk through the closing and recording at the town clerk's office.

Deep down, I know Del is right. I should go to the ceremony. Reopening myself to my past beyond what I've shared with Callan seems insurmountable. Without a doubt, Callan will encourage me to go. He rivals Del in the supportive category, but in different ways. Both may be right, but wrapping my brain around the necessity of accepting it isn't going to be easy.

When I arrive home, my guys are shooting around outside. I change and join them. I like the sound of "my guys." Over the years raising Caden, I lost hope of finding someone who would fit with us. A man who would accept us both, warts and all. Until I met Callan.

"Hey, guys," I call out when I step onto the court.

"Hi, Mom."

"How was school?"

Caden shrugs and returns to the drill he was working on—a normal answer from a high schooler.

Callan is walking in my direction. "Hi, gorgeous. How was your day?" He sets a brief kiss on my lips.

He'll know something is off. I have no choice but to say, "Not great. Well, I'm mixed. We can talk about it later."

"I'll hold you to that," he promises me.

"I know. I expect nothing less." For the next hour plus, the guys play one-on-one while I shoot around until my arms feel like rubber. Each shot has me tossing different scenarios in my mind. The worst thing that could happen—I feel their pity again. It's no secret that none of my teammates are my friends now. I expertly kept them at arm's length during college. Not one has reached out in the intervening years. No grudge here. It's what I wanted, a clean break. In my mind, all relationships are a two-way street. I may not be friends with my teammates, but Coach was supportive every step of the way. She didn't treat me differently, but I felt as if she understood my drive to do it all.

"Alannah." Callan's voice breaks into my thoughts.

"Hmmm?" I meet his gaze.

"Ready to eat?" he asks.

"Sure." I rack my ball and follow them inside. Given my state of mind, I didn't notice the casserole in the oven when I arrived home. Thankfully, the guys are chatting away about the first day of school and not engaging with me at all. Caden finishes his second serving before clearing his plate and heading to his room.

Once my son is out of earshot, Callan requests, "Time to share, sweetheart."

I rise from my chair and hand him the invitation from my tote.

He takes a minute and gathers his thoughts. "You're afraid they'll judge you again or differently." A statement not a question.

"Yes."

"Why do you care? You didn't care about the townspeople or your aunt and uncle when we woke up together. Why are these women different?"

I don't have an adequate answer. They aren't. In fact, I care about their opinion less than the others he mentioned.

He continues after sliding his fingers into mine. "I'll support you either way, but you should go. You're successful, raised an amazing son on your own, hold the three-point record, and your coach invited you. You may not believe it, but I do for both of us, you're exceptional. The rest of the world should recognize it to."

I have no words to quantify the rush of warmth and a smidge of pride from his words. "Like I told Del earlier, I'll consider it."

"Okay."

I appreciate he isn't going to push me, at least right now anyway. I have a week or so to RSVP.

"Can we plan other events?"

I wrinkle my nose. "Such as?"

"How do you and Caden normally celebrate Thanksgiving?"

I rise from my chair and skim my lips across his before setting our plates in the sink. Callan follows with the rest.

I reply while I wash. "Normally, we have dinner at Clem and Paul's after attending the high school football game. However this year, they're going to the Bahamas with their children and grandchildren for the holiday. Why?"

"Will you and Caden join me at dinner with my family in Connecticut?"

Without a shred of hesitation, I answer. "Yes." I set the last plate on the rack, turn toward him, and eliminate the space between us.

"No nerves are necessary," he assures me, reading me accurately.

"Of course they are."

His lips meet mine before I can voice any further concerns. He knows my thoughts before I can vocalize them. After a knee-weakening kiss, he pulls back slightly. "My family won't judge you because of Caden."

"Okay. I'm going to need more details between now and then about your family."

"Such as?"

"You never shared their names or much about your nieces."

He laughs. "Now work?"

"Sure. In the living room?"

He leads me out of the kitchen, and we curl up on my couch. "My father's name is Pádriag, which means Patrick. He oversees one of the warehouses for a global company. He has been scaling back his hours for the last five years. My mother's name is Gráinne. She goes by Grace. She was a stay-at-home mom when I was young. Now she works part-time at a bookstore."

"Both names are unique. Were they born here?"

"Yes, but they're first-generation Americans. Both sets of grandparents are from a small village on the coast of Ireland named Kenmare. They met on their journey here."

"That's fascinating. Your nieces?"

"Maeve and Quinn, born in that order. Patrick has primary custody."

"There's a story there."

"Yeah, but not mine to tell. As long as you don't mention his ex's name, you're good."

I tilt my head in question.

"Ciara."

"Understood. Do you have wedding stuff this weekend?"

He frowns. "Not tomorrow, but Saturday into Sunday is the bachelor party."

"What are you guys doing or are you sworn to secrecy?"

"Wondering how much trouble I'm going to get into?"

"No. I trust you. Some of your coworkers, not so much."

"Understandable. Greyson wasn't invited. It's a small group—the groom, me, Cap, Hagen, and Gugliotti. We're having dinner on Saturday at Smith and Wollensky, then attending the afternoon game at Fenway in the luxury suite."

"Smithson has good taste."

"Yeah, he does."

I snuggle deeper into his arms. "Thank you for not pushing me to decide tonight."

"You're welcome."

His response is the last thing I recall. Near two in the morning, I wake, set an alarm, and allow sleep to reclaim me.

CHAPTER SIXTEEN

CALLAN

The Smithson wedding festivities have severely decreased the amount of time I'm able to spend with Alannah. With extra preparation for their super-secret but unique plan for their first dance, tuxedo fittings, helping with the program and favors, I haven't spent more than our morning coffee with her in longer than I like. Zack is my brother-in-blue, but I need Alannah. I've fallen hard for her. However, given the rapid progress of our relationship, I haven't shared my feelings with her. Before I leave my house for the venue, I call her. Hearing her voice will settle me until I can hold her.

"Hi, beautiful."

"Hi. All set for tonight?" I can hear the smile in her voice.

"I'm headed to Savannah's and then the Cliff House."

"I can't wait to finish my research of my favorite outfit."

I laugh. "I think you might be forgetting an outfit to judge."

"Am I?"

"Definitely."

"Which is?"

"Gray sweatpants and a backward baseball hat."

"Dirty words, Callan."

"Making sure your research is thorough, sweetheart. Have I mentioned red is my favorite color?"

She exhales. "Liar."

"It's my favorite color on you."

"I haven't worn anything red yet."

"I'm confident in my statement before seeing how gorgeous you look later." I imagine her face flushing pink. "I can't wait to see you."

"Me either. I'm going to have Caden drop me off before he goes out with Del."

"I'll find you as soon as I can."

"Don't worry about me. Be a great friend. I'll be there when you're done."

She may not realize it, but I worry about her daily. Maybe worry isn't the right word. My goal is to care for her every need and most of her wants for the rest of her life if she'll have me. She doesn't need me to do anything for her. I want her to want me to.

"See you soon." I end the call and recheck the back seat of my SUV. Tux, shoes, tie, box of programs, spare everything for Zack, and gift for Scarlett. All there. I slip my hand into my pocket and verify the rings are secure for the millionth time today.

I take the winding road up to Savannah and Sam's where Scarlett is getting ready. They live in a gorgeous home near the Nubble Lighthouse. While the views in this area are spectacular, I would prefer a huge backyard. I knock on the door.

"Hi, Craven. Is everything okay?" Lia Cappelli, who is Scarlett's bestie and former roommate, greets me with a hug. She appears to be mostly ready except for shoes.

"Yes. I have a special delivery for Scarlett."

"Come in." Lia ushers me inside, and when I enter the living room, all talking ceases.

"Is Zack okay?" Scarlett asks, her voice shaky and concerned.

"Of course."

Her hand rises over her heart, covering the embroidered "Mrs. Smithson" on her robe, and she takes a deep breath.

"I didn't intend to worry you. Savannah knew I would be stopping by."

Scarlett shakes her head. "It makes sense why she didn't send Zack's gift yet. Let me get it for you." When she returns, I accept the narrow box from her and hand her the groom's gift. After a brief hug, I make my way outside to meet up with the groom.

The scene is significantly different with the groomsmen. The bride and her bridal party are nearly ready. Zack and Hagen are wearing sweaty workout gear and chowing down on a late breakfast. I appreciate they ordered enough for me.

"Hey! I'm getting married today!" Zack announces when I step into the suite. "Eat before your food gets colder."

I grin at him. "I know. This is from your bride."

Zack shakes his head and accepts the gift.

"Something wrong?"

Zack answers, "No. I'm not surprised she didn't listen. I don't have to open this to know she bought tickets to the painting exposition in Paris."

"That is how you know she's the one, bro!" Hagen adds. "She knows you want to go, and she's willing to join you." Hagen finishes his food and hops into the shower.

"How was she?" Zack asks.

"What are you worried about? Scarlett's your better half."

"I'm worried about her father doing something stupid. She invited him, his wife, and her younger brother. However, he didn't take well to her not asking him to walk her down the aisle."

"She was smiling and happy after I shared you were fine. Savannah forgot to mention I was stopping by. She was worried for a brief minute about you. No mention of her dad."

"Okay. I want this to be perfect for her. He's messed up plenty over the years. While he's made strides recently, I don't fully trust him."

Hagen emerges from the bathroom and Zack jumps in. When the photographer knocks on the door, we're ready for our closeups. With the pre-ceremony photos done, we wait in a small room with snacks. I peek my head out of the room a few times, searching for Alannah. I haven't been able to locate her in the attendees.

"Stop worrying about Alannah," Hagen states when I turn back into the room.

"Not worried. Anxious to see her, that's all."

"Aww, dude. You ready to join the club too?" Zack asks.

"Eventually. I was waiting to meet her." I turn my attention to Hagen. "What about you?"

Hagen shakes his head. "I have enough to worry about with Lilah. As I'm sure Alannah pointed out, dating as a single parent is difficult—more so with a young child." Hagen is tightlipped about Lilah's mother. The only information I have is he's a single dad. Not one word—good, bad, or indifferent—has been uttered by him about Lilah's mother, at least not to me. His statement would lead me to believe she wasn't truthful with him about what she wanted or who she was.

"She did mention it. However, you would need to go on a date or two to find the right woman."

Hagen shrugs. "Maybe. How exactly did that work out for you and the groom here?"

I drop my head. "Point taken."

The wedding planner calls us to our places. Given the small gathering, the wedding party isn't escorting guests to their seats. We take our places under the decorated archway near the water's edge. I check my pocket yet again for the rings and direct my attention to the guests. From the back to the front, I scan each row methodically. When I find her midway through my sweep of the far side of the room, my chest constricts. She's breathtaking. Her hair is swept half up with a few pieces framing her face. Red is my favorite color on her. The V-neck dress is floor length with a flowy skirt.

"I'm pretty sure I'm supposed to need breathing reminders, not you." Zack nudges me.

I have no response, so I hang my head and shake it side to side.

"Don't mess that up," Zack adds before Lia moves to the end of the aisle.

"I won't." When I recover, I catch her gaze, wink at her, and mouth, "*Hi.*"

She winks back and responds in kind. I spend each second of the ceremony staring at Alannah until it's time to hand over the rings. After the officiant announces the happy couple and their first kiss, I dutifully follow to the bridal suite for more pictures. Nearly an hour later, the photographers excuse everyone except the bride and groom from the bridal suite.

"Time to find my husband," Savannah states, taking off at a brisk pace.

I see it happening in slow motion, and I can't stop it. Savannah's heel gets stuck in a crack in the sidewalk, and she crumples to the ground. Hagen and I catch up to her and check her out.

"I'll go find Sam," Lia states before rushing inside, more carefully than Savannah.

Hagen starts with basic questions. "Did you hit your head?"

"No. My ankle is on fire though. Scarlett is going to kill me!"

We have been working hard on Scarlett's first dance plan, including dance classes. "She won't. We'll figure it out," I offer, despite not having any idea how to fix the problem.

"We need to get her inside, locate some ice, and find Lia. Then we'll figure out the dance issue." Hagen states.

We help Savannah stand; she has one arm around me and one around Hagen. Hobbling, we make our way through the main entrance.

Sam is waiting with an ice pack and a frown on his face. "*Cara mia, what am I going to do with you?*"

Savannah smiles and then drops her head. We set her down on a tufted bench near the restroom.

"Thanks, guys. Good luck with the dance issue," Savannah offers.

Hagen and I join Lia near the entrance to the reception hall.

"Any ideas," Lia asks.

"Yes, give me a few minutes." I open the door and step into the elegantly decorated ballroom. Scanning the room, I find my gorgeous woman chatting with Maggie Washington and Kelsey Ramirez, but her back is to me. One attribute of her dress I didn't notice before is the dangerously sexy, low back. My fingers itch to caress her ultrasoft skin. "Good evening, ladies," I say, approaching them.

"Hi, Craven," Maggie and Kelsey state in unison.

My hand slides across her midback, and I curl my fingers around her side.

"Hi, Callan. Is everything okay?" Concern is evident on her beautiful face.

"Yes and no. Caden is fine. Will you come with me?"

"Of course. I'll catch up with you later, ladies," Alannah excuses herself from the conversation.

I lead her, our hands linked between us, into a small alcove off the main lobby. After verifying we are shrouded in semi-privacy, I draw her against me and kiss her. My feelings drip from each swipe of my tongue. Breathless but temporarily sated, I add space between us. "You are stunning. Red is officially my favorite color on you."

She smiles. "I missed you too. Until you mentioned the gray sweatpants, I would've finished my research today. To date, you in a tailored tuxedo is officially my favorite. What's going on?"

"Savannah twisted her ankle a little while ago. Any chance you learned to tango in your dance class?"

She tilts her head in question as to where my information came from. "Yes. How do you know about that?"

"Caden shared you took dance lessons and taught him to waltz. Savannah was my partner for this first dance thing. Will you dance with me?"

"Which tango? What song?" she asks.

At least it isn't a no. "Have you seen the movie *Scent of a Woman* with Al Pacino and Chris O'Donnell?"

"Of course."

"Okay. The choreography is the same, but the music is Michael Bublé's 'Sway' instead. The pace of the song is a bit faster."

"How much time do we have?"

I glance at my watch. "Thirty minutes, tops."

"I'm in, but I need to refresh my memory and practice."

"You're amazing. Let's go then." I send a text to Hagen informing him I found a partner. Then I hand her my phone and take her hand. "If you open the browser, I saved the dance to practice in one of the tabs." When we reach the bridal suite, I note Hagen and Lia are gone. No idea where they went, but... I shuck my jacket and wait for Alannah to finish watching. For the next twenty-plus minutes, we practice open steps and forward and backward crosses.

The concentration on her face is sexy. Her determination combined with the sensual movements makes me want to strip her dress off here and now. I'm so lost in how she feels in my arms, I don't hear or notice we're no longer alone.

"Damn! You two make the tango look sinful," Lia offers when the music stops.

Alannah's face blushes fiercely. Soon thereafter, Zack and Scarlett return to make their grand entrance. The wedding planner informs me she will announce Savannah's name as originally planned, and then Alannah can join me to dance.

"Thank you so much for stepping in, Alannah," Scarlett states.

"You're welcome. I'll have to thank my bestie for the dance lessons when I get home."

Scarlett laughs. "My husband...." She pauses, wrapping her head around the fact Zack is officially hers. "My husband thought I was nuts.

We couldn't possibly ask our friends to do this, and they wouldn't accept. I'm glad he was wrong and you're willing to join us." Scarlett hugs Alannah.

"I'll meet you inside near the edge of the dance floor," Alannah whispers and places a light kiss high on my cheek. We line up to make our entrance.

CHAPTER SEVENTEEN

ALANNAH

I slip into the ballroom and take my place where instructed by the wedding coordinator. Am I really doing this? I'm out of my mind! *Breathe, Alannah!* We can handle this. It'll be fun, especially with Callan.

The DJ's voice crashes into my head. "Ladies and gentlemen, please welcome Lachlan Hagen and Lia Cappelli of the bridal party." The DJ continues announcing, but I tune him out.

Callan sets his hand on my forearm. "You can back out if you want to," he murmurs as he sidles beside me.

"No, not at all. I'm just nervous I'm going to mess up."

Callan draws me closer and escorts me across the dance floor. "As Lieutenant Colonel Slade stated in the movie, 'There are no mistakes in the tango, not like life. If you make a mistake and get all tangled up, you just tango on.'"

I nod and take my starting position beside him while Scarlett and Lia move beside their partners. Callan's gaze never leaves mine from the second I drag my hand across his chest and circle around him.

"Please remind me to thank Delilah for gifting you dance classes for your birthday," he whispers near the shell of my ear as he drags his hands up my outer thighs.

My brain is spinning in opposite directions. The steps are scrolling through my mind, but at the same time I'm cataloging how sensual and sultry I feel. The ache between my thighs has increased to a throbbing need requiring a release—one I can't have for at least a few hours. The sheer fact there's a roomful of our coworkers—for Callan—and our acquaintances, I push from my mind. It'll only make me lose focus.

"Are you as turned on as I am?" Callan asks when I lean on him and we dip to the side.

"Yes." My voice comes out raspy, low, and laced with desire. "How long is this reception?"

He laughs, and we twirl around the dance floor with the bridal party. Callan turns me away from his body and draws me in close with our arms crossed. "Try not to kick me with those sexy heels."

"It was once."

He offers me a panty-melting grin—as if my panties aren't already useless. In fact, wearing them is pointless when he's within touching distance of me. The unmistakable need to have his hands on me is palpable.

I add, "I'll do my best."

Successfully, we make it through without me kicking Callan again. We're nearing the end of the dance and the final dip.

"Can we do this again—" Callan brings his mouth near my ear. "—at home?" He dips me, and my gaze sears into his.

"Definitely."

The roar of the applause surrounds us. It isn't until I'm upright and my fingers are threaded into Callan's do I realize the others stopped dancing at some point. Heat builds in my cheeks.

"Can you escort me to my table?" I whisper, hoping to end the standing ovation. More accurately, hoping it truly is for the bride and groom and not us. Thankfully, the applause slows when Zack and Scarlett make their way to the head table.

I'm not seated with Callan, nor would I expect to be. Scarlett placed me with Sam Morgan because Savannah is at the head table as well. Kelsey, Maggie, and their husbands are also seated with us.

"You two were amazing! How long have you been practicing?" Maggie exclaims when we approach.

"Savannah twisted her ankle earlier. I stepped in about twenty minutes ago," I share.

Surprise covers Kelsey's face, and she replies, "The sexual tension between you is impossible to miss. You're fully clothed, and it got exponentially hotter in here."

Callan leans in so only I can hear him. "I'm sorry, but I have to go sit over there."

I turn and reply, "Nothing to be sorry for. They aren't wrong. It was hot as hell. I can handle them." I press a kiss to his cheek, and he takes his place with the bridal party beside Zack.

Luckily, the meal takes precedence over the tango. It's magnificent. Hands down the most delicious meal I've had at a wedding in my life.

While the happy couple make their rounds to the tables, Callan leads me outside onto the patio. He sweeps me into his arms near the edge of the stone. The crash of waves against the nearby shore is nearly as intoxicating as how I feel about Callan. I've fallen hard for him, but my fear of losing another significant person in my life has me holding back.

"Thank you again for stepping in for Savannah."

"None are necessary. It was a little nerve-racking, but it was fun. I will take you up on dancing more at home. Mr. Felter wasn't as good a partner during the classes."

Callan laughs. "I assume he was an older gentleman, not the type of partner Delilah was hoping you would end up with."

"Exactly. I'm glad her fixups failed."

Callan kisses me lightly. "Me too. Ready to head back inside?"

"Sure."

Callan wiggled out of giving a speech because Zack's sister Nadine wanted to do the honors. She didn't want to be part of the wedding party but wanted to give a speech because their mother passed away recently. Childhood stories and a sheen of sadness falls over the guests while she speaks. Savannah's speech is poignant and to the point. Once they finish, we spend the rest of the evening dancing the night away.

After Zack and Scarlett exit, the remaining guests leave as well.

"Ready to go home, gorgeous?"

I shake my head. "Your home. Del is staying overnight."

"What my lady wishes, she shall have."

"Sweet but corny, Callan."

He shrugs. "I need to grab my bag upstairs, and then we're set."

Bag in hand, he leads me to his car. He shucks off his jacket and places it along with his bag in the rear storage area.

Unlike the last time with a similar dress, Callan wastes no time baring my thigh and skimming his fingers from my knee dangerously close to my still pulsing center.

A chill of the best kind covers me from head to toe. "If you don't stop, we won't make it to your house."

He glances over at me, dips his finger beneath the edge of my panties, and pushes forward. "I don't plan on stopping. What are you worried about?"

"Not worried. Never had an orgasm in an SUV before."

"You're about to." His fingers curl, and he hits the spot within me only he knows will make me shatter within a minute.

White-hot pleasure shoots through me. "How are you driving—" A jagged breath cuts off my words. "And…." I can't even finish my question. My inner muscles pulse around his fingers, and my release starts to uncoil in my lower belly. Tremors spiral outward from my core to the tips of my fingers. One hand clamps around his wrist while the other encircles the door handle. "Callan!" falls from my lips as I turn to look at him.

His gaze remains forward on the road, but he has a sexy, devilish grin on his chiseled face. He pulls into his complex, but he doesn't stop teasing my swollen nub and keeping me on the edge of another climax. He slows enough to reach up and open his garage door. After pulling in, he closes the door behind us. "I'm guessing you haven't had sex in a car either."

I shake my head as my eyes flutter closed when his fingers reenter me.

"Interested?"

I focus on his face and reply, "Absolutely, but don't stop."

The small smirk on his face tells me he intends to do exactly that. He withdraws his fingers, leaving me feeling momentarily hollow, and hurriedly squeezes through to the back seat. "Come here and I'll finish you off improperly."

I slide my leg over the center console and hover, pulling the other through.

He sets his hands on my hips and perches me on the console. "Are you attached to these lace panties?"

I raise an eyebrow. "No, why?"

Without a second thought, he shreds the sides and pulls them from my body. *Sweet mercy!* With a wink, he sets one sequin-heeled shoe on either side of his thighs. When he said finish me off, he didn't mean with his fingers. He scoots forward on the seat, grips my ass with his hands, and drags his tongue flat across my dripping center. Each swipe of his warm tongue strokes the undercurrent of bliss waiting to be unleashed from the drive here. Again. He's unrelenting and ravenous as if he can never get enough. He brings immense pleasure spiraling out of me. My entire body trembles to the point I thread my fingers through his hair and attempt to wiggle away.

His refusal sets off a cascade of unmatched tremors.

"Callan!" His name echoes in the passenger compartment of his SUV. I loosen my hold on his hair when the aftershocks slow to mild. Is he done? No. His mouth meets mine as he sets my feet on the floorboard. Then he draws me into his lap. Without breaking our kiss, I fumble with the buckle of his pants. I may have successfully unbuckled them, but…. I laugh. "We didn't think this through, did we?"

"Doesn't matter." He resets me on the console, drops his pants and boxer briefs, and hauls me into his lap. "Problem solved."

I hope I never get used to how we feel. "Almost." My fingers expeditiously unfasten the buttons of his shirt.

"To maintain balance," Callan starts before coaxing the straps of my dress down to my arms.

"Balance, of course." With a hand on his shoulder, I add space, stroke him once, and align us. Sinking down in small increments is heavenly. When I take him as deeply as I can, I pause to adjust.

"You good?"

"Better than good. Haven't had sex in this position before either."

"Take whatever time you need." His eyes never leave mine. He dips his head and circles my aroused nipple with his tongue.

Containing my sigh is impossible.

"Noted, gorgeous."

He repeats the movement again, and I mirror him with my hips. His groan is all the encouragement I need. Our pace ratchets up to feverish in a matter of minutes.

"You feel amazing wrapped around me," he murmurs against my breast.

"You feel indescribable deep inside me."

Lifting and crashing down, he meets me thrust for thrust until we splinter into a million tiny shards of heaven at once. After catching our breath and partially redressing, at least for him, we make our way inside and straight to the master bathroom to clean up.

Where his kitchen needs updating, his bathroom is a dream come true. An open Carrara-tiled shower, complete with heated floors and towel rack, dominates the space.

I slip out of my dress and lay it on the chair near the fireplace. After I do, I actually peruse his bedroom. The walls are a medium gray with dark furniture, including a huge bed and sitting area near the fireplace complete with perfectly situated chairs and a love seat. It appears the only room he hasn't updated is the kitchen—odd for a passionate chef, unless these rooms were worse. I shake away my thoughts and ask, "Can I have a shirt?"

"Help yourself. They're in the second drawer, but you won't need it until I take you home. Do you have plans tomorrow?"

"No."

"Good, because we're not going to be sleeping much." He disappears around the corner and returns with two bottles of water.

My reprieve is only until I finish the water. Callan spends the next hour mapping my skin with his mouth, and then I do the same. Twice more through the night with a short nap, we tangle up his sheets and steam up the mirrors in his bathroom.

Wakefulness creeps into my body slowly. I catalog how I feel. Spots deep within me are sore that never have been before. His bed is much more comfortable than mine. Not only because he's curled around me, but his sheets are nicer and the mattress softer.

"Morning, beautiful," he mumbles against my shoulder blade.

"I never want to leave your bed. It's so comfy."

I feel his grin on my skin. "Not opposed, but it isn't realistic. Are my super luxurious sheets and plush mattress the only reasons you don't want to leave my bed?"

"No. I like waking up with you, but...."

"It's soon for Caden."

"Maybe." I twist to look at him. "What is normal?"

His smile adds to his mussed hair and morning scruff. "Hell, if I know. The only woman who has been in my home, forget my bed, in the last few years is you."

"Same." I cover my face at my mistake.

"Don't get nervous on me now."

"I mean—"

"I know what you meant. However long it'll take for you to be comfortable is fine with me. I'm willing to drive to your place for coffee instead of the Perk. The kisses are much better. Val is cute, but she isn't you."

I shake my head and snuggle closer. Before he allows me out of bed, we chase another round of body-bending orgasms despite the escapades of last night.

"Want to go grab supplies and make brunch at your house?"

"Not really. I don't have clothes or panties."

He grins at me. "Not sorry at all."

"Neither am I, but I'm not willing to go grocery shopping."

"Fair enough. I'll order groceries to be delivered to your house, better?"

"Yes."

We take a shower together, but we don't make love again. *Love? Shouldn't I share my feelings with him first? Idiot. You have been sharing your feelings with your body and actions. You just haven't said the words.* It's not something I should blurt out randomly.

Callan offers me a pair of shorts in addition to the shirt. I hook the straps of my shoes after gathering my dress from the chair. Before we leave, I send a quick text to Del.

Me: We'll be there in twenty. Please occupy Caden.

Delilah: Walk of shame. I love it.

Me: No shame. Poor planning on my part.

Delilah: I've got you. Love you.

Me: Love you.

Callan pulls into my driveway and sets his hand on my arm. "Don't worry. He's a teenager. I'm sure he can take a guess why you were out all night."

I hang my head. I do my best not to think about whether Caden and Kyla were sexually active. Caden has been forthright about his desire to wait until he's older to have kids. "Not worried. Del will handle the inquisition after you leave thoroughly enough on his behalf, I'm sure."

Once I'm inside, I walk straight to my room. I'm grateful Del was able to get Caden upstairs.

Quickly, I change my clothes and join Callan in the kitchen. "Are you opposed to me keeping your shirt?"

"No, it looks better on you anyway." He presses a kiss to my temple as Caden steps into the kitchen.

"How was the wedding?" he asks.

"Fun. Thanks for the tip about the dance classes. It helped out," Callan responds before I can.

Caden shrugs. "Welcome. Glad you had a good time."

The doorbell chimes with our brunch fixin's. Callan retrieves them and gets to work.

"OC, you should move in. Breakfast is much better when you're here. Sorry, Mom, no offense."

My son's suggestion swims in my head. I'm not offended by the breakfast slight. He isn't wrong. I finish doing my part by brewing three coffees.

After an amazing brunch, Del takes off and Caden heads outside to practice.

Over the next few weeks, I need to do my best not to freak out about meeting his parents. The last set of parents I met—sort of—were Daniel's and well....

CHAPTER EIGHTEEN

CALLAN

It's been a few weeks since Smithson's wedding. For the most part, the only thing I don't do at Alannah's is sleep. I drive over each morning and have breakfast with them. After work, I return and teach Alannah to cook something new or cook for them. Although, we have carefully crafted stories after a few slipups. I want to wake up with her, but she isn't ready.

I've never brought a woman to meet my family, and my brothers have been digging for information since I told them about Alannah and Caden. I gave them the basics. My family can decide they're amazing in person like I did.

Today though, I'm having coffee solo in my house. The quiet is unbearable. I feel as if parts of me are missing when the three of us aren't together. After a workout and a light breakfast, I pack my SUV and head to Alannah's earlier than necessary. I'm confident she's freaking out about meeting my family.

I hate texting, and yet it's my brothers' preferred manner of communication.

Patrick: *Are you really bringing a woman and her son to dinner?*

Me: *Yes. Why?*

Patrick: *Prepare yourself for the inevitable questions.*

Me: *Such as?*

Patrick: Marriage and more grandchildren.

Me: Not worried.

Patrick: She's important to you.

Me: Seriously, have I brought a woman home before?

Patrick: No.

Me: Then there's your answer.

Patrick: See you later.

If I thought my phone would be quiet, I was wrong. After I park in her driveway, my phone vibrates again.

Liam: Should I hide the knives?

Me: Not funny. What are you worried about?

Liam: Mom is going to lose it if you truly bring a woman home.

Me: Why would I lie about that?

Liam: You never have before.

Me: I know. That should show my interest in her and her son.

Alannah and Caden are it for me. I refuse to second-guess my decision to invite them. Although the warning from my brothers may go deeper. I haven't seen my family regularly since I moved to York. I see them a few times a year at most. I don't choose not to visit. They choose not to visit. I have a career, and after being rebuffed by my family to visit more than once, holidays are what I can make work. Yes, I choose to work most holidays, which allows my coworkers with kids the chance to request them off. My parents are semiretired and have more flexibility. Only Patrick and the girls have visited me, though the entire family has an open invitation.

Caden is on the stoop waiting for me. "Morning, OC."

"Morning. How freaked is she?"

"Over the top," he informs me.

"Is it today or tomorrow?"

"Both. Today is about her future and tomorrow is about the past. The events terrify her in different ways."

"Did she tell you that?"

"Didn't have to. Mom is happy with you. Meeting your family is a big deal—something we've never done before. Attending Coach's ceremony tomorrow is reopening a box she closed to protect us—well, mostly me."

"How do you feel about it?"

"I like you for us. You don't push me too hard but offer solid advice when I ask. You keep your word and show up whether it's meals, picking me up from camp, or helping with my recruiting video. No one has stepped up for me or her before. I know you aren't my dad, but you act like you are, and I appreciate it. I'm working on an upgraded name. OC is too impersonal now, and Callan isn't right either."

"Thanks, Caden. Let me know when you decide. I'll be here for both of you until your mom says otherwise."

He stands and bro hugs me.

"Are you packed and ready to go?"

"Yeah, my bag and dress clothes for tomorrow are by the front door."

"Good job. I'll see what I can do about your mom."

Caden smirks at me. "Good luck."

I take a deep breath and search for Alannah. She isn't in her bedroom, office, or the kitchen. Then I hear it. *Swish. Bounce. Bounce. Swish.* Outside on the court, Alannah is retrieving the ball again. She's not dressed to play basketball. She's wearing a mid-length skirt and a jacket. I noticed her shoes by the back door.

"Morning."

When she hears me and turns toward my voice, I eliminate the space between us and close my arms around her.

"Is it today or tomorrow?" I murmur against her neck.

"Both."

Caden was right.

She adds a sliver of space between us. "What if your family hates us?"

"They won't. Alannah and Caden Kramer are amazing. I see it, and they will too."

"How can you be so sure?"

"I'm happier than I've ever been with you and Caden. Nothing else should matter."

"Is it that easy?"

"For me it is. I wish yours were here so I could wow them. The best I can do is continue to impress Paul and Clem. I mean my strong arms for hugs and your smile seem to be enough. As they should be." Sharing I've never brought anyone home isn't the best plan right now. It will only make her edgier. "Want to talk about tomorrow now?"

"No, I need to freshen up so we're not late. It would be a terrible first impression to make."

I know we're not out of the woods as far as her feelings about meeting my family. However, we're making progress at least.

Caden is handling the music while we set off for my parents' house. After he chooses, he asks for a family history. I share the same information I have given to Alannah.

We make a quick stop for coffee and snacks for Caden. As we drive, we laugh and belt out song lyrics. I have to admit, Caden's taste in music is nothing like his classmates'. He chooses music from the late nineties and early two thousands mixed with current hits.

I notice Alannah's gaze is trained on the GPS. Her hand grows clammy the closer we get to our arrival. I pull down my childhood street and offer, "I promise, it's going to be great."

She acknowledges me and exhales slowly. I park on the street and guide them to the front door. It swings open as I raise my hand to knock.

"About time, Uncle Callan," my niece states.

"Hello, Maeve. Nice to see you too." I know this isn't Maeve, but I've always messed with her and her sister. Quinn has more freckles.

"You know I'm Quinn, right?"

"Of course I do! Quinn, please meet Alannah and Caden."

"Wow, you're tall," she points out. I'm not sure if she means Alannah, Caden, or both. "Nice to meet you. Just a tip, Grandma has been pacing since we got here."

"Thanks for the insider information."

"Welcome," she replies and scampers off.

She's replaced by Liam. We bro hug, and I introduce everyone.

"Nice to meet you."

"You as well," Alannah offers in response.

"Why don't we get you some drinks, and then you can meet everyone else?" Liam offers.

"Sounds perfect."

I thread our fingers, and we follow him into the kitchen.

"Hi, Mom and Dad. Please meet Alannah and Caden."

"Callan, you failed to mention she's beautiful," Mom comments.

"Thank you. Pleasure to meet you, Mr. and Mrs. Craven," Alannah says before nudging Caden.

"Yes, nice to meet you."

"I'm Maeve. How old are you?" my nieces asks, taking over the inquisition.

Caden crouches down. "I'm seventeen. How old are you?"

"Only ten." She shrugs.

"Ten is pretty good. You can do some stuff, but you don't have to do everything for yourself."

"I like you. You make sense."

"Thanks, Maeve." Caden raises his hand for a high five, and she complies.

"Welcome."

We finish the introductions, and my mom leads us into the living room with our drinks. "Dinner will be ready in about thirty minutes. Let's get to know one another a little better. How did you meet?"

"We met at a charity game for the police department. Caden volunteered to help, and then I did as well," Alannah answers.

"Lovely. What do you do for work?" my mother asks.

"I'm an attorney."

I note my father paying attention to her answers more intently.

"What type of lawyer?" my brother Patrick asks.

"I run my own small transactional practice, mainly real estate and estate planning. I handle some litigation, mostly in family court."

"How nice. What about you?" my father asks Caden.

"I'm a senior in high school. Not really much else to tell."

The adults laugh. I'm not sure what my father is driving at. I'm aware of his disdain for lawyers, but it's mostly those who handle insurance issues and motor vehicle accidents. Caden is a good kid. All my father needs to focus on is that. We're saved by the timer in the kitchen.

"Callan, will you join me in the kitchen please?" my mother requests.

"Of course." I lean down and press a kiss high on Alannah's cheek. "Breathe, you can handle this." I nearly spill my feelings at the end but don't.

She nods, and I dutifully follow my mom. Patrick joins us as well.

"Callan, please carve this," Mom directs. "You've never brought a woman home before."

"I haven't been with a woman who I wanted to be with long term until now."

"She's important to you." It's a statement, not a question.

"Both of them are."

"When you shared you were bringing guests, I was taken aback. Now I see why. You look settled and happy."

"I am, and it's because of them."

"You weren't kidding, bro," Patrick states.

"About Alannah, no, otherwise I wouldn't have invited them."

"I look forward to getting to know them better," Mom replies.

"Thank you." I bring the carved turkey to the table while the others filter in from the living room.

We take our seats at the table overflowing with dishes containing traditional holiday fare—turkey, stuffing, potatoes, green beans, and, of course, bread. Alannah is on my right and Caden on my left. Over dinner, the edge of our earlier conversations fades away. My family is chatting about current events and football. Her hand is perched on my thigh, and Caden is on his second plate of food.

After we eat, we each wash our dishes and then chat more on the back porch. Alannah and Caden are laughing about something with the girls when my brothers pull me aside.

"Dude, real talk, where did you meet her?" Patrick asks.

I shake my head. "We met exactly where she said we did."

"Does she have a sister?" Liam asks.

"No, she doesn't."

"Damn!"

The three of us laugh and continue catching up. Sometime during my conversation with my brother, I lose sight of Alannah. When Dad summons us for dessert, I find her, Caden, and the girls giggling in the kitchen. I catch her gaze and smile at her. She returns an equally happy smile. Over an hour later, loaded down with extra dessert helpings, we make our way toward our hotel for the night.

When Alannah accepted her coach's invitation, we booked a hotel for tonight. Unfortunately, I'm working on Saturday, so our trip to Boston will be short. We check in, and Caden collapses onto the bed closer to the television.

"Cool if I eat more dessert, Mom?"

"Have at it, but leave me—"

He grins at her and sets one of the containers aside. "I would never take the last of the chocolate dessert. I value my life."

I reach over and offer him a fist. "Well done, Caden."

"Thanks, DC."

"DC?"

"Dad Craven or Dad Callan, both work."

"Cool. Thanks."

Alannah hasn't said a word since requesting the chocolate dessert. Instead, she scoops a spoonful of the mousse into her mouth, seemingly lost in her thoughts. Caden finds football on the television and settles against the headboard with extra dessert.

I climb onto the bed beside Alannah. "Are you okay?"

She doesn't say anything, which is unlike her, but she does drop her chin slightly. If I wasn't looking at her, I would've missed it. When she scoots closer and sets her head on my shoulder, I press a kiss to her temple and wait for her to share. Like a typical teen, Caden falls asleep sitting up, watching the game a little short of an hour later.

"He's asleep. Want to share now?"

"Meeting your family was nerve-racking."

"I'm sorry."

She squeezes our linked hands. "It started off awkward, but then it shifted. What did you say to your mother? I swear she and your father have a secret language. He was much nicer after you carved the turkey."

I laugh heartily. "They do have a secret language. We could never figure it out. She put me on the spot. I never invited a woman to dinner, holiday or otherwise."

"I didn't know."

"I know. I didn't tell you, given you were already nervous."

"Normally, an omission would piss me off. I'll allow it this time only."

"Understood. You won them over."

"I'm glad. Your nieces are a hoot. Their mom doesn't sound like a very nice person."

"Ciara didn't want to be a mom but agreed to have a baby with Patrick. They had twins. She left when they were three. They have no contact with her."

She frowns. "How sad."

"Do you want to talk about tomorrow?"

"No, I'm good."

"I'm sorry, what have you done with my Alannah?"

"I like that."

"What?"

"'My Alannah.'"

"Me too."

She kisses me deeply as if her son isn't less than three feet away from us.

I pull back whisper, "You can't kiss me passionately right now."

She pouts. "Why not?"

I raise an eyebrow as if she truly doesn't know why.

"He's sleeping."

Shaking my head, and request, "Please tell me why you're good with tomorrow all of a sudden."

A glorious smile grows on her face. "It's because of you."

"Definitely share your revelation."

She rolls her eyes. "I realized the weight I'm putting on this event is too high. We're happy and thriving, the three of us. I don't care what my former teammates, who I have no current relationship with, think about me or my choices since the last time I saw them. Coach invited me, and she was understanding and supportive."

"I'm proud of you."

"Thanks. I am too. What did your brothers say?"

Now it's my turn to roll my eyes. "They asked if you had a sister. When I shared you don't, they commented on my improved demeanor."

"Happy to help."

"What time do we need to be at the arena tomorrow?"

"Two. The ceremony is before the game. Tip time at four."

"Okay. Anything you want to do in the morning?"

"Not really. The Christmas tree won't be revealed until next week."

"Then we should come back so you can see it," I offer.

"Maybe we should." She pauses to collect her thoughts. I've learned to wait her out. "Thank you for not giving up on me this morning."

"I never will."

Alannah kisses my lips lightly, then burrows into my side. Hours later, I wake to an awful infomercial on the television. I shift lower and allow sleep to reclaim me. Today started off rocky but worked out in the end. I'm looking forward to many more holidays with Alannah and Caden.

CHAPTER NINETEEN

ALANNAH

Surprisingly, my nerves haven't resurfaced in the light of a new day. Callan is sound asleep beside me, and Caden is sprawled out in the other bed. I turn and snuggle closer to Callan and close my eyes again.

After a huge room service breakfast, which Caden deemed "the best thing eva!" we make our way to campus. On the way, my phone chimes.

Delilah: How was meeting the parents?

Me: Pretty good.

Delilah: I'm proud of you for attending today.

Me: Thanks.

Delilah: I want more details about dinner and today when you get home.

Me: Fine.

"Delilah?" Callan asks.

"Yeah."

We arrive earlier than necessary but park near the arena. "Want to walk around for a bit first?"

"Sure. Where did we live?" Caden asks.

Callan lifts my hand to his mouth and kisses the back.

"We didn't live on campus. We can drive by the complex after the game."

"'Kay."

The three of us make a loop around campus and check in a few minutes late. Immediately, the media director is spewing directions at us.

"You two will sit in the third row while Miss Kramer will be in the front row with the other record holders. There will be another seat for you beside your family during the game. Coach will be seated on the court and make a short speech before the current players join her."

"Do I need to do anything?" I ask.

The frazzled woman replies, "You need to stand and wave to the crowd when the announcer calls your name."

"Great. Thank you."

She shows us our seats, and we chat until Coach steps onto the hardwood. Clearly, she didn't forget me, considering she invited me. However, I didn't expect her to seek me out first.

"Hi, Coach. Congratulations on your farewell season."

"Antoinette, it's wonderful to see you again."

"You as well. This is my boyfriend, Callan, and my son."

"Pleasure to meet you, Callan. Caden, nice to see you again as well. You weren't nearly this tall the last time I saw you."

She remembers his name.

"Nice to meet you," my guys reply at once.

"Do you have any basketball skills, young man?"

Caden instantly blushes. "Some."

"He's being modest," I admit.

Coach points to a tall, blond teen standing beneath the basket to our left. "He could use some extra practice."

"Thanks." Caden takes off.

She turns her attention back to me. "Is your shot still on point?"

"Yes," Callan answers without hesitation.

"Well, let's see it." With a flick of her hand, two racks of basketballs appear.

I take a few shots, which rim out before they start falling in quick succession. Callan feeds me a new ball as I make my way around the arc. When I finish the two racks, I note Caden defending the young man at the opposite end of the court.

"I shouldn't be surprised, should I?" Coach asks.

I smile at her. "It's part of who I am. Who is Caden playing against?"

"My grandson, Nicolas. He's also a senior and joining the men's team next fall."

"Good for him," I offer.

"Thank you. We're proud of him finding his way. Thank you for coming. I know it wasn't an easy decision. I need to get into the locker room to pump up my team."

"You're welcome."

When she walks away, Callan steps beside me and links our hands. "How are you?"

"Glad I'm here. You don't know how much I appreciate you for pushing me to attend, even if it was slight."

FOR LOVE & BASKETBALL 217

"I do, but I don't mind hearing it as well."

I kiss him lightly before we make our way across the court to watch Caden and Nicolas play until the last possible second. Callan and Caden take their seats when I do. Many of my teammates in attendance are cordial. Some are overly polite, as if they recall how horribly they treated me. Whether it was Caden or the perceived special privileges, doesn't matter. I'm fine with where I am in my life. I don't need half-hearted apologies from people I don't know anymore. The ceremony proceeds as planned.

"Antoinette Kramer, four-year starter and holder of the Boston College record for most three-point field goals in a career," the announcer states.

I stand, wave to the crowd, and make my way over to Coach and hug her. "Congratulations again."

"Thank you."

"You're welcome."

I retake my seat until tipoff. Then I join Callan and Caden for the game. My alma mater holds their own for most of the game, but in the end come out on the losing end.

"What do you say to pizza before we head back?" Callan suggests as we exit the arena.

"The answer to pizza is always yes!" Caden replies.

We laugh and make our way off campus.

I direct Callan toward the complex where we lived. He slows near the entrance. "We lived in the end unit on the right for four years."

"Cool."

I'm not sure what type of reaction I was expecting, but I suppose "cool" from a teenage boy about a home he doesn't remember is sufficient. We laugh and joke over delicious pizza before heading home.

Caden hops out of the car and hurries inside.

"Are you coming in or do you need to go?" I ask.

"I would prefer to live here," Callan admits.

"I know, and I want the same thing. I'm sure it isn't fun leaving nightly—most nights."

"No, but I'll do it until it's the right time. It's fast by most definitions."

"True. Coffee by the fire?"

He nods, grabs my bag from the trunk, and we head inside. I exchange my heels for bare feet and start our coffee. Callan slipped outside to start the firepit. When I join him, the fire is warm and cozy.

Without hesitation, he sits in the corner of the couch and opens his arms to me. I set the mugs on the side table and curl against him, my head resting on his chest as his arms collapse around me.

"You aren't going to be able to drink your coffee snuggled against me like this," he states.

"Fine by me."

"Are you and Caden free for the YPD holiday party?"

"Should be. Let me know when it is. As long as he doesn't have a game, we'll be there."

"Are you going to Clem and Paul's for Christmas?"

"No," I mumble. "Christmas is only Caden and me, always has been. Will you join us? We have a huge breakfast and then open gifts. It's later now than it was when he was younger with a lot fewer gifts."

"Yes, I would love to. Why?"

"He doesn't get up."

Callan laughs. "Why fewer gifts?"

"His cost per item has increased substantially."

"Makes sense. What does he want this year?"

"A new computer and bigger television for his bedroom."

"At least his priorities are straight," Callan quips.

When he finishes his cup, he unclasps my barrette and runs his fingers through my hair. It's soothing. His heartbeat against my temple lulls me to sleep. The last thing I recall is Callan removing my dress and tucking me into my bed… alone.

Early the next morning, I tug on my robe and stumble to the kitchen for a cup of coffee. As I near the bottom, Del barges in through the front door, followed closely by Paul and Clem.

"Good morning, everyone. To what do I owe the pleasure of your company this early?"

Clem pulls out one of the stools and says, "You should sit, dear."

I comply, but say, "You're scaring me."

Callan. Did something happen to Callan? They wouldn't call my family before his.

Clem continues, "There was an article about Coach Sowell in the Boston Globe this morning."

"As there should be. The event was wonderful and well received. It's too bad they lost the game."

Paul sets his hand on my shoulder. "They wrote about you as well."

My heart is in my throat. *Caden.* I'm off the stool and bounding upstairs before I hear another word. I peek into his room and see he's sound asleep. Retreating as quietly as possible, I return to my guests.

"Is it bad?"

"No, it's matter of fact," Del answers.

"However, it contains lots of facts we shielded you from," Paul adds.

I take a bit more time to process. "Okay. It's no problem. I won't read it. I've made it this many years without seeking out deeper details. It won't change because a major newspaper has picked up the story again. It'll die down before the next news cycle."

"As much as I would love to maintain the shield for you and Caden, I don't think it'll be possible," Clem adds softly.

"You've read it?" I ask the three of them. Their facial expressions show the same emotion… fear.

"Yes. It wasn't until the end that I realized you need to read it as well," Del states.

"No, it doesn't change anything. My parents and Daniel are gone. No details will impact today."

Paul takes my hand in his. "It might."

Del rounds the island, sets her phone in my hand, and stands in front of me.

I read each word about Coach Sowell, my teammates, and other record holders who were also mentioned. Nearly three quarters of the article is complete before the accident is mentioned. The details aren't graphic—simply stated facts of a two-car accident caused by an impaired motorist resulting in seven deaths and one survivor. Then the article lists the names of the fatalities: my parents, Daniel, Cathy Mathewson, Mark Mathewson, Chloe Mathewson, and Sadie Craven. I reread her name a few times before continuing through the text naming me as the sole survivor.

Bile rises in my throat. I push Del away and rush to my bathroom. Though I haven't eaten, I lurch and empty what little contents remain in my stomach. After the urge to hurl lessens, the sobs begin. I slide along the shower door to the floor and draw my knees against my chest.

No, I will not question his integrity. He wouldn't do that to me. He wouldn't lie to me. I believe he didn't read the reports. *Right? Without a doubt!*

Time passes slowly. The sobs decrease to short breaths and an unyielding ache in my chest. A soft knock draws my attention, and Del peeks her head inside.

"Can I come in?"

I nod, and Del joins me on the floor. "Does he know?"

"No. He was only a teenager as well."

"What are you going to do?"

I shake my head. "I don't know. I...."

"You've fallen for him." Her words are succinct and wholly accurate.

"Yes." Unequivocally. This information may prove insurmountable for us going forward.

"Does he know?"

All I can do is shrug.

"What is your plan for Caden?"

The sobs I successfully pushed down resurface, and I lose control of my emotions.

"I've got you."

"He is the first—" I inhale sharply. "—man who wanted both of us. What happens now?"

"I'm sure it's 'wants' not 'wanted.' Does it matter to you?"

"I don't know. I'm happy for the first time in my life. I was happy. Why now, why him?"

Del scoots forward and throws her arms around my shoulders.

The minutes pass with me swimming in my thoughts. Is Callan going to run too? What about his family? Will they still accept me? Caden?

I'm not sure how much time elapsed before Clem knocks on the door. "Caden is up. Do you want us to take him to breakfast?"

"Thanks, that would be nice," I manage.

She slips away. My son can't see me like this. I need to get myself together and organize my thoughts. I need to figure out if I can handle being with Callan going forward.

"What the hell am I going to do?" I ask the universe, though Del is still here.

"You need to talk to Callan."

"And say what?"

"Everything you're feeling."

Del's right. I know she is. The pit in my stomach has me moving toward the toilet again. Like before, nothing comes of it.

Clem knocks again. "It appears breakfast was taken care of. Caden is happily downing colorful donuts in the kitchen. There was a pastry for you as well."

"Thanks, Clem."

"Time to get off this floor, splash some water on your face, and eat breakfast sent by your man," Del urges.

"Then what?"

"Baby steps," she answers.

I push to my feet and freshen up. It would've been smart not to look in the mirror. My face is red and blotchy. My eyes aren't much different. My heart… there aren't enough words to describe the agonizing pain. The ramifications of the article details will be devastating. Despite wanting to forget I ever read them, I join everyone in the kitchen and prepare a cup of coffee.

"Morning, Mom. Do we have plans today?"

"Nope." I keep my response short and steady.

"Cool. I'm going to get ahead on my schoolwork with the season starting this week."

"Okay."

My son disappears to his room. Paul, Clem, and Del continue to hover.

"You don't have to babysit me. I'll be okay."

Paul throws his arms around me and hugs me tight. After adding some space, he declares, "You're one of the top two strongest women I know. Before you do anything rash, at least hear him out. Then remember how you were feeling about him before you knew the details. If any couple can figure out how to navigate this, it's you and Callan."

"Thanks, Uncle Paul."

"Of course."

Clem hugs me as well. "I couldn't have said it better myself. You two are good for one another. You'll weather this storm and any others in the future."

I hope they're right. I'm not so sure. "Thanks."

Paul and Clem show themselves out, leaving me and Del in the kitchen.

"Unfortunately, I can't stay. I'm working this afternoon."

"Thank you for coming, Del."

"You're my bestie for life. I love you, Lan. Don't give up on him so easily. He's going to surprise you."

"Love you too, Del."

"I'll call you tonight. If you want to pour it out with a sleepover, let me know."

I nod, and she leaves. Despite the possibility of getting sick again, I warm the pastry from Callan. It's not the pastry; it's the note that gets me.

Alannah,
I wish I could be there to share this in person. I'll see you tonight.
xoxo, Callan

How can I reconcile my love for this man with the fact I was present on one of the worst days of his life? I survived, and his sister didn't. Tears well in my eyes. I set the pastry aside and curl up on my couch, hoping this entire morning was a dream. Deep down, I know luck isn't on my side right now.

CHAPTER TWENTY

CALLAN

I overslept. Not only do I not have enough time to work out, but I won't be able to bring breakfast to Alannah and Caden. Instead, I order it. I hurry out the door and straight to the precinct. Thankfully, I clock in on time and take my seat at the desk. I don't mind desk duty. For the most part, the public is usually polite and willing to listen.

I redirect a few calls. Then I sip my coffee and eat my breakfast. I hear my phone chime while I'm sorting the mail.

Caden: Thanks for breakfast. Are you coming over after work?

Me: Yes, why?

Caden: Mom is upset about something. Something big. She needs you.

Me: I'll be there as soon as I can.

Caden: Thanks, DC.

Me: I'm here for both of you.

Right now, I wish it was my weekend off. I switched shifts with Gugliotti so I could attend the ceremony with Alannah. Part of me is upset she didn't reach out to me herself. Then again, she knows I'll be there after work and likely doesn't want to bother me.

The time passes moderately during my shift until right before lunch. My phone chimes again.

Mom: How could you bring her and her son into my home?

Me: What are you talking about?

A link to an article comes through. I skim the beginning. It's about the ceremony. Then I reach the part my mother is pointing me to.

Alannah is the survivor. Now Caden's message makes sense. Big doesn't begin to cover the depth of this revelation. It could be catastrophic for everyone involved.

While I hate text messages, I reply in one. *Me: I didn't know.*

Mom: I expected better from you.

Mom: She and her son are no longer welcome in my home.

There isn't an adequate response to her statement. Alannah didn't choose to survive instead of Sadie. Alannah wasn't at fault for the accident. Chloe's dad was. I will not choose between my future and my parents.

The phone rings with an internal call. "Craven speaking. How can I help you?"

"Blake will be there to replace you within the next ten minutes. Please come to my office."

"Will do, Cap."

Concern and anxiety ripple through me. I can only imagine how Alannah feels. Does Caden know? Ironically, I don't care about me. I'm worried about them.

Blake pulls me out of my head. "Afternoon, Craven. Cap sent me to relieve you."

"Thanks, he called too." I step around him and make my way to Cap's office. "You wanted to see me?"

"There isn't an easy way to ask this… did you know?"

My eyes close, and I shake my head. "No, I didn't know, and neither did Alannah."

"How is that possible?" he asks.

I explain the circumstances and why I chose not to read any coverage, similar to Alannah but for different reasons.

He steeples his fingers when he thinks about things. "I've known Antoinette for quite some time. She isn't going to take this well."

"No, she isn't. I fully expect for her to push me away when I show up later."

"Is that what you want?" Cap asks.

"No, not at all."

"Good. Not only are you happy, but so is she. Blake will finish out your desk shift if you want to take off now."

"Thanks, Cap."

"Good luck, Craven."

I nod curtly, grab my bag, and hurry to my car. I consider whether flowers are the right way to go and decide against it. I don't want to wait any longer to hold her and assure her we'll be fine.

I park in her driveway and knock on the front door. For longer than I would like, no one answers. Caden bounds down the stairs and opens the door.

"You're early," he states and bro hugs me.

"You sounded concerned." He doesn't need to know Cap made my early arrival possible.

"I am." He looks over his shoulder and whispers, "She thinks I didn't hear what was going on down here after I ate. I read the article despite knowing she'll ground me for the rest of my life."

"How do you feel about it?"

"It's sad, but honestly no one else will truly understand the pain better than you two. I'm sure it's different because she was your sister, and we lost my dad and grandparents. The fact it was at the same intersection has to mean something."

Alannah sweeps into the living room, and Caden clams up.

"Callan. What are you doing here? I thought you were working."

"I was. I came to see you. We need to talk."

Caden retreats upstairs without another word.

Alannah raises her arm, ushering me into the kitchen. "There isn't anything to say. The only thing I want is for you to hold me and tell me it doesn't matter. Yet… I know it does."

I step closer to her and take her hands in mine. Her eyes flutter closed briefly, as if my hands surrounding hers will be enough. I want it to be, but I know it won't be. "It doesn't matter."

"How can you say that?"

"It's the truth. A wise young man reminded me of this fact. Only you and I can understand how the other feels."

"He knows?" Her voice comes out anguished and strangled.

I draw her closer and set her hands on my chest. She curls against me as my arms surround her.

"Yes, he overheard you and, I assume, Del this morning. Then he read the article."

Her shoulders drop even further. I'm surprised she hasn't pushed me away. "Paul, Clem, and Del busted through the front door early this morning. I was working out how to share this with Caden." Her words are mumbled against my chest, exactly where she belongs—burrowed against me, willing to face this news with me, not alone. Silence blankets the room. Anxiety and tension wrack her body to the point she's trembling. I tighten my hold, hoping to absorb some of her distress. My hope we may be able to walk out of this unscathed is dashed a few moments later when she pushes me away.

"Why doesn't it matter I survived and Sadie didn't?"

"You were not at fault. Mr. Mathewson was."

Fire bursts in her narrowed eyes. "How do you know his name? Did you lie to me?"

"No. I promised you I would never lie to you, and I haven't. My mother sent me the article this morning. I never read anything before today. You were in the wrong place at the wrong time. Losing Sadie put a lot of things into perspective for me."

"Such as?"

"Tomorrow isn't promised. Sadie could've been anything, but it wasn't meant to be. I don't believe in fate per se, but you and Caden were meant to survive to walk beside me, to be a family with me. Now isn't exactly how I wanted to tell you, but"—I close the gap between us enough to cup her jaw with my hands and drag my thumb over her lower lip—"I love you, Alannah. I love Caden. It isn't going to change because some unfortunate mass of twisted metal tied our families in tragedy fifteen years ago. I didn't know when the simple touch of your hand made my heart pound, and it doesn't matter now."

"It does. I can't allow you to choose us over your family. I would give nearly everything to have mine back for an hour."

My stomach knots as I ask, "Me? Would you give me up?"

She doesn't hesitate or waver in her answer. "No."

"Then why do you expect me to do it?"

"You have exponentially more to lose. I refuse to allow you to regret choosing me and my son."

I exhale slowly. "You don't get to decide for me. I will make my own choice. I will never regret falling in love with you and our amazing son."

Her eyes widen, and her mouth falls open. For the first time, I've rendered her speechless.

I don't give her the opportunity to speak. "I won't give up on us. You and Caden make me a better man and who I'm meant to be."

"Which is?" she manages, barely above a whisper.

"Your other half and his father." A single tear rolls over the ball of her cheek. I swipe it away with the pad of my thumb. "Take some time to grapple with this information. Wrap your head around the fact I'm yours and these details don't matter to me. I'll be waiting. Don't take too long, or I'll camp out on your porch until you talk to me." I press a kiss to her forehead. "I love you, Alannah."

As painful as it is and the last thing I want, I release her and walk toward the front door. I briefly consider talking to Caden but decide it isn't smart. I hope I didn't imagine it, but I would bet my life I heard her say, "I love you, Callan," as the door closes.

Leaving isn't sitting well with me, but if I learned anything about my gorgeous woman, it's that she needs time to process. Alannah needs to dissect it, put it back together, and yank it apart five different ways before she'll accept my words. I don't blame her. It's a lot to process.

I pull into my garage and shut off the engine. Memories of making love to Alannah here flood my mind. I push them away because it makes my heart ache more than simply leaving her. I make my way inside, drop my bag on the floor, and fall into a chair on my back deck. My phone vibrates against my thigh, but I ignore it. Yet, while I attempt to settle myself, the notifications become incessant. When I finally look, I have a host of messages. Why is it people don't understand that I hate texting?

Caden: I don't know what to say.

Me: Nothing to say. If you need me or your mom does, I'm a call away.

Caden: Thank you.

Me: Your mom needs time. I promised to give it to her.

That isn't exactly how it went down, but it's an adequate explanation for his purposes.

Caden: Okay.

I'm not sure what else to expect from Caden. He's in a tough spot now. I can only hope he realizes I'm true to my word. If he needs me, I'm there whether Alannah comes around or not. No, her not coming back to me isn't an option. Unwillingly, I glance at the next few messages.

Patrick: How could you bring her and her son to holiday dinner?

Patrick: Please tell me you didn't know. Lie if you have to.

Patrick: They met my daughters. Maeve can't stop talking about her.

I shake my head and move on to my other brother's messages.

Liam: The sole survivor, seriously? Was she knocked up at the time?

Liam: Mom and Dad deserve better than this from you.

The two messages from Liam hurt more than I expect. Hurt isn't the right word. His words are laced with disrespect and lead me to believe they won't accept Alannah and Caden. They did at dinner but won't in the future. It shouldn't matter if Alannah was already pregnant. I know she was, but it doesn't matter. Choosing Alannah and Caden has nothing to do with my parents and everything to do with me.

Instead of responding, I set my notifications to silent, and I'll only answer calls. Within thirty minutes of my arrival at home, there's a knock on my door. My heart skips, but I know in my gut it isn't Alannah.

"Up for some company?" Smithson and Gugliotti are standing on my porch with bags of snacks.

I open the door wider for them to enter. "I appreciate you guys, but don't you have wives and families you would rather spend time with? Plus, I won't be good company."

"We do, but we've been where you are. Sort of. And we're not expecting you to entertain us," Smithson admits.

Smithson messed up royally during an incident with his mother after Scarlett's graduation from nursing school. He's a groveling expert—not that I need to grovel. Gugliotti's situation was a little different; he needed patience from the beginning while waiting for Lina to realize what was right in front of her. I didn't do anything wrong, but their support means a lot to me.

"Feel like sharing more than we already know?" Gugliotti asks while he unpacks grinders, chips, and iced teas from the bags.

"Not really, but I will." While we eat, I catch them up, including my conversation with Alannah and the disrespectful texts from my family.

"I'm not defending your family, but you can understand why it would be shocking, right?" Gugliotti asks.

"Sure, but disrespecting them isn't okay, shock or no shock. It isn't as if Alannah was in any way responsible for the accident. The sheer fact I brought her to meet them should've been enough for them to choose their words better."

Smithson chugs the rest of his iced tea. "True. What is your plan?"

"With my family? I have no clue." If they force me to choose, I'll choose Alannah and Caden without a second thought. I'm not ready to share my thoughts with the guys yet, considering I haven't had the opportunity to share them with Alannah, not those exact words at least.

"What about Alannah?" Smithson asks.

"When did we turn into a bunch of guys who talk about crap?" I laugh. "She needs time, and I'm going to give it to her. It may kill me, but I'll do it."

"Welcome to the club, man!" Gugliotti slaps his hand on my back.

"Thanks, I guess. Not really a great place to be at the moment."

"No, but she'll come around," Smithson offers.

I need her to trust my word. I was wholly honest with her. The details don't change how I feel and won't going forward.

I kick the guys out a little while later and consider going for a run but decide against it.

I pick up my phone and hover over her name. Scrubbing my hand down my face, I set my phone aside and search for a notebook. To be true to my word, I can't call her right now, despite the pull to do so. With a small notebook in hand, I lock up and write to Alannah before allowing sleep to claim me.

CHAPTER TWENTY-ONE

ALANNAH

My alarm startles me. *Damn!* It's already seven fifteen. How many times did I press snooze? I throw on my robe to check on Caden. When I make it into the kitchen, he hands me a cup of coffee.

"Morning." He's dressed and ready for school.

"Morning. Thank you," I grumble.

He nods and grabs breakfast.

The simple fact Callan isn't here makes my heart constrict. It's been twelve hours max, and I miss him.

"Want to talk yet?" he asks.

"No, but thanks."

He rounds the island and hugs me. I know he wants to talk about Callan, but I need to finish examining the situation myself first. My son is good at keeping his emotions in check. Me, not so much. Keeping the tears at bay is difficult, but I pull it off.

"I'm going to come home after school, then go back for my game. Have a good day, Mom. Love you."

"Okay. I'll meet you at the game. Love you too."

Once I'm ready for the day, I hurry to my office and sequester myself.

Delilah: Are you free for lunch?

Me: Yes, but I don't want to talk about Callan.

Delilah: No promises. Am I still invited?

Me: Of course.

Delilah: I'll bring something chocolate from Chef.

Me: You're the best.

I'm trying as hard as I can, but pushing Callan out of my mind is impossible—much like ignoring my attraction to him the day we met. I finish drafting paperwork for the selectwoman and review estate documents for Mrs. Brinson. My pace, however, is slow and my mind drifts. At exactly noon, Del is knocking on my door.

"Hey, girl!"

"Hey."

She sets lunch on my desk and immediately hugs me. Del isn't really an openly affectionate person. It means I look like hell.

"I look bad enough for a hug, huh?"

Her lips are in a tight line, and she nods a few times. Thankfully, she doesn't push me to talk about Callan at least.

"Are you going to the game tonight?" she asks.

"Always. Are you free?"

"Yeah, I can join you. Scott is…."

"It's okay. Scott is?"

"He's taking his nephew James to an event in Boston."

"Cool." Our conversation ends there, and we're surrounded by silence.

"How are you feeling?" she asks cautiously.

"I don't want to talk about him."

"I didn't ask about him. I asked about you."

"It hasn't been an entire day, and I'm miserable."

"You know it means your feelings for him are deep and worth fighting for."

I sink lower into my chair. "I keep going back to the same spot. His family will basically disown him because of us. I can't allow him to choose us."

"How do you know that?"

"Gut feeling."

"You would rather lose the love of your life because his family is short-sighted?"

Is he? Without a doubt. "Losing his family because of us will be a huge blow, Del. Without talking to him, I know his family is pissed. They weren't keen on my job. Adding on the accident and how it played out...." I shake my head.

"His family probably needs time to process, like you."

"I hope you're right." Thankfully, Del drops her questions. I don't think I can handle much more without breaking down... again.

She cleans up the mess and leans against the door. "I'll see you later. Love you, Lan."

"Thanks. Love you." The instant the door closes, I can't hold the tears back any longer. I manage to lock the outer door before I collapse on the couch in my office. I replay my talk with Callan in my mind. He didn't hear me. If he did, would he have left? Yes. Time, it's what he knows I need. He's the only man who sees me, all of me—quirks and idiosyncrasies—and still he wants me. Is it possible our love is strong enough to handle the fact we lost family members in the same car wreck? Us... probably. No, definitely. His family... I'm not certain. What about Paul and Clem? Caden?

I pull myself together and pick up my office phone. "Hi, Clem."

"Hi, dear. How are you?"

"Not great. Is Paul there as well?"

I hear muffled words.

"He'll be right in." After a few moments, she adds, "He's here."

"There isn't an easy way for me to ask this question. How do you feel about the article? I didn't ask yesterday, and I should have."

Clem speaks first. "No, you shouldn't have. Over the last fifteen years, the only person who brought my sister's smile to your face was Caden... until Callan came into your life."

"Did you know when I introduced you to Callan?"

"We didn't put it together immediately, but yes, we knew about the connection before you."

"But—"

Paul adds, "No buts. It was an accident, Antoinette. The fact you and Callan ended up finding one another all these years and states away only means one thing. You're twin souls."

"And if his family doesn't feel the same way as you?" I ask.

"Handling his family is up to him," he replies.

"No."

"Why not?" Clem asks softly.

"It isn't how a partnership works. How can he choose us if his family doesn't approve?"

"A relationship with equal partners means give and take. When he chooses you and Caden and his family isn't on board, it's their loss. It also means he's willing to put your family first. The family of the three of you, not you and Caden."

"Sounds simple. Is it?"

Paul answers emphatically, "In our experience, yes, if you choose one another. No relationship is rosy every day. The hard days make or break a couple. It seems you and Callan are tackling a major divide early on."

"Thank you for listening."

"Always, dear. We'll see you at the game," Clem adds. They have never missed a season opener since Caden started playing basketball.

I end the call and attempt to finish my tasks before the game. At nearly five, there's a knock on my office door.

"Can I help you?"

"I have a delivery for Alannah," the young man states.

"I didn't order anything."

"Are you Alannah Kramer?"

"Yes. Who is it from?"

He checks the tag. "Kelsey, Maggie, Lina, and Scarlett."

I extend my hand. "Thank you. Hold on, let me get you a tip."

"No need. It's been taken care of. Enjoy your dinner." He disappears down the hall.

Why would they send me dinner? I don't really know them. I shake off my thoughts and open the package. There's absolutely no chance the ladies know my favorite dish from the Inn. I create a group text and thank them.

Me: Thank you for dinner.

Kelsey: You're welcome.

Scarlett: Happy to do it.

Maggie: Of course.

I dig into the side salad before devouring the lobster macaroni and cheese. While I appreciate the gesture, I have a sneaking suspicion Callan is behind my dinner. I consider reaching out to him as well, but I'm not ready to address anything else. With mixed feelings, I clean up and make my way to the high school. As with every game, I send a text to Caden.

Me: Have fun tonight. Love you.

Sometimes he answers, sometimes he doesn't. I paste on my biggest smile and step into the gym. Thankfully, Paul and Clem have secured our seats. I show my season pass, get my hand stamped, then join them in the stands.

"Feeling any better?" Clem asks.

"Not really, but thanks for listening earlier."

Paul throws his arm around my shoulders. "We're here for you and Caden."

I search the court for my son and find him chatting with one of his teammates near the base line. It appears Caden is explaining a play to him, considering his hand movements.

Del plops herself on the bleacher in front of me. "I made it!"

I laugh and return my gaze to where Caden was. He's moved since I looked away. My heart is in my throat, and knots form in my stomach. My son and my... Callan are flying through their personal handshake. I can't read lips, but it looks pleasant. *He came to his game.*

Del nudges me. "You shouldn't be surprised. He loves you both. He made promises he clearly intends to keep, despite the current break you and he are on."

I level my gaze at her, then cast it upward to the ceiling and exhale sharply. My emotions are all over the place. No man has put us first. Callan shows up for my son while he's giving me space to figure out how to deal. He's beyond everything I ever wanted for us. How do I get over the fact his family will never accept us?

The referee's whistle draws my attention. I refocus on my son's final season opener instead of the turmoil in my head and heart. I'm able to tamp down my thoughts for the first half of Caden's game. His team is ahead by six at the half.

"Are you going to talk to him?" Del asks.

"I can't. Not yet." I look up and see him walking along the edge of the court into the lobby. As he passes, he greets a bunch of students and staff on the way. Most notable is Kyla. Her arm is in a sling but isn't in a cast any longer. He stops, and they exchange a few words. Callan's response brings a frown to her face, but then she drops her head. As if he can feel my gaze on him, he turns and looks in my direction. A half smile starts to appear on his face, but then he nods and continues out the door.

"Oh, girl," Del mumbles.

I have no response. The constant dull ache in my chest is enough for me to handle. Talking to Del won't help. I just realized that how I feel right now was my normal before I met Callan. I feel hollow, distressed, and alone.

The second half passes in silence, at least among myself and my family, with limited cheering exceptions. The boys pull out a three-point victory at their home opener. I make my way down to the court and watch Caden disappear into the locker room.

"Have a good night," Clem states as we part ways in the parking lot beside my car.

"You too," I reply, but my eyes are searching for Callan. I feel him. I find him one row over. Unmoving, we stare at one another. The space between us feels insurmountable. Twenty yards away. He's waiting for me to move. It's protective. I appreciate the gesture, but it's painful as well. We should be going home together. "Thank you," I murmur and yank open my door before I determine if he heard me.

The rest of the week passes and plays out exactly the same way. Meals arrive when I would skip them. Callan is conspiring with the PD wives to take care of me, and I don't hate it. He's present at Caden's games, including an away game nearly a thirty-minute drive away. My resolve nearly breaks daily. When I get out of bed on Saturday morning, I find Caden watching cartoons with a box from the Perk perched on his lap.

"Morning, Mom. Your breakfast is on the island."

I take a deep breath. "Did you see Callan this morning?"

"No. He texted me breakfast was on the porch. Are you ready to talk about him yet?"

"Not really. I'll listen if you have something to share."

"Okay. I'll meet you in the kitchen." He shuts off the television and gathers the box.

While my coffee brews, I warm the chocolate croissant in the microwave.

"My intention is not to hurt your feelings. You're back to being lonely and unhappy, like you were before you met DC."

My son using Callan's upgraded name is a gut punch. I didn't consider how Caden would feel about me taking the time Callan offered. For the first time, I put my feelings first. "Your observation is wholly accurate." I pull my breakfast out and take a bite.

"You do more for me than any of my friends, most of whom have two parents. Not only did DC take care of you, but me too. I'm not saying your reasoning is invalid. How you feel about the fact his sister died on the same day as Dad and your parents is how you feel. If DC doesn't see it as an issue, then I'm confused as to why he isn't still part of our life."

Not my life. Not his life. Our life. "It's complicated."

"Not from my perspective. Do you love DC?"

No reason not to tell him the truth. "Yes."

"Does he love you?"

I quell the tears welling in my eyes. "Yes."

"Why isn't that enough?" he asks.

"Given how things ended with Kyla, you should be able to answer your own question."

"It isn't the same. Kyla chose another guy. Well, she wants me back. It isn't important. The details about the accident that happened before I was born shouldn't impact your relationship today."

"They don't for Callan, but they do for his family."

He considers my words for a moment. "Was the accident your fault?" he asks pointedly.

"No."

"Then I don't see the problem."

I explain how I surmise Callan's parents can't separate our survival and the loss of their only daughter.

"You and DC aren't together because his parents can't see he cares about us more than their pain."

"Arguably."

"You don't want him to choose us because he would lose his family if he does."

"I don't want him to regret choosing us and we lose him later anyway."

"Huh. DC was wrong. He said eventually dating would get easier."

I laugh. "Do you want to ask anything else about Callan?"

"Not really."

"Want to talk about Kyla?"

He shrugs. "She broke up with me to test the dating waters. Andre was dating her and someone else. She claims they were exclusive. Now she wants me back."

"How do you feel about dating her again?"

"Not sure. I don't know if I can trust her. All I can say is she didn't cheat on me, but something made her decide she needed more than what we had."

"I'm proud of you. You're wise beyond your years, Caden."

"Thanks." He finishes his breakfast and camps out on the couch to watch movies, given the dismal weather outside.

I make another cup of coffee and curl up in the window seat with my book.

CHAPTER TWENTY-TWO

CALLAN

The last thing I should be required to do is defend my relationship with Alannah. However, I'm thirty minutes from my childhood home, and I've requested my brothers' presence as well. I fully expect a hostile environment. In fact, it would match the dark, gloomy weather outside. I have a key, but I knock anyway.

"Callan, nice of you to visit so soon," my mother greets me.

Although I'm taken aback, I say nothing. Maintaining my composure is key for me to get through this discussion with my family.

"Dad."

"Nice to see you, Callan. To what do we owe the pleasure of your company so soon?"

I frown. "I want to have a frank and honest discussion about Alannah and Caden. I mentioned this in my voice mail."

"She isn't welcome in this house. I figured you would break up with her," Mom states matter-of-factly.

"No. The issue isn't with her or me. It's the four of you. All I ask is you hear me out. If you can't see my position, then I'll have to make decisions for my future and who is welcome and who isn't."

"I see." Mom closes the door behind me.

I follow her into the kitchen and see my brothers with coffee in hand at the island. We exchange curt nods.

My parents take a seat.

"We're listening," Patrick states.

"First, although it truly shouldn't matter, I didn't know until Mom sent the article. Until last week, I haven't read any reports, articles, or commentary about the accident. Neither did Alannah. Her aunt and uncle shielded her when they took her in. I have dissected all the information I could pull together in the last week. I need to hear your reasons for your fierce opposition to her and her son."

"You pulled the reports?" Patrick asks.

"Yes, it was necessary. I'm a trained police officer, regardless of my choice to work in the school system. I need unbiased, detailed, emotionless, and objective information to form a complete opinion of a situation."

"She was already pregnant?" Liam asks.

"Yes, why does it matter?" I put my brother on the spot.

"I suppose it doesn't."

"Was the young man in the car Caden's father?" Patrick asks.

"Yes."

"The other couple were her parents?" my mother asks.

"Yes."

These questions aren't important. "Have any of you read the accident report?"

I receive a chorus of noes in response.

"You're relying on your recollection and news reports."

I receive four yeses in response. "It appears my trip was a waste of my time and yours." I pull out my phone and forward the information to all of them. "Now you have the same information I have. Please read it. Then I would like to discuss it."

"Why?" Dad asks.

"Alannah and Caden are important to me. If you can't see past the unfortunate fact they were in Mr. Mathewson's path that night, then...."

"You would choose them over us?" My mother's voice shakes as she asks the question.

Yes. "I hope it isn't necessary for me to choose. Perhaps given my age at the time of the accident and your decision to throttle our access to information"—I gesture between my brothers and myself—"I see Alannah differently than you. To restate, I didn't know until well after we met and started dating who she is. More importantly, I determined for myself that she's nothing short of amazing. She survived and thrived. Not only did she raise Caden while playing basketball in college, but she successfully put herself through law school. She runs her own practice and has been raising him alone. I can't imagine what else you could possibly believe is necessary in a woman who would be worthy to step foot in your home."

No one utters a word. I turn on my heel and walk straight back to my car. I wasn't exactly hoping for an instant change of heart, but a conversation would have been preferable to the dialogue over the last thirty minutes.

I pull out of the neighborhood and grab a coffee for the ride back. Like I'm giving Alannah time, I should offer the same to my family. The sole problem with the premise is I miss her smile, her laugh, the way she soothes my nerves by threading her fingers in mine… I miss her. The ride passes without a notification or indication of progress with her or my family. I meant what I said, the time I'm willing to offer her has an expiration date. A date that is rapidly approaching. I will not allow her to endure another anniversary alone. The only positive of today is it isn't raining here yet. I park in my garage, change, lace up, and run until my legs ache.

When I return home, I drag myself into my kitchen for dinner before showering and collapsing into my bed. I write more to Alannah and call it a night.

Bright and early—well, not bright—I roll out of bed and nearly fall to the floor. My legs are stiff and sore from running too many miles after driving round trip yesterday. However, skipping the run wouldn't have allowed me to sleep last night.

I order lunch for Alannah from the deli around the corner from her office while my coffee brews. Those are the only things going right for me today. Rain pours from the sky as I pull into a spot and catch up with Hagen heading inside.

"How are you doing, Craven?"

Miserable. "Okay. How's Lilah?"

"Too smart for her own good."

I laugh. My mind wanders to what our little girl could look like. Almost immediately, I shake the thought away but Hagen notices.

"She still taking time?" Hagen asks.

"Yeah."

"How long has it been?"

I could tell him down to the minute. "Nearly two weeks."

"It can't be easy for either of you." He considers his words, then adds, "Any of you."

It's awful. "No, it's not." We stow our bags and head in for roll call.

The first shoe to drop is Greyson will be joining me at the high school today. *Great!* With keys in hand, I make my way to the motor pool.

"Ready, Greyson?"

"Yup. Ready for an easy shift."

I frown at him as he takes the passenger seat. "Why would you think a shift at the high school will be easy?"

"It can't be hard or taxing to walk around the school all day and keep a bunch of teens in line."

"Uh-huh."

Greyson looks in my direction. "What?"

Mother nature isn't happy today. It's still pouring, and thunder rumbles in the distance.

"We're you a good kid in high school?"

"No, not really."

"Please follow protocol today. We do more than monitor the halls." I check in with Michelle at the front office and direct Greyson to make rounds on the western side of the building.

While I walk the east side interior, I see Caden talking with Kyla near the gym after first period. I offer a polite nod and continue walking.

"DC, wait up!" he calls after me.

I slow my pace. "Hey, Caden. How are you?"

"I'm okay. Thank you for coming to my games. I'm sure it wasn't easy with everything going on."

I stop walking, and Caden does as well. "I won't abandon you or your mom."

Another loud crack of thunder rattles through the building. Then the lights flicker and go out. "Let's go." I pull my flashlight from my hip and escort him to the community resource office and key him inside. "Please stay here."

"Okay. Be careful, DC. Mom may not have told you yet, but she's working it out in her head." Caden is squarely on team Alannah and Callan staying together.

Apart isn't an option for me either. "I will. I know. Stay here."

He nods. I close the door and contact Greyson with the walkie. "Greyson, status."

"I'm outside room 204."

The emergency lights illuminate.

"I'm calling this in. Stay where you are until further instructed."

"Got it."

"Dispatch, this is badge #132."

"Go ahead."

"There's a power outage at York High School. Emergency lights are on, but the generator hasn't restored power. We'll follow procedure and move students into classrooms."

"Roger. Power outages are citywide, including the courthouse and government buildings."

Fear slices through me. Is Alannah at the courthouse today? My chest tightens, but I reply anyway. "Roger." I make my way toward the main office while using the walkie to contact Greyson. "Greyson?"

"Yup."

I shake my head at his lack of professionalism. "Move any students in the hallway methodically into the closest classroom from west to east. I'm going to the main office and then will do the same from east to west. When you finish the second floor move up to the third."

"Yup."

I hurry down the main hallway to the office. "Principal Kisel," I call out.

"Here, Officer Craven."

I locate her in a dark corner of her office. Her face is barely illuminated by her cell phone. "Can you give me a status update?"

"I'm on hold with the electric company. If the estimate is longer than two hours, I'll dismiss the students."

"Understood. Officer Greyson is clearing the second and third floors. I'm going to clear the main floor and larger areas. Then I'll return here. Please keep me updated."

"Okay, thank you," she replies.

I walk the corridor and verify the bathrooms are empty as well. Next I move onto the auditorium. I find two seniors kissing in a dark corner.

"Let's go."

Begrudgingly, they follow me to the nearest classroom. After dropping them off, I check the gym and finally the locker room. "Greyson, status?"

"Second and third-floor corridors clear. All students in classrooms," he replies.

"Good job. Please report to the main office."

"On my way," Greyson replies.

Walking back to the main office myself, I check on Caden. "You good?"

"Yup. Is power out all over town?"

"Yeah. How do you know?"

"I texted Mom to tell her I was fine. She's in her office, and there's no power there either."

Alannah is fine, physically at least. The tightness in my chest loosens marginally. "Good. I'll be back when I know more. You'll probably be dismissed early."

"Sweet. I'm fine here, DC."

I nod and close the door. Principal Kisel is speaking loudly and forcefully to whoever is on the other side of her call across the hall. "I need to get my students home safely. Make it happen."

"Craven, what's next?" Greyson asks as he approaches.

"We wait," I answer him. "How can we help?" my question directed at the principal.

She turns in my direction. "Honestly, your presence has been quite helpful. The bus company will be sending buses within the hour. Until then, the students are to remain in their classrooms."

"Understood. Just so you're aware, Caden Kramer is in our office. We were talking when the power went out. I put him in there."

"I'll make note of it. I'll use the intercom to dismiss the students in an orderly manner. If it isn't working, we'll use the bullhorn."

"Okay."

Greyson and I patrol the building while we wait for the buses to arrive. As quickly and orderly as possible, we escort the students out of the building and send them home. Students with cars are dismissed once the buses pulled away.

I see Caden walking toward the exit. "DC, I'm heading home. Mom is still at her office."

I appreciate the unsolicited information. "Okay. Thanks. Drive safely."

"Will do."

"Caden?"

He turns back, "Yeah?"

"Please text me when you get home."

He nods. "I will after Mom."

I smile as he walks away.

After the staff and principal leave the building, we return to the precinct. I grab my bag and check my phone.

Caden: I'm home, but it's a disaster here. Can you come over?

Me: I'll be there in ten minutes.

As fast as possible, I rush to Alannah's. The destruction in her front yard isn't terrible. A tree near the sidewalk uprooted and fell onto her grass—fixable with a chain saw and some work. Luckily, it missed the house. Caden looks shell-shocked standing near the garage.

"The back is worse," he admits after throwing his arms around me.

"Did you call your mom?" I ask after releasing him.

"I texted her I was home, but I didn't tell her about this yet."

"Okay. Let's check it out."

Caden's description doesn't begin to cover the damage in the backyard. A massive tree fell from the rear neighbor's yard, crushed one of the hoops, and spans the entire court. Small branches, a few remaining leaves, and debris litter the cover of the pool and the patio.

"Mom doesn't really need more right now," Caden mutters.

"Is there something else aside from…." I can't finish the question, a question I have no right to ask. *Do I?*

"No. Her dissecting everything is enough for her to handle."

"I understand. Why don't you call her and ask her to come home? Make sure you remind her you're fine but there's some storm damage."

He calls her on speaker. The moment her voice surrounds me, my heart clenches. It was the first thing I was attracted to. Getting to know the rest of her was more than I ever wanted for myself.

"Hey, Mom."

Her voice is strained when she asks, "Are you okay?"

"Yeah. I'm fine, but there's some storm damage. You should come home."

"Okay. I'll be there as soon as I can."

He ends the call.

"Does your mom have a chain saw?"

Caden laughs. "She has everything."

Of course she does. "Can you show me?"

With Caden's guidance, I locate her chain saw and the gas. The tree in the front needs to be taken care of right away. Plus, it's Alannah's responsibility.

We're leaving the shed with the tools when she arrives home.

CHAPTER TWENTY-THREE

ALANNAH

Caden said he was fine. I keep reminding myself this as I navigate home. There are a few closed roads due to downed trees or power lines. I suppose it's a good thing it was a rainstorm and not snow.

My throat seizes when I see Callan's SUV in my driveway. As if taking care of us from afar isn't enough.

"Caden?" I call out when I step out of the car. The damage I can see isn't terrible.

"We're back here," he replies.

I round the garage and step through the gate. *Damn!* I nearly crumble to the ground at the destruction in my backyard. "Well, that's an impressive mess, isn't it?" My attempt to cover the shock is dismal at best and a failure as well.

Callan pins his gaze to mine. I'm not sure what I expected to see, but the unspoken—at least in this moment—love in his eyes nearly knocks me over.

"Hi, Alannah."

"Hi. Thank you for coming."

"Always."

The ache in my chest is unbearable. My breathing becomes labored and impossible to ignore. Despite me accepting time, he's here taking care of us. He's an exceptional man who wants a future with us. How can I get over the past though? Of my fear of the past ruining our future.

"What do we do about this?" Caden asks as he motions to the backyard.

"I'll call Mrs. Gilson and have her contact her insurance company about the damage for the backyard. The front yard, we have to take care of."

"I'll take care of the tree in front," Callan states.

There's no room for me to argue with him. I drop my head in acquiescence. Sure, I can cut the tree, but he's here and willing to do it. I have no doubt he'll be more efficient and have it done in a more reasonable time.

"Do you mind if I change first? I can go home and come back if you would prefer."

The notion he would leave to change so he doesn't enter our home is... exactly who he is. "You don't have to leave to change," I answer.

"Thank you." After retrieving his bag, he follows us inside and goes straight to the guest bathroom.

"Can I help?" Caden asks me when Callan emerges changed.

Keeping my vivid memories in check is much harder than I anticipate. His shirt leaves nothing to my imagination. That isn't true. It isn't too tight. It fits perfectly.

"Mom?"

"Huh?"

"Can I help?"

"If Callan doesn't mind."

"Not at all. You need a long-sleeve shirt and sneakers," Callan instructs.

"On it!" My son rushes out of the kitchen and bounds upstairs.

Instead of kissing him with abandon, which I need desperately, awkward silence settles between us. My fingers caress the necklace he gave me. Callan is looking anywhere but at me right now. If the ground could swallow me whole, it would be better than the emotional trench between us in my kitchen.

"Please send Caden out when he's dressed," Callan requests.

"I will."

He takes a few steps and turns back as if he needs to share something. With a shake of his head, he continues outside. Less than five minutes later, Caden bounces down the stairs despite the lack of electricity and rushes outside to help.

I would busy myself making dinner to avoid the swirl of emotions coursing through me, but no power equals no cooking. I change and join the guys outside. I would love nothing more than to get back to them both being *my* guys. Getting back to *my* is on me and I don't see a way to get there. By the time I join them, the tree is cut into six sections.

I walk across the grass, grab one of the sections, and carry it over to the cord holder on the porch. I'll split them later. Once the logs are moved, the awkwardness sets in again.

Caden attempts to break it. "Thanks for letting me help, DC."

"I appreciate the help."

After they hug, Caden heads inside. Aside from leaving us alone, there isn't anything he can do.

"I can put the chain saw away," I offer.

"I'll do it." He disappears around the house with the case in his hand. Protective, possessive Callan is lethal to my heart. He's being true to himself, and it's killing me. When he returns, he scoops up his bag from the front porch. When he's about an arm's length away, he reaches out to touch my hand. Before making contact, he lets it drop.

My body reacts as if he actually touched me. Heat and awareness trickle through me.

"Please don't try to clean the backyard alone."

"I won't. Thank you for coming, Callan."

"Always. Good night, Alannah." With a slow exhale, he turns to leave. Callan sits in his SUV until I'm inside the house.

I lean against my front door and slide to the floor, pulling my knees to my chest. It doesn't dull the pain in my heart or head. *How do I get over the fear he'll change his mind?* He's proving he won't every single day regardless of the fact we're broken up—sort of. What more do I need?

Assurance.

I need assurance.

There are no assurances in life. Of all people, I know nothing is promised, and so does Callan. I scramble to my feet and search for my phone. It's dead. Great!

"Caden, is your battery backup for your phone charged?" I ask from the base of the staircase.

"Not anymore."

"Okay."

I scribble down what I want to say and climb into my bed. Can't do anything else. At some point overnight, our power is restored. My flashing alarm clock indicates it's been back on for about four hours. I drag myself to my kitchen, plug in my phone, and wait to see what time it is. Barely five in the morning. No reason to go back to bed at this point. I check the contents of my fridge, then stare at my phone, willing myself to send a message to Callan. I accepted the time he offered. I need to reach out first. Yet, I can't bring myself to press send. I'm terrified to choose wrong. Does it matter? Caden is equally attached and affected by our separation. *Ugh!* It doesn't help the anniversary of the worst day of my life is in a few days.

Resolved I can't fix it now, I wake Caden and get ready for work. My son rushes downstairs and checks the front porch like he has been since the first breakfast delivery. Not only does he find breakfast but a gift bag as well.

"I assume this is for you." Caden hands me the gift and breakfast.

I accept the bags and set the gift aside. "Thanks."

He grabs a bottled water and the donuts from Callan. "I'll see you at my game."

"Have a great day, Caden. Love you."

"Love you too, Mom. You should open the gift."

"I will." Eventually.

I lock up and make my way to my office, purposefully leaving the bag on my bed. Once everything is reset in my office, I order groceries for delivery and review two files for this morning's appointments. Lacking focus, I go in search of a fresh cup of coffee. Two meetings later, the coffee is cold, and I'm interested in pressing send on the many texts to Callan I've saved over the last few weeks.

Cara enters my office right before noon, gives me my messages and mail, and leaves for the day. Near one there's a knock on the outer door. I expect to find a young delivery person on the other side of the door with lunch courtesy of Callan. I'm shocked to find Grace Craven there instead.

My stomach bottoms out. "Is Callan okay?"

"As far as I know. He doesn't know I'm here. May I come in?" she asks.

I open the door wider and then close it behind her. "Would you like water or a coffee?"

"No, thank you."

I offer her a seat in the conference room. Uncomfortable silence stretches between us, but she showed up unannounced, so I wait for her to speak.

"Did you know my son drove home last weekend?"

He did? Why? "No, I didn't. Callan and I are…." Broken up? Taking a break? All it'll take is a call from me. "Callan offered me time to figure out how to handle the facts of the accident."

"I see. He requested a meeting to discuss the facts, and we rebuffed him, all four of us. I assumed his presence meant he broke up with you—a notion he dispelled immediately. He left without much talking other than a fierce defense of you and your son as well as an admission he would choose you if forced."

Oh, Callan. "I would give nearly anything to change the past. However, life doesn't always work out how we want. I would've preferred to stay in my clueless bubble as it pertains to the accident. I didn't know when we met. I wish I didn't attend Coach's farewell ceremony; then I wouldn't know now. The fact is, I do know. I walked away from the accident with no parents and my son without his father. I can't fathom losing Caden. I would be…. It's why Callan and I aren't on the same page. I refused to allow him to choose us. I tried anyway."

"You would walk away?"

"As painful as it has been, we can't be the reason Callan doesn't have his family in his life."

Grace is quiet and pensive for longer than I expect. "I'm staring at the possibility of losing a second child because of one accident fifteen years ago. My son doesn't say things he doesn't mean. He will choose your family."

"Callan is an exceptional man. Aside from that fact, I can't offer you anything else. How you and your family handle his statement is up to you." What it means for mine is another matter—something I don't plan on discussing with anyone other than Callan.

"Thank you for the courtesy of answering the door. I need to have a conversation with my husband and sons."

"You're welcome. Have a nice day."

I close the outer door and lock it before pulling out my phone and scanning the texts I saved to Callan. I opt for something else entirely.

Me: Can we talk?

This time I press send. I gather my tote and head home. Caden arrives and goes straight to his room to get some homework done before his game. Hours and a grocery delivery pass. I get worried and angry at the same time. As much as I don't like involving other people in my life, I text Smithson.

Me: Have you seen Callan today?

Smithson: No, but he's hiking. He does it every year.

I'm sure Zack knows about the accident. Callan probably has no signal and isn't ignoring my texts.

Me: Okay. When will he be back?

Smithson: Late on Sunday.

Me: Thanks, Zack.

Smithson: Everything okay?

Me: Hopefully it will be. Thanks.

Smithson: You're welcome.

I throw together a sandwich and eat on the way to Caden's game. Knowing he's hiking means he won't be at the game. I can't help but be upset he's letting Caden down. Then again, I have no right to feel that way.

We're in a weird limbo I created. I hate it. I call and leave a voice mail asking him to call me when he can, considering his dislike of texts.

When I enter the gym, Caden trots over to me, which is an unusual occurrence. "Coach Ortega is here."

"That's great! He said he would attend a game."

"DC isn't coming tonight." His tone is sad but understanding.

"How do you know?"

"He told me while we were cutting the tree. Something about an annual hiking trip."

"Oh, okay. Even though I texted you like always. Have a great game. Love you."

"Love you too, Mom." He rejoins the warm-ups, and I take my seat in the bleachers.

I doubt it has anything to do with Coach Ortega, but Caden and his team look like it's playoff time, not within the first few weeks of the season. At halftime, Caden has twelve points, four assists, and three rebounds. I check my phone again, hoping for a response, but I don't have one.

"Hi, Miss Kramer." Kyla takes a seat beside me.

"Hi. How are you?"

She shrugs. "I got the cast off, but the physical therapy stinks."

"At least you're making progress."

"I guess so. Can you give Caden a message for me?"

"Is he not replying to you?"

She exhales sharply. "I think he blocked me after Andre said some untruthful things."

"I see. What would you like me to tell him?"

"Please tell him I'm sorry and I would like to talk to him in person."

"I will, but it doesn't guarantee he'll contact you."

Her head drops in understanding. "Thanks. I know." She climbs down the bleachers and rejoins her friends.

The second half starts exactly as the first ended. Crisp, clean passes and shots hitting the bottom of the net. Tonight's game is one of the best I've seen my son play. It's amazing to watch. After the final buzzer, Caden waves me over to the sideline where he's speaking with Coach Ortega.

"Coach Ortega. Nice to see you again," I greet him.

"You as well, Miss Kramer. I would like to set up a meeting with you about Caden's future at our university. Perhaps over the holiday break?"

I cast a look in my son's direction. The glee on his face is like mine when I was choosing a school. It also brings a pang of sadness up for me. "We would be happy to set up a meeting."

He hands Caden his card. "Please contact my office to set up a time. Great game tonight, Caden."

"Thanks, Coach!" Caden shakes his hand before he walks away. "What did Kyla want?"

"She wanted me to give you a message."

"Which was?"

"She's sorry and would like to speak to you in person."

"Okay. I'll meet you at home." He hugs me and hurries downstairs into the locker room.

I'll take any and all hugs from my son—postgame sweat included. My phone chimes in my purse. I scramble to pull it out, only to be disappointed it isn't Callan. After the short ride home, I change and reach into the gift bag.

Alannah,

I promised I would give you time. However, I was also clear it was a limited offer. I miss you. I miss us. I miss our family. Each time I thought of you or wanted to send you a message I wrote it here instead of impinging on the space I offered. I'll be back from my annual hiking trip for Sadie late on Sunday.

Callan

If you had opened the gift, you wouldn't have had to contact Zack. I dislike people knowing my business, but I needed to know if I lost him permanently. Before I get to read the first entry, Caden calls me from the kitchen.

"Mom?"

"I'm in my room."

He stands at the threshold.

"What's up?"

"Can Kyla come over?"

"Sure. You know the rules."

"Yup. Thanks."

"You're welcome." With my door open, I curl up in my chair near the window and start to read Callan's entries.

Offering you space to figure out if you still want us was one of the hardest things I've ever done.

Each entry is dated. Some are simple, everyday texts from "Good night, Alannah" to "I miss sharing my morning coffee with you" and "I miss the way your hand feels in mine." The sentiments are sweet and echo most of the things I miss about him. Then there's one from last weekend, presumably after he went to see his family.

I'm asking you to worry about my feelings, yours, and Caden's. How my parents and brothers feel about the circumstances is on them. Perhaps if you were at fault, it might matter to me, but you weren't. Don't let their feelings ruin what we have built so far.

I close the book and move into the kitchen when Kyla arrives. While I don't eavesdrop, the tone and volume of their conversation seem amicable. Slightly more than an hour later, she leaves. Like me, when Caden is ready to share with me, he will.

"I'm going to play video games with Jonah. Are the tree people coming tomorrow?"

"Yeah."

"Good. I need my court back." He gives me a side hug.

"Me too. Good night, Caden."

"Night."

I lock up and climb back into my bed with the notebook. I miss how I feel safe within his arms. He knows the absolute lows of my life, and he wants to be with me. Comparing his words to mine of the texts I never sent is uncanny. They are nearly identical until the entry from a few days ago after the tree fell.

I hate I felt asking for permission to be in your home was necessary. Not even the moment we met did you feel like a stranger. Even though Caden called me for help, I felt like an outsider. Worse than that was not being able to comfort you. I know you well enough to know the damage to your backyard was difficult to see. Please know I wanted to take it off your plate and handle it for you. I wanted to fix it, all of it, not only the fallen tree in the front. You are the strongest person I know. I want to be there for you. I want you to rely on me for big things and little things, every single day.

I close the book around my finger and lay back against my pillows. I consider going to my secret thinking spot, but it's late and dark. Stopping the deluge of tears is impossible. Tears for no longer living in the clueless bubble, tears for those we lost, as well as sobs and heaves for me, Caden, and Callan. The anguish and tears pull me into a fitful, dreamless sleep.

CHAPTER TWENTY-FOUR

CALLAN

I'm grateful Caden was willing to call me when he saw the damage at his home. He could shut me out in deference to his mom. It's one thing to be present at Caden's game and see her at a distance or verify she gets to her car safely. However, being near Alannah and unable to touch her is another level of hell. I can't go back to before I knew how soft her lips are or how her body molds to mine when she's in my arms. Being away from them is torture. My trip couldn't come at a better time, although the last thing I would choose is for her to endure another anniversary alone. I suppose she's never alone because she has Caden, but I wanted to be there for her.

Despite my lack of good sleep, I drag myself out of bed and recheck my gear. At first the trip was a way to remember Sadie. She went camping with her bestie. Each year since I went away to college, I hike Acadia around the anniversary of the accident, up to and including the day of. It offers me a chance to disconnect and avoid unnecessary calls from my family. Immediately after Sadie's death, my parents made a production of remembering her at the exact time they were notified she was gone. It took me two years to realize it wasn't healthy for me to remember her that way. Perhaps my way isn't the best way either, but it works for me.

I would've invited Alannah and Caden, but given the strained nature of our relationship, the opportunity didn't present itself. Also, Caden has games I'm sure he wouldn't choose to miss. Instead, I dropped off breakfast and the notebook containing each word I wanted to share with her while we're on a break. I laugh out loud at myself paraphrasing *Friends*. Our break will be coming to an end as soon as I get home. It's time for her to decide. As I explained and reiterated in my words to her, the time I offered is limited. It expires when I get home. She may smash my heart into a million infinitesimal pieces, but if we're over, I need to move on from the limbo we're treading in.

The drive isn't terrible. As I near the exit for the park, I pull off into a local grocery store for supplies. The cabin is sparsely furnished without television or internet. I need food though. An hour later, stocked with food for the next few days, I pull into the driveway of the secluded cabin. Purposefully I shut off my phone. Smithson knows where I am and how to reach the rental agent in an emergency. It isn't as secluded as I would like. I have neighbors about three hundred yards to the east. I stow the groceries, change into my boots, and walk out the front door with water and my thoughts.

The trail I chose today is purposefully only a few miles. Tomorrow I'll tackle the Precipice Trail, which is steep and described as treacherous. Ironic, I know.

Two hours later, my clothes drenched in sweat and my thighs shaking, I climb the front steps of my cabin. After a lukewarm shower, I make an easy dinner and eat it outside on the back porch, which boasts an unmatched view of the surrounding mountains.

Sleep proves easy after traveling and hiking today. The next morning, the sun is peeking through the drab curtains, hitting me squarely in the face. I probably should've closed those last night. Resolved to hike for Sadie, I roll out of bed, dress, and leave for the day.

I make my way to the entrance to Precipice and find it's closed for unsafe conditions. It's late in the season to be climbing it. Two years ago, it was closed as well. Shifting gears, I walk to the beginning of the South Ridge Trail. It's the longest but easiest as far as terrain—not what I wanted. Midafternoon I return to the cabin. After cleaning up, I make an early dinner and power on my phone.

A few notifications come through. The first thing I see is a voice mail icon and a few text messages. I scan the texts first.

Mom: We're ready to talk about Sadie. Please call us.

Liam: I'm sorry. I was an asshole.

That's putting it mildly, bro. The third message makes my heart plummet to my feet.

Alannah: Can we talk?

I check the voice mail, which is also from Alannah. Her sultry voice warms me despite the fact it's a recording. "I sent the text before I read the notebook. I…." A few moments of silence come through before she adds, "Please call me when you get home."

Call her. No, I'm going to her right now. With a quickness I didn't know I possessed after two days of hiking, I pack and hurry out of the cabin. The cracked miles of pavement can't pass fast enough. The last few days have been both cathartic and torture. There's something to be said for being absolutely alone with your thoughts. Though I was clear before I traipsed through Acadia, now there isn't a question in my mind. Alannah and Caden are my people, and I'm miserable without them. Before we met, I thought I was happy. I was wrong, dead wrong. Choosing them may sacrifice my family, but I need to live for me, not my parents. The messages from my mother and Liam may mean they've made similar strides in the last week. I was merely moving through each day, waiting for her. Alannah's text, actually her voice mail, leads me to believe she's come to the same conclusion.

Nearly four hours later, I pull into her driveway, rush up the steps, and ring the doorbell.

The door swings open and she's... wearing leggings, my T-shirt, and an unbuttoned flannel. She looks like she hasn't slept well in too long. Her skin is sallow, and despite the meals I sent, she looks like she lost weight.

"Callan." My name falling from her lips increases my desire to kiss her breathless.

"Can I come in?" I have flashbacks from when we first met.

"Sorry, please come in."

Purposely, I keep space between us when I step inside, despite my aching desire to slant my mouth over hers and confirm this conversation will go well.

"I was outside by the firepit. Want to join me?"

Silently, I follow her. She said she wanted to talk. This isn't going how I thought it would. Then again, she didn't say what she wanted to talk about. We take seats on the couch against the opposite arms—the space reflecting the steps backward we've taken in the last few weeks.

My gaze meets hers before she asks, "Did you cut your trip short for me?"

"Yes."

"Why?"

I raise an eyebrow at her. "You asked to talk."

"I understand better than anyone needing to be away for the anniversary. While not many people know about your sister around here, everyone knows me and Caden."

"I would've invited you, but…." I leave the reason hanging.

"So many times, I almost texted you."

"What stopped you?"

"Fear."

"What are you afraid of?"

"So many things. Everything."

I wait her out as she hasn't finished her thought.

She scoots forward a little and reaches her hand in my direction. I surround it with mine. The electricity hasn't lessened; it's stronger.

"I felt drawn to you instantly. You listen and aren't concerned with what others will think taking up with a single mom. I didn't share immediately, but I fell hard and fast for you. You make me feel whole. We fit, and we have from the moment we met. I was confident you and I could be together for the rest of our lives."

Was? My thoughts catch in my throat.

She continues, "I was prepared to spend time with your family to prove my single motherhood and job don't make me a bad person. How I feel when I'm with you is terrifying and exactly what I've been searching for. The type of love my parents had—selfless, enduring, and unwavering. I was sure about us, until the article. The article had me rethinking if you and I could be together. If knowing Caden and I survived and Sadie didn't… would be insurmountable for us. I can understand how it could be. To some extent, I understand your parents' anger about who I am. Then you offered me time, which I took. Truthfully, it was one of the hardest decisions of my life."

I'm on edge. *Why does she keep saying 'was'?* This conversation is not going how I thought it would. "And now?" I manage.

"Now, is up to you. What I mean is, you never stopped taking care of us regardless of my choice for space. The meals, knowing I wouldn't eat enough. Using Kelsey, Maggie, and the others instead of your own name was smart. Although, I saw right through it. Showing up for Caden, the tree damage cleanup, all of it. It means you're in this with us too."

"I didn't—"

She extends a finger from our linked hands and raises it to my lips to interrupt. "But believing you might regret choosing us is solely on me. I would give anything to have my parents here to meet you—except you. If I can't see myself without you, how can I expect you to?" She inhales sharply. "Your mother came to my office to talk to me. I told her I wouldn't force you to choose. It was a boldface, all caps lie. I don't share my choice to lie to her lightly."

I tilt my head in question. "You told me precisely the same thing."

"I know. I don't want you to *have* to choose. To hell with whatever anyone else thinks. I want to be selfish and happy with you. You said you loved me, and I hope you heard me then. I love you, Callan."

"I love you, Alannah. I want to be selfish and happy with you too."

"Really?" The disbelief in her voice rocks me.

I haul her into my arms and hold her. Her breath against my neck and her coconut shampoo teases my nose. "There was never a single second when I wasn't going to choose a life with you and Caden." I catalog her curves against me before she speaks again.

"You have never felt like a stranger to me. I know that doesn't make sense."

"It does. I felt the same way when I heard your voice the first time. It's as if you were imprinted on my heart before we were introduced. I wasn't looking for love when I found you. I was looking for peace. I met you and took a risk. Your reluctant yes led me to you and Caden. I found calm and healing in two people. Our love is a Carl and Ellie kind of love, and I refuse to relinquish it while I'm breathing."

She lifts her eyes to mine, and I slant my mouth over hers before she can speak another word. Every ounce of angst, pain, and tangled emotion from the last three weeks flows away from us. Panting and breathless, she adds a sliver of space between us.

"Who are Carl and Ellie?"

"You've never seen the movie *Up*?"

"Can't say I have."

"Well, we're going to watch it together, and then you'll understand who Carl and Ellie are."

"Okay. I need to amend my statement about your clothes."

I frown at her. "What do you mean?"

"Until today, you in a tailored tuxedo was my favorite. I'm changing my mind. Gray sweatpants and a backward hat are hot as fuck."

"I see. Are you sure it isn't because we haven't kissed in a while?"

"I'm absolutely sure."

"Is Caden here?"

"No, he's out with Jonah and Silas."

"How long until he gets home?"

"At least a few hours, why?"

I bring my lips to the shell of her ear and whisper, "I would prefer all night to reacquaint myself with you, but I'll take a few hours."

Goose bumps erupt on her skin from my proximity and my words.

Her gaze levels with mine. "You should take the entire night and every night after tonight. We do prefer breakfast prepared by you."

"Is breakfast the only reason?"

She giggles softly. "No, not even close."

"I have one condition," I murmur.

"What?"

"We trade your mattress and sheets for mine. The rest is perfect as it is."

"Deal. Let's go make use of our alone time." She's on her feet and turning off the firepit faster than I anticipate.

As we reach the bedroom, I waste no time stripping off each stitch of my clothing and hers, except her shirt. After a long minute burning the image of Alannah in my YPD shirt and nothing else into my mind, I lift it over her head and climb over her.

I intend to go slow, but Alannah has other plans. With strength she hasn't utilized before, she hooks her leg behind my knee and switches our positions.

"In a hurry?"

"Yes." Her voice comes out desperate and needy.

"Fast first. Then slow."

With my hands on the flare of her hips, she lowers herself over me in one measured movement. A slow exhale later, she sets her hands on my chest and we move together toward our first feverish climax of the evening. Each thrust pushes the anguish of the last few weeks away. Each kiss seals our belief in each other about our future. She spasms around me, and I burst into her as she falls over the edge.

She places a few open-mouth kisses to my chest before resting her head. I sweep her soft tresses away, uncovering a gorgeous, satisfied smile on her face.

"Ready for a slow round two?"

She lifts her head and stares at me. "Yes."

I spend the next hour painstakingly worshiping Alannah before she returns the favor. Then we careen over the edge of carnal bliss for the second time tonight. Reluctantly, thirty minutes before curfew, we drag ourselves out of her bed and curl up on the couch. Alannah catches me up with the happenings over the last three weeks, including Caden's upcoming meeting with Coach Ortega.

"Do you think he's going to pick SNHU?"

"Don't know. He applied to both schools where he had offers and SNHU without a written offer. I think he was prepared to go there without a basketball option."

The front door opens, and Caden steps inside.

"Hey, Caden," Alannah greets him.

"Mom, you're up. Hey, DC."

The palpable relief on his face is enough for me right now. I don't need a drawn-out explanation. It's clear Caden was worried about his mom. He also knew informing me would get him into trouble. He's probably right.

"Did you fill him in yet, Mom?"

"I started to, but you can if you want."

"Nah, it can wait until Monday. Glad to have you back, DC."

"Happy to be back," I reply.

"I'm going to bed. Same schedule tomorrow, Mom?"

She takes a deep breath. "Yes."

I realize as she inhales why Caden doesn't want to talk now or even tomorrow. The clock has flipped. It's officially the anniversary of the worst day of our lives. Then it occurs to me, I don't know how she remembers her parents and Daniel. You would think I'm jealous of him. I am, but not in the way you think. I wish I met them earlier. All I can do is give them the best of me going forward.

"Can I ask you something?"

"You can ask, I may not answer," she says cautiously.

"What is our schedule for tomorrow?"

"Our?" Her voice trembles as she asks.

"Yes, you'll never be able to get rid of me now."

"I never want to be without you again. We make a trip to the cemetery. Then we sit at the Nubble Lighthouse. I share the last year of Caden's life with Daniel in my head and make intentions for the upcoming year."

"You do this together each year?"

"I go each year. Caden has joined me more often than not. I don't force him. Paul and Clem have their own way to remember my parents. Del always works, and we catch up a few days later. It's always been me and Caden on the anniversary. What about you?"

"I created the camping trip in Sadie's honor. Honestly, I couldn't find her grave if I tried. I was only there on the day we buried her. Next year, we can do both my tradition and yours." Our ways of remembering those we lost are quite different, but also exactly what we need.

"I would like that," she offers.

"Me too."

Without additional words, she locks up and we burrow in her bed until morning.

CHAPTER TWENTY-FIVE

ALANNAH

Waking with Callan, especially today, should make me pause. It doesn't.

"He would understand," Callan mumbles against my shoulder blade.

"How I love you is different and exponentially more than Daniel. I loved him, but it was an immature type of love. I would have sacrificed my happiness to give Caden what he deserved." I turn in his embrace and kiss him deeply.

"How much time do we have?" he asks.

I crane my neck to look at the clock. "Maybe an hour, but you need to go home first, don't you?"

He frowns.

"It'll be one of the last times. You're welcome as soon as you can pack your stuff."

A devilish grin appears on his face. "It won't take long."

"Why?"

"Only the master bedroom furniture and the television belong to me. The rest came with the house."

"Now it makes sense."

"What makes sense?"

"The kitchen doesn't suit you and your talented closet chef skills at all. I assumed you simply didn't get around to renovating it."

He laughs. "If the house belonged to me, the kitchen is the first thing I would fix. You did an amazing job on yours."

Ours. "Thanks. I'll make you a cup to go."

Slowly, he untangles himself from me and pads to the bathroom. I tug on his shirt and my robe. As the cups finish brewing, Callan meanders into the kitchen. He takes a heavy gulp from his cup.

"Morning," Caden mumbles as only a teen can do when he shuffles into the kitchen.

"Morning."

"Morning, DC."

"Caden," he replies.

My son grabs a bowl, milk, and spoon and takes a seat at the island. Then I notice Callan shoving his phone in his pocket.

"You okay?" I ask Callan.

"Yes and no. We can talk about it later. I need some time to process."

"Okay."

"I'll be back as soon as I can," Callan states after setting his cup in the sink. With a quick kiss, he's out the front door.

"Did DC leave last night?"

"No. Were you serious when you asked him to move in?"

My son turns to me. "Absolutely. DC is awesome. Is he moving in?"

"Yes, he is."

"When?"

Right now! "As soon as he can."

"Sweet. I'm going to get dressed."

A little later than normal, I brush a few leaves and debris from the top of my parents' grave and set the flowers down. Caden is six rows ahead of us, standing at Daniel's grave instead. Callan's hand is linked with mine, but he says nothing. After a few long moments, I take a step toward Caden. Callan follows.

I can hear Caden talking, but I can't make out the words. When I do, I stop advancing toward him.

"You okay?"

"Yeah. Offering him some privacy. Want to talk about what was bothering you earlier now?"

Callan shrugs. "My parents and brothers read the information I provided. With that knowledge, they're willing to reconsider their acceptance of our relationship. Slowly—Liam's words. However, I'm angry. I shouldn't have needed to prove you weren't at fault. Introducing you to them should've been enough. How deeply I love both of you should've been enough."

My heart nearly splits in two for him. "What are you saying?"

"The easiest way to explain it is, I'm hurt my family didn't accept you and Caden at my request and only my request. They want to talk. I'm past talking. They are either fine with us or they aren't. I need more time to accept they aren't ready, I guess."

"Then you should take it if it's for you. Don't if you think you should wait for me."

He turns more fully in front of me. "Please explain."

"On some level, I understand how they feel. I don't agree, but I understand. You choosing us was difficult for your mother to hear. I could tell your choice astounded her. Now they're ready to flip back to acceptance quickly to get you back. We decided to be selfish together. If you're not ready to forgive them for not welcoming us as you would have liked, then you wait until you are."

Caden has been silent for a few minutes, standing before his dad's burial site. He turns to face us and asks, "Is Dad going to be mad at me?"

We take a step closer to my son, and he throws his arms around me. "For what?"

His words are muffled against my shoulder. "For needing DC. For calling and treating DC as if he's my father. For loving DC as if he is my dad?"

"No. Of course not."

"How can you be so sure?" my son demands.

"Daniel would want both of us to be happy. He and I didn't have a chance to find out if we were meant to be married and raise you together like we planned. Daniel would want you to have an amazing father figure in your life, even if it isn't him."

Caden releases me and hugs Callan. "I love you, Dad."

"I love you, Caden."

Our little family stands in silence for a few minutes before we leave the cemetery. Wordlessly, Callan drives to the Nubble and parks. It's the offseason. There's plenty of parking, and the area is vacant. Caden hops out and takes a seat on one of the stone benches while I opt for the rock facing the majestic structure.

Callan leans against the rock beside me and threads our hands together. "Do you want me to go back to the car?"

"No. I'm at a loss for what to share. Sharing how Caden was doing in the past was a way to keep Daniel in the picture, at least in my mind. Now it doesn't seem necessary for me to do it considering the conversation we had with Caden earlier."

"Understandable. Quiet remembrance is fine too. Why here?"

I squeeze his hand in mine and sidle closer. "My parents got engaged and married here. It's where I told them about my pregnancy. This place with the stunning views and soothing waves has heard the good, bad, and awful news of my life."

Callan presses a kiss to my temple but says nothing.

"Why did you pick Acadia?"

"It isn't about Acadia exactly. Sadie went camping with Chloe and her family. I decided a log cabin in a forest with tons of miles to walk and traverse was the best way to honor her."

"It's sweet, Callan."

"Ready to go home?"

"Our home. Absolutely."

It takes Callan three evenings to move over all his belongings, except his bedroom furniture. With my help, we changed the mattress and sheets. He wasn't wrong, his are more luxurious. Smithson is going to help him move the bedroom furniture after the holiday. Today he's working at the school, the last day before holiday break, and the YPD holiday party is tonight.

I hurry through the morning at the office and then head home. The quiet in my house offers me time to wrap some gifts for my guys. With the wrapping done, I take a long shower and start working on my hair.

Del: I'm out early. Want help?

Me: Yes please!

I'll take any excuse for more girl time with Del. The door swings open within minutes.

"Were you already here?"

"Yup," she answers.

I laugh, and Del gets to work on my makeup. You would think I would've picked up enough tips over the years. I probably have, but if she wants to use me to practice, she can.

"How was the anniversary?"

"Same, but better."

She wrinkles her eyebrows at me.

"Having Callan beside me made it a little easier to handle. It seems silly, I know."

"Not really. Humans aren't meant to be alone. It took you a while to locate your person, that's all."

"Yeah, it did. Still joining us for dinner on Thursday?"

Del smiles. "I can't. Scott invited me to have Christmas dinner with his entire family."

"Oh, I'm excited for you!"

"Me too."

Del puts the finishing touches on my hair and makeup. Then she nixes the dress I chose for tonight. She pulls an aubergine wrap dress from the closet, indicating it's a better option.

Later than I expect them, Callan and Caden rush through the door one after the other and fight for the hot water. Little do they know, there's plenty of water for both to shower at the same time on different floors. Under an hour later, my guys are ready to go to the party. Caden opts for dress pants and a polo. Callan is similarly dressed, except he chose an Oxford shirt with the sleeves rolled. Who knew I found his forearms exceptionally attractive?

We arrive at Morgan's for the YPD holiday party. It's the perfect way to begin our holiday festivities.

"You know where I'll be," Caden informs me.

"Stalking Kelsey's desserts?" I ask.

"Yup." Then he's gone.

Callan laughs beside me. "Can't blame him. I would be right behind him if it wouldn't be frowned upon not to mingle at least a little."

I shake my head. "I know."

The first group of people includes Smithson, Scarlett, Grant, Maggie, and a tall blonde I don't know. I would bet she's Grant's sister given they could be twins.

"It's nice to see you again," Scarlett states.

"You as well. How was your honeymoon?"

"Tropical island perfection. There's something to be said for leaving drab, cold weather and heading to white sand beaches and sunshine with your husband."

"I'll keep it in mind," I reply.

"How are you, Alannah?" Maggie asks.

"I'm well. Thank you again for the meal. It was above and beyond."

"You're most welcome."

"I wonder, though, how you knew my favorite meal from the Inn?"

Maggie rolls her lower lip between her teeth in a curious reaction to my question, then releases it. "Lucky guess." The tall blonde sets her hand on Maggie's arm. "I'm sorry. I would like to introduce Eva, Grant's sister. She's considering a move here."

"Pleasure to meet you, Eva." As soon as the words leave my mouth, a tiny blonde girl with ringlet curls wipes out near Eva's feet. Her plate of decorated holiday cookies scatters on the floor. Tears instantly flow from the little girl's eyes.

Eva bends down and checks her out. "Hi, I'm Eva."

"Lilah."

"Are you hurt?"

She shakes her head furiously with a magnificent pout on her face. "My cookies are though. Daddy won't let me eat them off the floor."

"Why don't we get some new ones?" As Eva asks, Grant cleans the mess on the floor.

A smile grows on Lilah's face. "Yes. Thank you." Her voice is still tear-logged. She takes Eva's hand and leads her toward the dessert table.

"She's gorgeous. Who is her dad?" I ask Maggie.

"Hagen," she replies.

Putting a face with the name in my file is helpful. The conversation around me continues while I watch Eva and Lilah walk to the dessert table. As Kelsey assists the little girl get new cookies, Hagen approaches them. Lilah animatedly explains what happened and appears to introduce Eva as her new best friend.

We mingle and eat delicious food for the rest of the evening. Caden spends most of the time coloring with Kelsey and Maggie's kids. He looks giant with them, but he's extremely patient. His patience is surprising, especially since we're decorating our tree when we get home tonight. Some people have a tradition of decorating as soon as possible. I refuse to add holiday cheer to our home until after the anniversary.

"Hey, gorgeous, ready to go?" Callan grabs my attention.

"Sure, if we can pull Caden away from the little kids."

Callan laughs. "He'll be fine with it." We motion for him to join us. "Ready to decorate the tree?"

My son scowls. "I guess. The forced labor hauling the decorations up from the basement, not so much."

"You'll survive," I add.

He shrugs and casts a look at Callan.

"What are you two up to?"

"We have no idea what you're talking about, sweetheart," Callan draws me against him and kisses me.

Unconvinced but not willing to discuss it further, we make our way home. I'm glad I didn't press them. When I was a child, my parents and I went to a pick and cut lot and searched for the perfect tree. The first Christmas after they died, I was numb and unsure how things would pan out. I don't recall much about the first one other than my parents were gone. When I was out of college and living on my own with Caden, tree farm traipsing wasn't truly an option. I'm sure Séamus would've joined us if I asked, but I didn't want to impose. Normally, Caden and I drag our fake tree from the basement and set it up. My guys decided to surprise me this year.

"Mom, can you go inside and make the hot cocoa?" Caden asks.

"I'm sure you two are up to something now."

Callan tugs me closer. "We are, but it's a good surprise. I promise."

While I busy myself in the kitchen, the guys bring up supplies from the basement. Then they slip out the front door again. When I finish making the cocoa, which is likely not as good as Callan's, I see they have set up a real tree in the living room and it's ready to decorate.

I nearly drop the tray. "How did you…? When did you…?"

"We have our ways." Caden smirks as he replies.

"Seriously though…."

Callan smiles. "I asked Caden what he recalled of your earlier Christmases and the stories you shared with him about your childhood. A real tree was prevalent in the stories. Earlier today, we cut one down at the tree farm near Wells."

"No tears allowed, Mom," Caden scolds.

Callan swipes them away with the pad of his thumb before bringing his mouth near my ear. "Our first Christmas together is going to be perfect."

"Thank you both." I pull Caden closer and hug them. With holiday music playing in the background, we decorate our first tree together. Nearly, two hours later, the three of us admire our work before turning in for the night.

CHAPTER TWENTY-SIX

CALLAN

On Christmas morning, I wiggle out of our bed without waking Alannah near eight. As quietly as possible, I prepare a feast for breakfast. It could go either way if Alannah is upset with me for stealing her tradition. However, she admits my cooking skills are better than hers. When I'm almost finished, Alannah wanders into the kitchen.

"Merry Christmas, beautiful."

"Merry Christmas, Callan. How did you sneak out of bed without waking me?"

I wink at her. "I have my ways."

I trap her against the counter and nuzzle her neck while she attempts to make coffee. Rather than fight me, she sets down the coffee and turns to face me.

"How much more time am I going to need to add when I have to get to work?"

I grin at her. "At least twenty minutes." Our lips meet, and her coffee needs are forgotten. We fall into our own little bubble until the timer for breakfast sounds. I groan and reluctantly release her. "Can you wake Caden?"

"No way. You want him up before noon, you're taking the risk, *Dad*." She puts emphasis on my newest title.

I pull the French toast casserole out of the oven and set it on top. "Please make some coffee for me."

"I will. Love you. Good luck up there."

Trudging upstairs, I nudge Caden.

"Everything okay?"

"Yup, breakfast is ready and there are gifts to open."

"Five minutes," he mumbles and starts to move out of bed.

I exit his room before he can change his mind. Without a word, I rejoin Alannah in the kitchen. I've had one sip of my coffee before Caden appears.

"How on earth?"

Our still sleepy son smiles and replies, "Dad is a better cook than you. Sorry. Love you." He gives her a side hug on his way to the table.

Alannah shakes her head, grabs the casserole, and takes her seat. We make a major dent in the food I prepared—French toast casserole with vanilla-infused syrup, scrambled eggs, and toast, along with bacon and home fries.

Caden leans back after clearing his second plate. "Best holiday breakfast ever!" He extends his fist in my direction.

As I bump it, Alannah swats his other arm, and they dissolve into laughter. The sound of her laugh and the increasing frequency I hear it makes me smile. I'm well on my way to seeing her smile and laugh daily for the rest of my life. It takes Caden legitimately ten minutes to open his two gifts and significantly longer to install and set them up.

Early afternoon, I wander downstairs and find Alannah curled up by the fireplace. "Want to share, beautiful?"

"Nothing to share. I'm content and enjoying how it feels. What about you though?"

I sidle close and surround her with my arms. "Normally, I offer to work. It gives my coworkers, like Washington and Hagen, the opportunity to spend the holiday with their kids."

"That's nice of you. You didn't offer this year?"

"Not exactly. I didn't ask for the day off, but I didn't offer to pick up a shift either."

"I understand."

Her tone is off. "What's going on in your gorgeous mind?"

She shifts to face me more fully. "I never asked before... when is the last time you spent a Christmas with your family?"

Without hesitation, I answer, "Before I moved here. However, the same rules applied at my old department as here. I offered to work. As much as I hate to admit it, losing Sadie fractured our family."

She tenses in my arms.

I continue, "I mean, it broke the relationship between parent and child. My parents weren't overly strict or overly lax before the accident. They were fair. However, after... strict or iron-fist rule would be apt descriptions. It made the rest of high school difficult. It's why I went away to college, which I've already shared with you. I needed to find my own life, and I did. My parents will never be the same people they were before they lost Sadie. Neither will I. With therapy, I've been able to acknowledge, grieve, and channel it into something better. My parents, and to some extent my brothers, haven't fully moved on because they still live nearby. It's one reason for their reaction to you and Caden."

My family and I have made progress in our relationship since the article. Anything short of completely embracing Alannah and Caden isn't acceptable to me. I informed them of that, and we have had multiple conversations. My parents and brothers are attending therapy to deal with losing Sadie. Hopefully, it will help mend our relationship as well.

Two months have passed since our first holiday season together. "Ready, gorgeous?" I ask.

Alannah comes around the corner dressed in a long, off-the-shoulder dress. "I'm ready, but I don't know for what."

I laugh. I purposely left out many of the details for this evening and the planning over the last few months. It'll be worth it.

I close the passenger door behind her and drive to our first destination— a private dinner at Morgan's. I'm grateful Delilah was able to secure tonight for me. She also gave me insight into Alannah's favorite dishes prepared by Chef Morgan.

I pull out her chair and opt for the seat beside her instead of across from her. After our server returns with our drinks, we talk about our days at work and our upcoming plans for spring break.

"Caden is going to get his wish. We're going to Florida, and he can warm his toes in the white sand before he plays basketball for Coach Ortega."

"I can't wait!" I admit.

She raises an eyebrow. "Why?"

"You lounging on a chaise in a string bikini... um, yes!"

She laughs and shakes her head. "What makes you think I wear a string bikini?"

"You should. You're gorgeous."

Crimson appears on her cheeks. "What am I going to do with you?"

I lean closer and whisper, "Absolutely anything you want."

Goose bumps erupt on her skin, and she exhales slowly. "You can't say…. Callan, we're in a fancy restaurant."

"I'm aware. Did it ever occur to you that I like seeing you flustered and off-kilter?"

"Like when we first met?"

"Yes. Word choice errors and nervousness are my kryptonite."

She tugs her lower lip between her teeth. "No, they aren't."

"They are, when it's you. I love I'm the only person who can trip you up."

Her nose wrinkles up. "Me too."

We enjoy our meals. I chose the filet mignon, and Alannah opted for lobster macaroni and cheese. According to Delilah, if it's on the menu, it's her first choice. After a delightful dinner, complete with chocolate *mille-*

feuille, we make our way to the second part of our date. I climb the winding road toward the ViewPoint Hotel. It's as close as I can get to the Nubble Lighthouse and pull off my plans.

"Are we not going home?" There's a slight hitch in her words.

While I'm confident Alannah trusts me with Caden completely, I haven't taken any liberties with his schedule, like planning an overnight date without her consent. "We aren't staying overnight. We're here for an event."

I pull into a spot, round the car, and offer her my hand. When we reach the main entrance, we're immediately escorted to the viewing area. I arranged for us to watch *Up*, complete with a comfortable couch, pillows, blankets, and a gas firepit table for warmth. It's a tad chillier than I would like.

Snuggled together on the sofa, the movie starts on a large screen for the two of us. The movie enraptures my gorgeous woman. From the look into Carl and Ellie's marriage, the trials and triumphs, and the sadness of Ellie's passing, a picture of what our love is plays out in animation. My promise to explain why we are Carl and Ellie is nearly fulfilled.

"You weren't kidding," she murmurs against my lips as the credits start to roll.

"No, I wasn't. We are them. I know you can take care of yourself and Caden, but I want to be beside you in case you want support. We are an amazing team, from fixing steps to cooking meals to dealing with fallen trees."

She smiles and drops her head slightly.

I cup her face and lift her gaze back to mine. "I want to plan a life with you. Where do you see your practice in five years? Where do I want to go with the department? How many tiny humans with my eyes and your smooth three-point shot will we welcome into our crazy world?"

She tilts her head to the side.

"Our circumstances are unique—ones I wouldn't wish on my worst enemy. We can take our terrible shared history and mold it into a spectacular future—together. I hope our difficult times are in the past and our future plans can be obtained. If not, I'm confident we can handle anything laid at our feet." I shift, press a kiss to her forehead, and move onto one knee on the ground in front of her.

Her hands immediately cover her face.

"Alannah."

She doesn't move her hands.

I peel her fingers away from her face. Her emerald eyes meet mine.

"Alannah, will you promise to get flustered at least once a month, never back down in a game of H-O-R-S-E, and walk beside me for the rest of my life?"

"Yes."

I slide a cushion cut ring with a micro pavé band on her finger before kissing her breathless. "There's one more thing."

Her lust-filled gaze rises to mine. "I don't need anything else."

"While we were securing the perfect evergreen, I asked Caden for permission to marry you."

"You did?" A few tears roll over the balls of her cheek.

Swiping them away, I answer, "I did."

She lifts her left hand and cups my face. "Thank you." She brushes her lips across mine and lowers her hand.

"You're welcome. There's more. While we were out, he shared a secret with me. I requested and received permission to share it with you. I need to preface my next few sentences though. For the next ten minutes, I need to retain you as my attorney."

She frowns.

I grin at her. "What I mean is, the information is confidential and can't be discussed with anyone other than me or Caden until we get married and you're officially invited as a member."

"Okay," she states with skepticism in her voice and her head tilted sideways.

"I met Caden within a week of starting as the resource officer at the school."

"At the beginning of his junior year?" she asks.

"Yes. There have been rumors of a list of eligible first responder bachelors floating around."

She nods. "I've heard the rumors."

"First, those rumors are true. There is a list, and I'm on it."

A huge smile grows on her face, and she turns her left hand in my direction as if I could forget sliding my ring on her finger not ten minutes ago. "Not anymore."

I laugh. "Technically, I'm on it until we get married."

"Well, we need to make it official as soon as practically possible then, but what does your inclusion have to do with Caden?"

I continue, "Patience, my stunning fiancée." I take her hand in mine and kiss behind my ring. "Caden heard the rumors as well from his classmate who works at the Perk—interestingly, the worker who replaced Scarlett. Last winter he had a conversation with Kelsey and requested help to set us up."

"Caden fixed us up?"

"Yes, he did. Well, he saw our potential and asked for assistance from Kelsey without knowing she was a member of the Matchmakers' Book Club."

"Why Kelsey?"

"From what Caden shared, he figured she would be best able to help because she's married to Cap. Looking back, it makes sense now why he assigned me to the boys' basketball games instead of the girls' games. At the time, Caden didn't know she and a few other women we know and trust are part of a book club who meet, maintain the list, and help foster relationships."

"I gather Maggie, Lina, and Scarlett are also members?"

"Yes, they are."

"Now the chitchat at the football game and the extra meal makes sense after the article."

I nod.

"Did Savannah really twist her ankle or was the tango carefully orchestrated as well?"

"No, Savannah did hurt herself. The tango wasn't set up for you to step in, but I'm glad you did."

"Me too. It was fun and hot as hell."

"Yeah, it was." I kiss her lightly. "We should discuss our wedding and plan accordingly. Whether it's next month or next year, eventually my name will come off the list."

"What kind of wedding do you want?" she asks.

"It isn't the party I'm worried about. It's the outcome. What does your dream wedding look like?"

"Smallish and elegant. Maybe at Clay Hill or the beach."

"Perfect."

"The first possible opening they have," Alannah suggests.

"I agree. Then we can grow our family."

"Any chance you want to start now?"

I kiss her deeply, escort her to our home, and spend the rest of the night and into the wee hours of the morning practicing.

Thank you so much for reading *For Love & Basketball*!

I hope you love the Matchmakers' Book Club. Which first responder will they match up next? Order *For Love & Cookies* now so you don't miss it!

Check out Lia's HEA in *Chasing Someday* coming soon!

Did you love *For Love & Basketball*?

Thank you for taking the time to read it. I hope you loved it!
If you liked this book or another one of my books, please consider posting a review.
A short line or two will be perfect! It helps indie authors like me get noticed. I appreciate your support and feedback.

COMING SOON

Two new stories are coming soon!

A York Beach Novel

The Cappellis

Chasing Someday

A Blackthorne Novel

Protecting Our Family

MY BOOKS

YORK BEACH SERIES:

A New Beginning with You

Taking A Chance on Me

Just One More

Kiss You Like You're Mine

Only with Him

My Once in a Lifetime

THE CAPPELLI FAMILY:

Chasing Forever

Chasing My Sunshine

Worth the Chase

Chasing after You

MORGAN BROTHERS SERIES:

One Unforgettable Favor

Until I Kissed You

Always Have, Always Will

BLACKTHORNE SECURITY

Protecting My Forever

Protecting Our Future

Protecting Us

Hers to Protect

MATCHMAKERS' BOOK CLUB

For Love & Coffee

All my books in one place: www.nicolevidal.com/books

www.ingramcontent.com/pod-product-compliance
Lightning Source LLC
Chambersburg PA
CBHW072345020726
47506CB00004B/1011